TYRIK COGDELL

ANGEL *of* SILENCE

Tyrik Revolution Books

Special thanks.
This book is dedicated to my family
Gabriella, Logan, Brandon cogdell and most importantly my
beautiful wife Morningstar who push me when things
got hard for me, making sure I didn't quit on my dream
of one day publishing my own book.
Thank you I love you babe.

PROLOGUE

Before there was time, god created the heaven's and the earth. God who made the heaven's named it Zion then created the holy Angels to live among him to praise and glorify all that he had made. God had a son named Lucifer. It was said he was the most beautiful among all of god's heavenly angels. Lucifer also had the ability to play the harp. his talent and beauty was unequal in all of heaven, Lucifer was loved by all. Lucifer being the most beautiful and loved among all of god's angels wasn't enough for him fore he has become envious of god's praise.

"WHY shall I glorify god? Am I not the most beautiful in all of HEAVEN? Am I not just as loved as him, no longer shall I worship and praise his name when I shall be treated as his equal." since that very moment those words was utter by Lucifer, all of heaven was divided in half.

There were the faithful ones whom chosen to continue to worship god, there Lord and savior whom bless them with eternal life of happiness.

Then there were the fallen ones whom chosen Lucifer the most beautiful and charming Angel in all of heaven, whom has shown them all the forbidden fruits god has forbidden them to taste. The pleasures of lust and adultery, the joy and arrogance of pride, The excitement and trills of gambling.

Lucifer has become the living embodiment of everything

that god declares evil with in the world. This rift between god and Lucifer created the first war in all of creation. A civil war in heaven between father and son, god's archangels against Lucifer fallen angels for control over heaven and all of creation.

The holy war between god and Lucifer lasted for centuries with the blood of angels shed across all the valleys of heaven's kingdoms.

In the end after countless of deaths Lucifer brother the archangel Michael the general of god's army stood over the defeated Lucifer with the aide of his father god. Because of Lucifer betrayal god cast him along with his fallen angels out of heaven in to the core of the earth where there physical bodies shall remained imprisoned until the day of Armageddon.

they're souls were still free to roam around the earth but there were no longer the souls of an angel. Lucifer was no longer the most beautiful angel whom played the glorious harp. His soul was now of the beast whom bared the curse mark of six hundred and sixty six, as well as his fallen angels who became demons who goals are to help persuade man to commit sin throughout the world.

As time went on god decided to create man in his image then created woman from the rib of man. They were known as Adam and eve, whom were created to give each other companionship for all of eternally in the garden of Eden.

Lucifer who now goes by the name Satan used his soul to take possession of a serpent, in order to persuade eve to eat the apple of life from the forbidden tree, whom god forbidden them to taste.

Adam and eve were trick by Lucifer to go against god's wishes. God was once again betrayed by love ones because of Satan's wickedness. A deal was struck between god and

Lucifer. To who may claim more human Souls in the end shall be the true victor of Armageddon.

Now the greatest war in all creation has started between heaven and hell, the war for the love and souls of humanity.

September 23, 2004 Upstate New York Maximum Prison.

Its lights out time where most inmates sleep's to escape the harsh reality of life in prison until there release or execution date but not Albert Houston this is his favorite time to reflect on all those old sweet memories. Like the infamous murders in that Manhattan hospital a few years back. What did one of those news reporters called it ? "the New York slaughter house, yeah that's what they called it." The two hundred and eighty pound Caucasian serial killer smiles to himself showing all his yellow decayed teeth in the darken cell. it was so simple wasn't it Albert ? All you had to do was find a hospital With just a handful of unarmed security guards. Remember that security guard's face expression just before we split his face open with the axes we pulled out our trench coat. Ooohh...we can't forget the best part of the day. Oh no we can't do that Now can we Albert? "No' no we can't. Best to believe it!" Albert answer himself as the sweat pours Down his face, drooling from the mouth as he remembers his fantasy. Remember how we made our way up the stairs butchering anyone we came near too. Hearing all those men and women crying and screaming for help as we made our way Down hall covered in enough peoples blood and gore that could make any man cum, Wouldn't it? Albert thought to himself.

Then we got to the sick ward. That's when the real fun started wasn't it!? Poor bastards was so sick they could barely move. We slaughtered those sick bastard So bad their bodies couldn't be identify without dental confirmation. Then there were the infants, you know how we love the kids. Best to believe it! They're parents put up a fight... yeah fuck all! They didn't give a shit what weapons we had. Even that mother who didn't get properly stitch yet after birth, that's why we only maim Them instead of killing them. we wouldn't want them to miss the show as we bash and chop up there fucking newborn babies. Killing is great but killing with a family as audience that's just... "Eeerrrah! Fuck yeah!" the serial killer moans out in pleasure remembering The looks of the maim parents faces as they cried and beg while I murder they're infant children. The thoughts of those memories cause's Albert Houston To ejaculate in his pants.

"I love a man who enjoys his work." Albert heard a voice inside his prison cell. "who the fuck!" Albert said, his eyes darts around the cell looking for the asshole He's about to kill. Albert's eyes are well adjusted to the darkness of his prison cell I don't see no one. Who has the fucking balls to fuck with us! It can't be a correction officer, not after what I did to officer Conner last year. Always had jokes didn't he, Always talking that one. Wasn't talking so much After we bit his lip's off wasn't he, best to believe it. maybe I'm hearing voices? No that can't be I don't have a problem killing people. Shit I love killing people, the screams, the blood and gore, people begging For their lives while pissing and shitting themselves from fear. Shit I'm getting a hard on just thinking about it, best to believe it.

"If there's anyone in this cell with me that hope's to live best to step the fuck Out, best to fucking believe it! "Albert warns his unforeseen company.

"Indeed Mr. Houston. Out shall I come." an voice answer from the darkness of Albert's cell. A tall slim figure emerges from the shadows of the cell. Right before Albert's eyes stood a tall Caucasian man with silk black hair and thin goatee, dress in very expensive black suit that would cost a correction Officer two months' salary to pay for.

"Mr. Houston I've been keeping a very close eye on you for some time now. I have to say I am very impress how you murdered those fifthly two people in that new York hospital two years ago excluding the thirteen people you killed and buried in your mother's backyard. Till this very day the police haven't found Those bodies. don't think I could of done better myself Mr. Houston." the well dress Man said to Albert.

For a very long time since Albert Houston was a child his chest tighten as his legs Began to shake, the serial killer known as Albert Houston was afraid. "who...who are you?" Albert ask nervously as he stuttered over his words While the sweat and adrenaline overwhelms his body.

Albert starts to smile, wondering is this a taste of fear he cause all those meat bags he butchered over the years as his heart began pounding in his chest Excited from this new sensation.

"I am one whom walked the earth before there was time. But I'm not here to talk about me Mr. Houston, I'm here to ask you to join my side Mr. Houston for the exchange to live for all eternally doing the things you love to do best? But I need a answer now, for our time grow short." the well dress man answer. Albert pause for a moment to make a decision about what the well dress man proposed but only for a moment. Albert smile starts to slowly widen from ear to ear showing All the yellow decaying teeth on a now happy psychopathic face. "Hell yes! you best to believe it!" Albert's shouts out rejoicing in the decision he made.

Suddenly the appearance of the well dress man starts

to change. His eyes turned a bright green that glowed in Albert's dark cell, his jaw seemed to extend Downward exposing teeth that would put a great white to shame. "welcome to the winning team Mr. Houston." his voice echo through Albert's ears as the well dress man disappears in to the shadows of his cell, leaving Albert Houston to his fantasy of murders yet to come.

CHAPTER ONE

Six years later. Upstate New York death row maximum security. Emotions are running high on this day because today is the day Albert Houston will be executed for the deaths of fifthly two people inside a Manhattan hospital in new York city eight years ago. the victims' families been waiting for this moment for eight years. Since Albert Houston was convicted of multiple counts of murder and attempted murder in court, to show him they're anger, they're rage and to watch the fear on his face before he dies, just like Albert done to them before their family and loved ones. "Look at you now! You son of bitch! Let's see you cry and beg!" One of the victim's father yell out to Albert. "I hope you feel every ounce of pain with that lethal injection before you rot and burn in hell you bastard!" a cripple Latina woman who was maim by Albert Houston killing spree also shouted out at the serial killer. The corrections officers try to settle the families down as Albert Houston looks up from his bed where he's strapped down by tight belts across Albert's legs, Waist and head in order to restrain Albert from escaping until he receives the lethal injection that will end his life. Then a disturbing smile ran across Albert's face.

"Heh heh heh! hey don't I know you? Yeah I know you. You're that pregnant bitch I chopped up and made you watch me butcher that whiny boyfriend of yours and that bastard newborn, they never could tell what sex it was when I was done could they? Heh heh ha ha ha ha ha ha!" Albert erupts in to a insane laughter that horrifies the entire room, bring it to complete silence. After an disturbing silence the warrant sends out The priest to hurry things along.

"Albert Houston would you like to ask god our lord and savior to forgive you for your sins as a last prayer my son?" the father ask. SPIT! Gosh of yellow spit hit's the priest in his eye from the rotten mouth of Albert causing the priest to kneel down in pain holding his right eye. "Fuck off priest! My soul belongs to Satan now!" Albert denounces the priest. Albert then looks at the nurse who is now preparing the lethal dose that will put Albert Houston to his untimely death. "I swear to Satan when I come back I'm going to kill all you son of bitches in here, You best to believe it! Especially you Mrs. Nurse Jones but first I'm going to fuck you like no one in the history of mankind has ever been fuck before bitch!" Albert said to her as he sticks out his tongue licking his chap lips while lifting up his lower torso up and down, up and down humping the air.

"Enough of this shit! Inject his ass already!" as the warrant shouts the command in disgust, nurse Jones ready herself to give Albert Houston the lethal injection in to his veins. nurse Jones slightly bends over to whisper in the ears of Albert Houston. "You can keep fantasizing while you burn in hell you sick ugly bastard. I added something a little special in your serum to personal make sure every ounce of this dose hurt like hell before you die." nurse Jones said injecting him with the lethal dose in the tube inserted in Albert's veins, entering his blood stream. Albert's body spasm violently, gagging on his own spit, his heart erupts inside his chest, his vision becomes blurry then dark, Albert Houston was no more.

Bronx, New York City. The Famous Play Mates Strip Club.

Where all men adult pleasure and dreams come true, single and married that can pay the cash. One of the clubs most loyal and regular customers is a well build African American thirdly two years of age man. Who comes to drank and spend his military money on naked strippers six days a week. His name is Jessie brown. Jessie sits in his usual seat in the front row Drinking his usual alcohol beverage jack Daniels. Jessie reaches' up to tip the five foot five one hundred and twenty pound Latina woman with a ass that would put a young Jenifer Lopez to shame. "Shake that ass watch yourself! Shake that ass watch yourself!" Music plays in the back round of the club giving their customers more entertainment enjoying they're filthy pleasures. "Yeah! Shake that fat ass for me bitch!" Jessie slurs over his words While putting his five dollar bill between the stripper ass cheeks. Jessie continues to drench himself in jack Daniels as the whiskey pours down his throat and shirt , waiting for the Latina stripper to turn around too look at her size c breast. Jessie already started fantasizing about them. "What the fuck!" Jessie screams out loud as he felled back out of his chair. Drenching his clothes with the bottle of jack Daniels he spill on himself. Jessie sits back up and looks at the Latina stripper again then blink his eyes. Not trusting his eyes, what he saw couldn't be real. Jessie looks again and see's three sixes branded in the forehead of the stripper on the stage revealing the mark of the beast. Wh...What the hell? Is this some kind of end of day's bullshit happening or something? Nah I'm bugging out.Too much Jack that's what it is. Jessie thought to himself, shaking his head trying to wake up from a bad dream.

"Hey mister you're OK? That was a nasty fall man." a

young Caucasian man ask Jessie. Jessie turns around to tell the young man who went out his way to see if he's alright while everyone else talked about him, That he was okay and properly just had too much to drink. But when Jessie turned to thank the man, his face was deformed. Half of his face was burned flesh; the other was of a jackal's face. Its eyes were pitch black like something straight from a horror movie. The things mouth seemed to water for my flesh as hot steam blows from its snout, it's massive claws reach towards me.

"Get the fuck away from me!" Jessie screamed as he scrambles back to his feet making an desperate run towards the strip club exit. Jessie seen many things over the years fighting secret wars over sea's that could give the toughest man nightmares for the rest of their lives but this...this was different...this wasn't human, this was something else. Jessie finally reaches the exit door, when suddenly it disappears along with everyone else in the entire club.

The once infamous playmates club was now gone, just a void of darkness. No strippers, no customers, no club, just him alone surrounded by complete darkness. "Mr. Brown aren't you tired coming to this strip club every day, just to go home alone? Fondling yourself to sleep wishing you had a life. Wishing you had some one to come home to? "Jessie heard the voice speak to him through the darkness. Jessie search around fanatically in the dark looking for the person who revealed his most shameful secrets that ashamed him every night of his miserable life.

"Who the hell said that?" Jessie yelled out in the darkness.

"I did Mr. Brown." the well dress man said as he step out of the darkness that envelope their surroundings.

All Jessie knows is this person knew things about him,

deep personal things that he never share with anyone before and now he wants to hurt the person Who reminded him of his deep shame. "I'll kill you!" Jessie filled with pure rage clinch his hands in to a tight fist then swings at the well dress man with all his might. Just to realize there Wasn't no one there as Jessie punches empty air. "What the fuck? I thought I...I thought I saw..? Jessie spoke confuse at what just occurred.

"You did Mr. Brown. If you will kindly calm down you might find what I have to say might be in your best interest Mr. Brown." The well dress man said as he reappear in front of Jessie.

"How the? What the hell are you? Jessie ask the man, trying to fight back the shock and chills that ran throughout his body. As a ex Green Beret soldier Jessie fought many small dirty wars for the united states government. Stuff that never made the news or publish in any newspapers, real dark black operations shit. Families, children murder, torture and even raped, Jessie seen and lived through it all, there was nothing that could surprise him, not until today.

"Who or what I am is not important today because am here to help you Mr. Brown. What if I told you your life can change overnight? No more lonely nights. All the money and woman you can have everything you always wanted in life." Within a blink of an eye a bright flash of red light glowed underneath Jessie feet and suddenly Jessie was surrounded by four beautiful women he ever saw in his life.

Black, white, Latin and Asian gorgeous beautiful women wearing nothing but thin see through lingerie, fondling Jessie's body just like his dreams. "wh..what is this?" Jessie could barely speak the words out of his mouth being overwhelm by the four beautiful women.

"Black, white, Spanish, Asian and Indian women all

shapes and sizes can be yours Mr. Brown. And the only thing you have to say is I join you and all this and more will be yours." the well dress man said but Jessie isn't paying attention anymore as the African American woman opens his zipper. She strokes him in a way he haven't felt since his nineteen birthday before enlisting in the military.

"Please say yes Jessie, please!" she moans in his ear as she strokes him faster and faster with her tiny soft hands.

"I...I "Jessie try's to answer but before he's able the Asian woman grabs and turns Jessie face towards her as she sticks her tongue down his throat. Jessie succumb to her, tonging her back while both the Caucasian and Latina woman takes his fingers and gently pushes them inside they're warm wet virginals. So warm and wet oh god I don't want it to end. Jessie pleads inside his head. "Please don't leave us Jessie. Please say yes...say yes Jessie say yes!" They all moan and moan for him. The pleasure becomes greater and greater until Jessie completely overwhelm with pleasure his body starts to erupt in climax. "Ah...Ahhh...yeah...yuh.." the four women disappear in the middle of his climax. Leaving Jessie vulnerable as he falls to his knees. "Please no...Where did they go? please." the now shaken Jessie brown begs the well dress man.

"They're be back Mr. Brown. The only thing you have to do is join my cause but I can see you're in no shape to answer right now. You have an hour to make your decision Mr. Brown." the well dress man said as he disappeared leaving Jessie on his knees surrounded by a small group of bouncers inside the strip club as if nothing happen at all.

"Please no...Don't leave me like this." Jessie whispers while he sobs and cries As life returns to normal.

Outside across the street from the play mates strip club. Two people wait patiently across from the infamous strip club. Dress in all white silk hooded robes with gold trims around the hood. On the other side of the street a huge strong bouncer throws out a drunken African American man on to the side walk from the playmates club. "That's him. That's the one I was sent for." the woman said to her partner. Her partner takes off his silk hood, showing his long straight black hair and bright blue eyes bearing a scar above his right eyebrow.

He watches across the street to see the man she's talking of. He watches in discussed as he witness the man drench himself in alcohol while staggering in the middle of the street, bottle still in his mouth. "sshh..Discussing. This is why humans are pathetic. Why he show such interest in them is beyond me. Look how consume in sin he is, are you still planning on disobeying your orders Natasha?" he response to his partner Natasha. "I know you would Norwell. That's why the all mighty has chosen this task for me to claim the angel of silence." Natasha and Norwell disappear from the sites of the living as Jessie drank his way back home.

CHAPTER TWO

While a small town sleeps in the comfort of their beds A storm approaches. Unknown to this small town and the rest of the world, This will be the worst storm in mankind history since god flooded the earth for forty days and forty nights wiping out almost all of life accept for a few chosen in the days of genesis. Fore this is not a storm of nature but a storm of pure evil, That will bring sorrow and death to all who crosses path with its unholy rain.

Kroom! Kroom! The thunder roars as it lights up the sky above the small town.

The ground shakes as it cracks open from the lighting strike that descended from the sky.

Deep dark smokes rises from the open crack splinter in to the earth. The small town remains silent in their sleep as something underneath Ground begins to move.

Something starts to pull up wards from the open crack in the earth. A large peach sizzling thing pulls it's self from the splinter earth. The peach creature collapse to the ground exhausted from freeing It self from the bowls of the earth.

Its body still smoking as if it just arrive from an inferno. Lighting erupts from the sky once more as heavy rain pours down from the heavens.

Rain pours down on the peach creature extinguishing its sizzling body. The body cools from the rain, revealing it isn't a creature but a man. This man isn't an ordinary man but a man whom committed countless of murders while pledging his soul to Satan.

This is a night of resurrections of the infamous mass murder known As Albert Houston.

Bobby Townsend is your typical forty year old married blue collar working man.

Yeah I know I'm married and all but a man have to do what a man have to do, it's only natural.

Bob thinks to himself as he wiggles around on his couch trying to find some kind of comfort. Come on! Look at this shit. I'm a forty year old man rolling around on this damn couch like I'm some damn kid and for what? So what my wife caught me Masturbating to some porn movie with my pants down my ankles. "If she would of gave it to me this morning before work I wouldn't had to do that now would I!" bobby shouts out loud hoping his wife would hear.

Kroom! Kroom! Bobby jumps straight up from his couch like a frightened Kitty cat from the sound of thunder roaring in the sky's above. "Damn weather. How in hell am I supposed to sleep with all this noise going on, unlike my damn bear of a wife upstairs!"

Bobby covers his ears almost pissing on Himself from the explosion outside his home. bobby downstairs windows cracks from the impact. "What the fuck is that!" bobby runs towards his now broken windows to investigate what cause the explosion outside his house. Bobby mouth drops open from shock. Of all the things he thought he might see he never expected to find a man shot dead by an lightning bolt a few yards from his house. "My God! I...I. Got to call the ambulance or something."

"Huh?" I just saw that man hand moved a little. No, maybe it's nothing. I heard that when some people die They're nerves jump causing certain body parts to move, giving the Appearance they're still alive. No what if he's still alive? If I leave him in this storm he will die for sure. With that thought in mind bobby decision was made. Dead or alive he was taking this poor man out of this terrible rain storm in to my house until the ambulance arrive.

Bobby makes a short run towards his couch and grabs his black blanket that he was trying to sleep in before the incident occurred. Bobby use to be an all American quarter back for the Westchester cougars in high school. I had over a dozen colleges offering me full scholarships to be there quarter back before my knees blew out during the state championship game, ending my promising football career. I ended up in a recovery hospital to repair my knee. This was the best thing that ever happen to me believe it or not. I met my future wife Julie claymore there. A young Virginia girl with a sweet Country ascent that moved to the New York suburbs for a better career choice As a nurse, god bless her soul. Although I might do stupid things now and then like masturbate. I never and would never cheat on my wife because she's my only true joy in life. Bobby confesses to himself as he used his natural abilities left in him to reach the wounded man less than five seconds time. "Jesus thank you he's still breathing." bobby thanked god. Bobby wrapped his black blanket around the naked man. Bobby easy picks up the man and carries him back to his house in a Cradle position.

"Don't worry mister you're going to be okay!" Bobby insures the man. Bobby gently puts the wounded man on his couch, soaking wet from the Thunder storm. Bobby rises off his knees from placing the wounded man on his couch, he notice's something about him, something familiar but Couldn't place it right away.

His face looks so familiar...where have I seen him before? "uuuuhhha" the hurt man moan as he regain his consciousness causing Bobby to forget where he might have seen his face before.

"Thank god you're a wake! Don't worry sir I'm about to call the ambulance. Just sit tight and take it easy okay."

"wa...water, water." he gasps liking his chap lips.

"Yeah sure. just hold on." bobby walks towards his refrigerator in the Kitchen, opens it to get the wounded man a fresh bottle of water. That face, wait a minute I think I remember where I seen him before. Damn he looks just like that serial killer that murder all those poor folks in that Manhattan hospital a few years back.

"Thank god he's dead because I would of thought that was him for sure." Bobby whisper to himself in relief knowing the serial killer known as Albert Houston was dead.

"You should always listen to your instincts, there usually dead on best to believe it." bobby heard the voice behind him. Startled, bobby drops the bottle of water and quickly turns around to face the wounded man behind him only to discover he wasn't wounded at all but a firm strong build man with the eyes Of a psychotic killer.

"No! You're dead!" bobby shouted in disbelief.

"Albert Houston's back from hell mister! You best to fucking believe it!" Albert smiles ear to ear showing off his infamous yellow teeth. Bobby quickly reaches towards his left and grabs a frying pan off the kitchen stove. Bobby swings the frying pan at Albert's face but his attempt at self-defense is spoiled. Albert easy grabs bobby left wrist then snaps it backwards, Breaking bobby's wrist.

"Aaahhh!" bobby's scream is muffle by the sound of the thunder storms.

"Look like we got a fighter here now don't we?! Now we can't have that can we!?" the crazy bastard Talk's to himself while he wraps his hands around my throat driving me to my knees. Oh god give me strength. He's so strong I..I can't break free. Bobby face turns purple as tears pour down his bloodshot eyes. Hard to breathe. Can't breathe. Albert Houston smile slowly disappears in to an face of lust, as the drool from his mouth fell on bobby's forehead.

"Gag...gah.." bobby gasp desperately trying to breathe.

"Yes that's it breathe. Breathe...fucking breathe." Albert moans. Sick..Bastard getting off..can't breathe. Can't ... bobby tongue hangs out of his mouth, his face becomes hot pink, eyes bloodshot red from lack of oxygen. Albert Houston licks his chap lips in lust. As Albert's excitement grows enlarging his penis. Albert strokes his lower half back in forth while he tightens his grip on bobby's throat. ...Julie.. god protect her...let her stay sleep and let him leave. Julie I love you...Julie...

"Bobby! Wake up bobby! I want you upstairs, I miss you!" Albert Houston eyes lit up with a sick joy.

"Bobby you have a wife? Don't you worry she won't be alone long. I'll give her one last fuck for the both of us, you best to believe it!" NO! Nooooo! Leave my Julie alone...

"Gahh..ugh..." Albert smile is the last thing bobby Townsend would ever see. His last thoughts was of his wife, as bobby gasp his final breathe.

"...Julie..."

"Empty! The god damn bottle is empty!" Jessie brown throws his now empty bottle of jack Daniel's across the living room, shattering it against the wall.

"Where the fuck is he? I've been waiting for fifth teen

minutes already damn it!" Jessie yelled still drunk from all the jack Daniels he consumed earlier at the strip club. Jessie gets out of his chair and stumbles his way in to the kitchen to retrieve another jack Daniels.

"It doesn't matter what the price is. I'll do anything to have a life like that. Anything you hear me damn it!" Jessie shouts again before pouring down A half of gallon of whiskey down his throat.

"You don't know what you're asking Jessie brown." a sweet soft voice said somewhere in his living room. Jessie heard the woman's voice and stumbles his way back in to the living room. Jessie isn't shock or surprise to see two people standing in all white robes in his Living room. Jessie drunken state of mind robes him of those sensations. "Your voice is beautiful; did he send you to me?" Jessie asked her while continuing to consume himself in whiskey.

"No I wasn't send by the one you speak of." Natasha answered. Jessie flop's down in his chair spilling some whiskey on his lap.

"Sign...well you and your friend there can leave the way you came in. I got an important meeting coming." Jessie waves his hand for they can go away.

"Disgusting human filth. Natasha be rid of him, he's already been consume by the sins of this world." Norwell whisper in the ear of Natasha.

"No Norwell he's just lost in sin, I'll show him the path of righteousness." She replies to Norwell as she took the white silk hood off her head.

"Jessie look up on me fore I am here to deliver you out of the darkness of sin and in too the light of righteousness." Natasha preaches. Jessie looks up to find his heart skip a beat causing a lost of breathe. Jessie haven't felt anything close to this since his high school first love Mary Dawson, but this is something more. This woman before him was the most beautiful person he has ever saw period. Yeah but I know how beautiful women really are. Just ask Mary Dawson. "You're the most beautiful woman I've ever seen in my life but I'm Too drunk to figure out all that light and darkness, whatever the fuck that means parting my French." Norwell clinch his teeth together trying to hold his anger in check.

"Natasha this is ridiculous!...this isn't your task, To plead like this." Natasha ignores Norwell protest as she walks towards Jessie.

"Natasha!" Norwell shouts but Natasha continues to ignore his pleads until she's a foot away from Jessie as he stairs up at her face in an drunken daze.

"Don't worry about me selling my soul. I've done it Plenty of times for the U.S. government. So trust me When I tell you there's no heaven or hell." Jessie drinks more whiskey.

"Hump. I also wonder why god made you humans." Norwell said more to himself than anyone else in the room. Natasha kneels down on one knee to meet Jessie eye to eye.

"Tell me Jessie what would it take for you to believe in god again?"

"Natasha. Natasha that's your name right?"

"yes it is." she reply back.

"Well may be I'll believe again if I saw a real life angel. Now you and your human hating boyfriend get out my house, you're fucking up my high." Jessie said to Natasha in a calm voice.

Natasha stands back up towering above Jessie as he sits in his chair. "Very well then Jessie brown." Natasha grabs the edges of her white silk robe. "It's okay Natasha it's god's will. You've done all you could do to save his soul." Norwell said. to his partner Natasha. Jessie try's to look up at Natasha but his vision is to blurry from the effect of the whiskey he consumed.

"wha..what are you ?" the air escapes from his lungs, his heart Erupts as his eyes swell with tears when Natasha drops her robe, Two feather wings expands throughout both ends of the living room Exposing an shining light emulating from her naked body, a body of A beautiful angel.

"I am living proof of heaven's glory. Make your choice Jessie brown good or evil, righteousness or darkness, God or Satan ?"

Shatter! The half of gallon of jack Daniels falls, shattering on the ground. Jessie follows and falls on his hands and knees. "Oh god what have I done! I'm sorry...I'm so sorry. Please forgive me. Oh. Oh god the things I've done in South America." Jessie sobs and cries for forgiveness as he holds on to Natasha's feet. Natasha rest her hands on his shoulders while he looks up at her Beautiful face with sorrow of tears in his eyes.

"All is forgiving because god has bless you in to his light, but we must now leave this place." Natasha answer Jessie pleads as she looked in to his eyes then all three of them vanish as another appeared from the depths of darkness.

"Mr. Brown I've come for your decision." the tall well dress man said as he appeared in to Jessie's living room. The well dress man stop's in his tracks and becomes very still. He then began to sniff the air like a wolf hunting its prey. "Angels. A demon can't never forget that sent of holiness." the well dress man kneels down and picks up an broken piece of Jessie's whiskey bottle.

"Wrong choice Mr. Brown. Those who cross the engineers pay's a great price which you will soon find out Mr. Brown, the Angel of silence." He then steps in to the shadows and disappears in to the darkness.

CHAPTER THREE

It's summer time which means there's no school or teachers telling you it's nap time when you're having so much fun. This is the best time of the year for Gabriella Shuford, bedsides Christmas and birthdays. The last few days Gabriella best friend from next door Daisy Smith has been coming over to play kick ball in her back yard. "look out Gabriella here I come!" daisy announce before kicking the ball at Gabriella as her blonde curry hair blows in the cool summer breeze. Gabriella manages to cut off the path of the ball. "I got it this time daisy!" Gabriella kicks the soccer ball over daisy's head, Over the back yard fence in to the middle of the street. "OH,OH! Gabriella you kick the ball in to the streets." daisy fans her left hand In dramatic fashion showing there's something wrong. "I have to tell mommy." Gabriella said. "No Gabriella, it's okay I'll get it." Daisy smiled then blink her right eye at her. "Daisy no! We aren't allowed to go in the streets remember?" "Yeah I remember but I'm six years old now. I'm big enough to get a ball out of the street's now Gabriella." "But. BUT.." "No buts Gabriella. Just open the fence door for me okay?" "Okay but be quick daisy." Gabriella said worried as she held the fence door open for daisy. Daisy smith look's both ways before she cross the streets just like her mother and father taught her. Daisy quickly picks up the soccer ball. "I got it Gabriella!" daisy shouted proudly. "Daisy get out of the street!" Gabriella yelled with complete terror in her face as a sliver car speeds down the street, crisscrossing on both sides of the lane of the two way street. "Daisy move! The car is coming!" Gabriella warns her best friend. Daisy can't respond to her best friend's warning because fear has Frozen her body, paralyzing her as daisy wait's for a ton of sliver steel to crush the life out of her. Daisy close's her eyes trying to escape the horror she's about to feel, hoping it will go away like some terrible nightmare. Daisy screams in horror that could be heard five blocks down the street as she feels a hard tug on her chest. Oh god I'm dead, OH god I'm dead. Daisy mind raced panicky. "Oowwww!" daisy howled as her thoughts spin out of control as her thin body is thrown to the curve of the street. Daisy finally opens her eyes to see her best friend Gabriella standing over her yelling something. "Daisy hurry! we got to go!" daisy heard her say. Gabriella's mother hears the girls shouting and the shrieking sounds of a out of control vehicle driven by some drunken idiot. Her name is Sherry Shuford. She's a nurse who works every morning accept weekends so she can have some alone time with her only daughter Gabriella. She is the only thing of importance to sherry since her husband died five years ago in the army leaving her daughter Fatherless and her a widow. Now some asshole is trying to make me motherless too. No I won't stand for it. Sherry thoughts race though her mind as she bust open the door to her back yard to see her five year old Daughter do the unthinkable. Gabriella ran towards the middle of the street and grabs her best friend daisy by the shirt and throws her to the curve of the sidewalk with the strength of a grown up. This cause's sherry heart to beat harder as she agonizes in fear. Although sherry was very proud of Gabriella heroics, she's now terrified that Gabriella's life in danger. Sherry love daisy smith with all her heart and soul, she wouldn't wish no harm to any child especially daisy but as a mother she would rather see Daisy in the middle of the street then her own daughter. "Gabriella, Daisy get inside now! Hurry!" sherry shouts out at the kids sprinting towards the fence door grabs daisy arm, pulling her in to the back yard not looking or stop running for a moment until she reach's Her little flower, the last gift she received from the only man she ever loved. "Gabriella grab my hand! Gabriella!" sherry reach her hand out. "Mommy!" Gabriella call's out to her mother while she tries to run towards her with all the speed and strength she can generate in her tiny five year old legs. Gabriella reaches her hand out towards her mother as the drunk driver Continues to speed out of control inches away from running over Gabriella. "I got you!" sherry yelled out grabbing Gabriella's hand, yanking her out of the middle of the street . "You're okay baby, mommy's got you, mommy's..." "Aaahhhh!" sherry screams in horror holding what use to be Gabriella's arm as the sliver car drags the now broken bloodied body of Gabriella down two more blocks before crashing in to a street light pole ending his drunken rampage. "Gabriella no! Nooo! God please don't take her away from me too...please." sherry pleads and begs god as she runs after her daughter's broken, lifeless body while still holding her severed arm in her hand. Neighbors and random people in the street gather around the murder scene. People scream in complete horror to witness this little girl's lifeless bloodied body dead on the streets that will haunt their dreams for months to come. Some people cried to see a mother lose their child in such away. while some just stared in shock, disbelief and sadly amazement. Others gave in to their anger as they drag the drunken driver out the shatter window of his car and gave him such a beating that would put him in coma for four weeks before his jail sentence. Sherry shoford doesn't care about any of that, she only wants her little flower to be okay again. Sherry drops to her knees and grabs her daughter lifeless body in to her arms and squeezes her in to her breast just like she did when Gabriella was first born. "Help...help me please! Oh god this can't happen! Gabriella please just hold on okay. Everything's going to be okay." sherry say's too her dead daughter, refusing to accept reality of her daughter's death in her state of delusion. "Please...please say something Gabriella...please. Oh god I'll do anything, just please, my little flower." sherry sobs and cry's holding her daughter tightly as Gabriella blood drench down her mother's arms and clothes. "Do you need help Mrs.shuford?" Sherry looks up with swollen watered eyes to see a tall handsome Caucasian man with black silk hair, trim cut goatee wearing a very expensive black suit. "Please sir I'll do anything just save my little girl please!" sherry pleads in desperation willing to beg anyone she thinks that could save her precious daughter. "If I save your little girl Mrs.shuford will you pledge to serve me you're very soul if I ask for it ?" "I'll do anything you want me to do mister, just save my little girl please, I'll promise!" sherry yell out still crying, the stress making her look twenty years older than she was. "Mrs.shuford put your daughter's right arm where it supposed to be and continue to hold her tight." the well dress man instruct her. Sherry doesn't ask any questions and do exactly what the man told her to do, no matter what her instants warns her not to do. A good mother would do anything to protect their child. "One day I will be ready to collect Mrs.shuford." He warns the weeping mother. "Just save my Gabriella already damn it! I've told you already!" "Very well Mrs.shuford I won't keep your reunion with your daughter apart any longer." He then place one hand on the girl's forehead, the other hand on the severed arm. within an blink of an eye all of Gabriella bruises and blood was gone, her severed arm was reattach with a light scar. "Mom? Mommy!" Gabriella shouts out in joy to see her mother again as she open her little eyes. "Gabriella! Oh thank you god and your angels!" sherry thanks' god in her excitement. Sherry hugs her little flower with tears of joy in her eyes. "Not god or his angels' Mrs.shuford. They're not the ones that you own." the well dress man said as his eyes glowed green before completely vanishing in to thin air as time unfreezes around them. No one in the crowed witness the well dress man or his miracle. Months from now people will be talking about how a five year old girl survive being run over by an drunken driver with barely a scratch. But not sherry shuford she's the only one who knows The truth about that day. Now she wonder's when that thing that looked like a man will come to collect her soul. Sherry watches her beautiful Gabriella sleep in her bed with no worries in the world. Gabriella is alive and every day that I get to see her I'm grateful, even with the terrible price I have to pay. Sherry is reminded of her deal with the demon all the time she look's in the left palm of her hand, where the mark of six hundred and sixty six branded in to her flesh. The things a mother will do to protect their children. Burns. It burns all over, like my blood is boiling from the inside. Jesus...it's...it's like that time in South America all over again. "Aaahh...fuck!" Jessie slumps down in the rainy streets of Manhattan from the burning hot pain spreading throughout his entire body. Natasha stood before Jessie and place her hand on his cheek, easing his pain. "I am sorry for the unpleasant pain you felt Jessie brown. I've forgotten how painful teleportation can be for humans." Natasha apologizes as she heals his pain. "Those pains bring back unpleasant memories? Would you like a drank Jessie?" a fake smile spread across Norwell's face as he prays on Jessie's weakness of alcohol that he uses to buries his pain and sorrow with. You humans filth disgust me with all their sins, hiding behind alcohol and drugs trying to escape the pain that most of you Inflected on yourselves. "Norwell why do you temp him!" Natasha snaps at Norwell. "If he's going to be a disciple of God he needs to plunge this sin of self pity from his soul!" Norwell snaps back. "Norwell this is not..." "It's okay Natasha." Jessie interrupted. "He's right. I'll be okay, I can handle it." Jessie spoke as he stood up from his knees, soak and wet from the rain. It's okay. Black out the pain soldier. Jessie tries to stay focus as old memories flood his thoughts as he remembers being held capture in south America by a small group of gorilla soldiers. Jessie remembers the hot damp humility inside his captures man made cave. The burned human flesh embedded in the wooden boards that covered the artificial cave walls. Remember how both of his hands bonded above his head by rusted iron chain's as his naked body hanged there, completely soak and wet with two iron claps attached to his chest that were connected to an old car battery charger. two soldiers threw another gallon of water on Jessie's body. "Hey American nigger give us the position of your American friends and I'll let you live." the commander said in bad English. PROOF! Jessie spit's a chunk of blood in the commander's face from his busted lip. "Fuck you!" The commander's smile's as he wipe's the blood off his face. "Good, good we haven't had a spirited nigger in a while." "wwah-hh!" Jessie screams in agonizing pain as bolts of electricity electrifies him throughout his entire body. Shit the burn marks on my chest still burns till this day. "Are you well Jessie?" Natasha ask Jessie as he stared in to space lost in old memories. "Yeah...I'm fine. Why are we in downtown Manhattan?" Jessie asked Natasha as he snap back in too reality from his nightmarish memories of his days as an soldier. Natasha points her soak hand across the street towards a small stone church. "There Jessie brown, is our sanctuary. All darkness is cast from this holy place. Here you shall learn the ways of the light which is our lord and savior Yahweh, God of all there is in heaven and earth." Natasha preaches to Jessie, grabbing his arm. "We must go now Jessie for the darkness seeks to taint what lies in your soul." Natasha eagerly pulls Jessie across the street towards the church. "Natasha hold on a minute I don't quite understand what..." "Listen!" Norwell yelled at Jessie interrupting him. "Natasha words are too holy for something like you to understand so I will lower my grace by translating it in a way that even you would Comprehend." "Norwell there is no need to be insulting!" she jumps to Jessie defense. "No...it's okay Natasha let him finish. I think I understand his feelings towards me." He's an angel too, so he properly knows all the sin I've commended in my life time. The army, the strip clubs. Jesus looked how they found me, completely drunk. just like the damn alcoholic that I am, how can he not be disgusted of me. Jessie looks down towards the ground feeling unworthy to be in the presence of god's angels. "Do not pity you're self for sins of your past. Embrace the light of your future with the lord and savior our heavenly father Jessie brown." Natasha lifts his head up to meet her eyes giving Jessie self worth once more as the rain continues to drench their bodies in front of the small church. "Like I was saying before this pity festival started. Natasha was trying to tell you this church will be your new home and more importantly no hell spawns like the engineer you were about to sell your soul to for a life time of filthy pleasures can't enter this church. Therefore he can't interfere with you learning how to use the abilities that god blessed you with but while you remain outside this church all of hell can go after you, is that explanation simple enough for you?" Norwell insults Jessie. Norwell fist's tightens, his angry face expression is hiding in the Darkness of his hooded cloak. "Yeah... I understand perfectly." I can't see his face with all this rain in my eyes ,with that hood he hide's his face under but I can feel his hate radiant Off his body like heat from a furnace. Enough hate to kill someone and am one to know because I've done Plenty of it. May god forgive me that I've done so much to make an angel feel like this towards me. "Come Jessie and Norwell." Natasha said as she open's the church doors. Norwell and Jessie walk's in to what would be there new sanctuary. Inside the church space was much larger then it appeared from outside. there were four rows of cherry oak wooden seats that could easy fit Sixty to seventy people on each side of the church. The center of the church had a large platform also made from cherry oak wood, A polonium stood in middle. There weren't a crucifix to be found inside the church to Jessie's surprise. To the far right of the polonium stood two large cherry oak double doors. "To whom enters thy sanctuary?" A strong woman's voice spoke through the double doors. "It is I Valery, Natasha and Norwell we've come with a special guest for you to meet." Natasha responded to the woman's voice behind the double doors. The double doors opens wide. A tall sandy brown curly hair Caucasian woman wearing thin Prada glasses with a silk white button down blouse that hug tight on her size D cup breast, and a tight long black shirt wearing black pump Prada shoes. In her right hand was an ancient bible, In her left hand she held a thick gold chain, trying to keep it from bouncing off her breast when she walk's. "Natasha! Norwell! It's been centuries! What's brought thy joyfulness upon thee?" Valery smiles over joy to see such old friends. "It's been to long my dear sweet Valery. I see you still have a taste for fashion." Norwell smiled for the first time since entering the realm of earth. "Thank you Norwell, a woman shall never lose thy joy in such fine material." Norwell brighten her smile. Natasha also smiles along as she pulls off her hood from her head. "It's is always a joy to embrace your light my dear friend." Natasha greeted Valery as she begins to introduce her special guest. "I have brought the one god have's sent me for Valery." "Hi Ms. Valery. I'm the special guest Natasha keeps talking about. My name is Jessie brown, I appreciate you welcome me in here like this." Jessie introduces himself while placing his hand out to shake hers. "Jessie...brown?!" Valery said his name coldly as her beautiful smile became a frown. Her eyes turned in to those of a seasoned soldier whom has accomplish many killing missions and about to commence another one. "Angel of silence thy shall slay thee in the name of our heavenly Father that thy serve!" Valery yells her warrior battle cry as she un Holst her golden chain that turned in to an swinging scythe. She's swings it at my head before I have chance to move. "Die spawn from Satan's seed!" KLANK! Inches from certain death an ancient sword blocks the Path of the scythe of death, which would have Clearly decapitated Jessie brown's head. Protects him with her sword, keeping Valery scythe from reaping her death prize. "What have thy done? Even now he sins for its master Satan as he speaks!" "What are you fucking crazy lady! I'm the one sinning? You just tried to fucking split my head open with a scythe, and you talk about me sinning because I'm fucking cursing you crazy bitch!" Jessie curses out Valery as Natasha and Valery continues there battle in a stalemate. None willing to make the next offensive move not wanting to maim or kill each other. "Natasha look how thee sin in thy sanctuary. He shows his true self." "Valery you tried to execute him. He's only human. It is natural for them to act in such a way in crisis situation like this." Valery slightly turns her attention towards Norwell. "Norwell why thee is standing still as a statue. You are an archangel be rid of him! Why thy haven't slay it yet?" Valery ask him. Norwell shrugged both of his shoulders. "My mission was not to be rid of the angel of silence Valery. If so I would have done so many hours ago...it is the duty of Natasha." Norwell answer somewhat amuse how stubborn Natasha has become over this human filth. "Thy have not fulfill thy oath to god! Now be rid of the angel of silence Natasha!" Valery pleaded. "I've pledge thy oath as a warrior of god's throne that I shall spread thy wings across thy sanctuary and come with all thy might if thy don't yield!" Valery gives her fellow angel sister one last warning. "NO I shall not yield Valery! I also shall spread the light of my wings across this holy sanctuary and bring it down with our battle cries, in to the belly of hell, with our blades stained with angels blood that would put the darkest demon to shame with the sins I shall commit to protect him!" Natasha stands her ground. "God entrusted me with the angel of silence to do what I theme best. To fight me is to fight god's wishes!" Natasha eyes tears up with sorrow to have to face a fellow angel, hoping her words will get through to her sister while showing she is willing to kill or die to fulfill what god has entrust her to do. All is silent in the sanctuary as the two female angels lock eyes. "....I've have error my dear sister may you forgive me Natasha?" Valery stands down as her scythe turns back into a regular gold chain. "Of course my dear Valery all is already forgiven." Natasha accepts Valery apology as they together extend both of their arms out and embrace each other in a hug. "Like hell! What kind of shit is this huh? You mother fuckers was sent to kill me like some god damn assassins! What kind of god do shit like that? I trusted you Natasha!" Jessie turns his back as he heads to exit the sanctuary door. "Jessie stop please I...I don't.." Natasha struggles to utter her words. "I don't what? I don't want to kill you is what you're trying to say is it? You're going to kill me if I walk out this door Natasha?" Jessie questioned her, his body now becomes harden, his senses and instincts are on high Alert, wired like the true seasoned soldier that he was but Jessie eyes tell a different story, A story of a man who been through too much sorrow in his life time and ready to put an end to it all. May be dying here would be for the best. Jessie thought "Jessie I am sorry for not telling you all there is to know." Natasha approaches Jessie as she apologies. "There is a war going on between light and darkness, good and evil, heaven and hell for the love and souls of humanity. For you are the precious gifts of god's love. There is only one or the other, god or Satan. staying here is choosing god, out there in the darkness is choosing Satan. Tears ran down Natasha's face. All Jessie's life no one had ever shed tears over him accept for his late mother Jennise brown. She was the only person who ever cared about me until she died from breast cancer when I was sixteen years of age. Although Jessie known Natasha for only a few hours, she has shown more emotion and love for him than anyone else he known in his entire life besides his mother... Jesus she was willing to die for me just a few minutes ago, what am I thinking? "Jessie.." Natasha calls him as he held her hand tightly. "Say no more Natasha. I chose you, I chose god." Both Natasha and Jessie eyes swell in tears of joy, hugging each other. All is joyous in Valery's sanctuary, All accept the angel who hides in the back shadows of the church. Allowing the darkness to dwell in his soul. Norwell hate grows like a cancer in his heart towards the human filth that contaminated his precious Natasha like a disease. Spreading pathos like a plague. But soon, somehow Natasha will be cleanse of this disease called the Angel of silence.

CHAPTER FOUR

It's a cold Chile night but you wouldn't know that if you were living in corrections officer commissioner's house. David McDonald sat on his plastic covered coach, dress in a white stained t-shirt and Boxer's on drench in sweat form having the thermometer on To high. "Phoww. Let's see what mess up shit is going on in the world today." The overweight commissioner passed gas as he turn on his television. "This is April O'Connor on T.W.X eight reporting live from a small private Community in upstate New York. Seven people were murder to night; three of the victims were also rape before being killed...I've just got a report that one of the rape victims... Was a child...the names and faces of the victims has been disclose for now until police can further investigate." McDonald heard on the news. "Jesus Christ man!" McDonald turned off the T.V Man that was some fuck up shit. Almost ruined my entire night. That commute aren't too far from here to, going grab a cold one and call It a night. CRASH! McDonald looked towards his stair case as he heard the breaking sound of glass coming from his bedroom upstairs. "The hell!" McDonald shouted as he walks up with caution towards the living room Stair case that leads directly to his bedroom. Damn it! It better not be Ms. Cunningham rotten, bad ass kids again. I swear if they broke my fucking window. "Ah shit!" he curses looking at shatter glass all over his carpet bed room floor. "Are you kidding me! Are you fucking kidding me!" McDonald yelled in anger. He pick up the brick with a note attach to it by a shoestring. "Fucking kids going do time in juvie for this shit...going leave me a note. Break my shit and taunt me! I'll show those little fuckers." McDonald opens the note as he reads his anger dwindle in to fear. The letter reads: Glad to see that you're still alive, you fat bastard. Told you and that sweet mouth nurse I'll be back best to believe it. ALBERT HOUSTON. "You boys think this shit is funny?" McDonald screams out his broken window. "Isn't no boy doing's commish." McDonald heard a impossible voice echo through his bedroom, it had to be impossible because that voice sounded like a dead man who died five years ago by lethal Ejection. A man named Albert Houston. It took all of the commissioner will power from shitting on himself. "Albert...is that you?" McDonald asked, voice shaken from fear. "Best to believe it. Hey commish how did you like my handy work on that little community back there, what's you call it?" "The Mitchell's apartment's complex. You did that?" "Yeah. Killed some poor bastard who thought he was saving me from Drowning in the rain, struggle him to death then fucked his wife and struggled her. Bitch died to fast, didn't get time to get off so I drop by their neighbor's house. Maim the father's hands and feet as he watch crying and bagging me to stop fucking his wife and daughter..... yeah...best to believe we took our time with that." Albert explained "You sick son of a bitch! How the fuck are you still alive?" McDonald yelled out as he walked over to his bedroom draw and started loading up his three forty five magnum revolver. You just keep on talking you stupid son of a bitch as I load my gun and blow your ass back to hell, for good this time. "Haven't you been listening? I came back from hell and I have all eternally to fuck and slaughter as many people as I want. Isn't it fucking great!" Albert gloats from a unknown space with in the apartment. I don't know how this bastard survived his execution but I do know that voice that's Albert Houston for sure. Unfortunate I can't pin down the location his voice is coming from, but there's only one way to get to this bedroom and that's up those steps and through this door. McDonald close's his bedroom door gently then takes ten steps back and crouch down in an marksman position, weapon loaded ready to kill. Completely ready for Albert's attack. Stupid asshole so full of your own shit. Should have killed me while I wasn't aware, You won't get that chance now. "Enough of the bullshit Houston! You waited five years for this. Come in fucking get it!" McDonald challenges. A exploding burst of glass shattered behind David McDonald. "you best to believe I will!" Albert leaps through the broken window landing directly behind McDonald. the warrant felt the tiny shards of broken glass pierce the flesh on his back and quickly spun around to face his enemy, completely disregarding his pain and keeping his nerves in check like the true professional he was. Unfortunate David's best wasn't enough to ward off Albert's Houston's attack. Albert's knife cuts deep, completely severed McDonald leg slicing through the joints of his knee. "Shit old man! I didn't think a fat bastard like you could move that fast. Only if you could of lost another eight pounds huh warrant?" Albert taught. "warrant?" Albert looked shocked to see the warrant on the ground holding his chest, wrenching in surreal pain. "The fuck! Don't you do it you fat bastard! Don't you fucking die on me yet! Best to believe I'm not done with your ass yet!" Albert Houston shouted at the dying correction warrant in disbelief. McDonald grabs and pulls on his bloodied t-shirt as he gasp for air. Then he laid still and everything was silent. David McDonald was dead. Albert Houston looked down at the now dead warrant's body stun. Albert Houston couldn't believe the warrant just died from a heart attack. You old fat fuck! I didn't wait five fucking years to watch you die from a fucking heart attack! "You fat pussy!" Albert slam's his butcher knife in to the decease McDonald's head with such force causing his forehead to explode in to chucks of flesh, jamming his blade in to carpet floor. "you got off real easy warrant. Best to believe we're going to have the best of times with good old nurse Jones." Albert Houston fantasize as he chop up the corpse of David McDonald to leave a message for all to see. The warrant was a bit oversize best to believe I had to cut him down a few sizes. ALBERT HOUSTON WAS HERE. Stan Johnson is an thirdly eight year man whom many people would considered obese, other than that Stan is no different from any other average American. I work a normal nine to five job and go to church three times a week while praising god every day of the week since I've been fourteen years old. So why is this happening to me? Stan thoughts flurried through his mind as his awkward body run's panicky down the streets of new York city. He can hear them getting closer, howling an unearthly sound yawning to tear in to my flesh. Demon hounds from hell and the only place I can be safe is in my old church, Valery sanctuary. The streets of lower Manhattan is completely deserted. Deep down in his soul Stan knows they're all dead. Slaughter and rip apart in the beds of their own homes. There's no one that can save him, only the power of god can save his mortal soul and only if he can make it to the sanctuary. "RRRAAAHAA!" the demons howls ran sheer horror down Stan's spine as he heard the hordes of hell rampaging down the streets ever so closer to devouring his flesh. Stan looks over his shoulders, the demons were close enough now that Stan could make out some of their features. There were six of them. It had the head of a lion with the body of an spike beast, its claws thick black and Sharpe enough to tear holes in to the cemented ground as they ran through the street's hunting him. No! No! They're catching up! God please help me I'm only a block away....I could make it... I can make it, I can make it. "Ggrrah!" Stan grunted in pain. one of the hell hounds tore in to Stan's back with its talon's ripping deep chucks of flesh. For the first time in Stan's life he felt an bolt of adrenaline pump throughout his body. He ignored the enormous pain that ran through every once in his exposed back, he ignored every fiber of his being that told him to yield, to give up. For the first time in his life Stan wasn't going to give in to the pain, he wasn't going to die. Stan large body picked up speed and ran as if he was a track and field star. Stan saw the front steps of Valery's sanctuary and jumps completely over the four large steps with an single leap, stumbling in to the church's door. God please let it be open! Let it be open! Stan prayed as he slammed his shoulder in to the double doors praying that they weren't lock. "Help me please! Valery! Valery!" Stan cried out, his heavenly legs finally giving out stumbling to the floor as the double doors gives in. "You are safe here Stan. No demons may enter through these doors." Stan heard the Familiar voice that he recognizes to be Sister Valery's and he knew all was well. Stan quickly lift's his head up to meet the precious woman, who just saved his life, To thank her for opening her doors to him. "What is this?" a confused Stan said as he witness every seat packed with people he knew, every day church goer's like him and with people he never meet in his life. All who were branded with some ancient mark on their foreheads. something told him it was the mark of god, Valery was the one who really shocked Stan as he watched her with awe and fear. he saw her standing before the podium wings spread across both ends of her sanctuary holding the scythe in her right hand. "Do not fear Stan Johnson fore on this day we all walk with god. Come to me child for your soul can be saved and live among the angels of god's kingdom." Valery summons him. "Yes! Thank you! Thank you god almighty my lord and savior, I want to be saved!" Stan shouts and prayed out to the lord as he walked towards Valery, all the pain throughout his body was gone, healed by this glorious sanctuary of god's kingdom. "kneel down Stan Johnson for the lord can give you passage." Valery commanded. Stan obeyed and kneel on both of his knees praying to the lord. Valery rise's her scythe high above her head. "Ask the lord to forgive thy sins with the spill of thy blood for the gates of heaven to be open for thy soul." Stan heard Valery's prayers and opened his eyes to witness a brand new type of horror. "No! Noo! Wait, what are you doing Sister Valery?" "I am saving your soul from the eternal pits of hell, for these are the end of days. Armageddon is upon us and we all must be judge." Valery explained. "I want to go to heaven but I don't want to die like this. I was always faithful to god. I went to this very church here four times a week, praised god every day. I'm a good person why can't my life be spared like the others who sits in this very church? Why?" Why are you doing this to me god? I praised and served you all my life...I didn't run and crawl my way here just to die anyway." Stan wept. Valery slowly lowers her scythe, stopping the would be execution of Stan Johnson. "Yes it is true Stan Johnson that you are a good person but only the most faithful can enter the kingdom of heaven without consequences. Stan you had worship the lord everyday but you did not followed all that he demanded of you, fore you have living your life as a homosexual without any guilt for thy sin. God is giving you another chance to enter his kingdom among the heavens with the end of your old life, you shall begin a better one in the gates of heaven." Valery explained as she weld her scythe of death above her head to descend it up on Stan in order to end his existence for he can begin a new one. "Time to choose Stan Johnson heaven or hell? Enteral salvation or eternal damnation?" Valery swings her scythe down to decapitate Stan's head. I don't want to die, oh, god I don't want to die but I can't burn in hell for all eternally. "Aaahhh!" Stan screamed in horror as he prepares for the scythe to end his life. ....Stan Johnson waits for the end, his eyes closed tight, and hands clinch to his thighs. And he waits and he waits but there was nothing. Stan slowly opens his eyes. To Stan's surprise he finds himself on top of the roof of Valery's sanctuary. "What? What the hell is going on?" a puzzle Stan said out loud to himself. "Well, it's a second chance at life Mr. Johnson." Stan heard an elegant voice answer him from somewhere above his head. he looked up and saw an angel with black wings descend from the sky on to the roof where he stood wearing only a well design pair Of black slacks and fresh cut goatee. "who or what are you?" a frighten Stan ask backing away from the black wing angel. "I am a angel whom can grant you a better life then what you been living. A world where you don't have to choose, a world where you can be free to be yourself." ".....more like a fallen angel, why should I listen to anything you have to say?" "I knew you were a smart man Mr. Johnson. You are correct I am a fallen angel. I am known as the engineer, I came here to offer you a better life." he admitted. "You're a demon how can you offer me anything that's good?" "I can offer you more then what she's offering you Mr. Johnson, and you wouldn't have to die for it nether." "And why should you die anyway Mr. Johnson. for what reasons? must you die for simply being gay. you didn't ask to be gay, you didn't want this. you were born this way Mr.johnson. just the way God made you, but yet he punishes you if you give in to who you truly are." Stan stood silent for the first time a loss of words, the engineer sees him desperately trying to find the right words to say as he continues on. "Don't lust, don't sleep with the same sex, don't sin god says but yet he made you yearn for these very things because it is in your blood, god design's you to be exactly what he says it's wrong to be. Human life is a constant struggle against your nature, god is nothing more than our torture whom enjoys watching us squirm trying to please his torturous demands." the engineer preach. for the first time in Stan Johnson's life, he finds himself questioning his faith. "you..you might be right but what difference does it makes, in the end you lose. Lucifer, you, all of you burn in the lake of fire for eternally in hell. I can't take that, I can't take that kind of pain...I rather die now and live in peace in heaven then living through that kind of torture for all eternally." Stan said surprising the engineer. Things wasn't turning out how he planned. if he was going to win Stan's soul he had to figure out something now. "What if I told you that the revelations ending in the bible was a lie?" A sarcastic smile rose up from Stan's face. "I would say you're a big liar Mr. Engineer or whatever your name is." I was wondering when you would show your true colors demon. Stan thought. "Whatever you may believe Mr. Johnson. We are not allowed to lie. We may manipulating the truth by throwing in our own personal views or simply leave certain parts of the truth out, remember Lucifer never lied to Adam and eve." he explained. "yeah he just forgot to mention the most important part, if you ate from the tree of life you will surely die. so tell me what truths are you hiding from me?" the engineer walks straight at Stan, Stan stumbles barely keeping himself upright "Don't be afraid Mr. Johnson but listen very carefully because you will learn what only a handful of people know in this world. Armageddon is not determine. heaven and hell both have their own versions of the bible but in both it is said there will be a last prophet whom name shall be called Dumah the angel of silence. the side the angel of silence shall chose will determine the fate of Armageddon. "I..I never read anything like that in the bible?" "Of course not Mr. Johnson the true bible was created by god's hands not man. it is an book of pure magic, it writes it's self when major events occurs in heaven, earth or hell. this book was giving to every angel in god's inner circle which included his son Lucifer. One was also giving to mankind many centuries ago. Men who were supposed to honor the word of god took what they wanted from the bible to give themselves power and hide the rest away from all of mankind." Stan collapse to his knees, crying in despair of hopelessness. "I..I can't believe this...I don't understand what do this prophet have to do with me?" "Mr. Johnson if the angel of silence die, god won't win Armageddon. if god doesn't win Armageddon you don't have to die, you will live for all of eternally here on earth being True to yourself with no judgment." "What? Are you telling me the only thing that's keeping you from winning the war is the Angel of silence?...why don't you just kill him?" "I can't. No angel or demon can harm the living but you're human, you can. He's a African American man named Jessie brown he now resides in Valery sanctuary the very place were standing on. The time has come for you to make your final decision Mr. Johnson." the engineer said as he ascended above the stars in the night sky. I don't want to die but I can't just kill some-one in cold blood. I'm not a murderer, I'm not a monster. shit I don't think I could kill in self defense, why would he tell me this? What the hell am I supposed to do now. "Engineer! Wait! Wait!" Stan pleaded out towards the fall-ing angel whom was beyond his sight not noticing the roof top underneath his feet were starting to cave in until it was already too late. "No! Noooo!" Stan felled through the crumbing roof slamming hard on to the sanitary wooden alter floor, badly bruising his back. "May god receive your soul in heaven amend." Stan looked up and saw Valery swing down the scythe of death that will end his life on earth. No I want to live! I don't want to die, I don't want to die! "No! I chose him! I chose Lucifer please!" Stan screamed as he raised up from his wet sheets body completely drenched in sweat. "Oh god...thank you god it was just a dream. Just a stupid nightmare." Stan thanked god as he took in an deep breath and exhale it. Stan then wipes the hot sweat off his forehead and notice Something swollen on his wrist. "The hell is this?" I must have hit my wrist on something hard somehow during my nightmare. Stan thought as he looks at the inner side of his left wrist to further examine it. A sick, dreadful feeling wash over Stan's body as he saw the mark of the beast six hundred and sixty six branded in to the flesh of his left wrist. that very moment he knew his visions wasn't some terrible nightmare but of the future that's yet to come and the only way from burning in hell for eternally, he have's to kill Jessie brown the angel of silence. Stan sat there in his bed crying, thinking for hours as his boss calls wanting to know why he didn't make it to work today. What they don't know is that stand Johnson won't be returning to work. Stan Johnson will never work again. Valery sanctuary., deep in the back room of Valery's private chambers. Valery stands still watching her special wall made from pure obsidian black stone. In curved inside the obsidian with purple gems were the names of all the falling angels Valery has slain in the great war of heaven, Two hundred thousand and seven hundred. Every time she looks upon this wall it reminds her why she has chosen to watch over the earth then serve in the kingdoms of heaven. so many brother and sisters I've sent to the ether, I was so consume in murder that even in earth my choice of weaponry became known as the scythe of death or the reaper. I don't know when I will find the strength to walk among kingdoms of heaven with so much blood on my hands. Valery thought. Valery heard the hard knocks on her chamber doors snapping Valery out of her depressing thoughts. she quickly closes the door to her private shame and approaches the more public domain of her chambers. Valery enters her main chamber that was made from the most finest riches of the world. the walls of her chambers was made out of pure black onyx. Valery office desk was also made from black onyx with gold edges and legs. her chairs were made from black croc skin with gold arm stands. Valery had three chandelier above her desk down to the entrance of the door made from pure diamonds. Her titles alternated from onyx and gold. Four six foot platinum lamps. One at each end of her chambers corners with black cobra skin as lamb shades. the office doors were made of cherry oak Valery's favorite type of wood. Every piece of mineral and fabric that was in Valery chamber's was over five thousand years old, which made every item in her office priceless historic relics. No human has ever witness the richest of Valery's inner sanctuary fore they might be consumed by greed. Valery sits down behind her desk, legs crossed as her arms rested on her golden arm-stands. "Come in Norwell." Valery answered the door.

"you knew it was me huh...this chamber it reminds me of home." Norwell looked amaze as he enter Valery chambers for the first time. "This room reminds me of the chapels of heaven, you never cease to amaze me Valery." Norwell sits down. "Yes thank you Norwell, it's been centuries since the last time I've walked inside heavens kingdom so I had to make my new home appear a little like heaven." Norwell smile quickly turns in to a frown. "I don't know how you can stand it Valery. For you to live among filth for all these centuries is beyond my comprehension, I've only been here for a few hours and already I feel contaminated by all they're sin and self greed." Norwell felt pity for his fellow angel as he admitted his dislike for the entire human race. "Do not feel pity for me Norwell, because there isn't anything to feel sorry about my fellow brother Norwell. I will admit at first mankind took some time for me to get used to. Violence, lust and greed is embedded in the Very flesh of mankind they are born to begot sin but I've have learned why god have such faith in them Norwell." "Is that so then please enlighten me my fellow sister for I surly can't see why god or anyone Else would have faith in such selfish sinful creatures." Norwell asked. "Remember mankind's very flesh and blood is embedded with sin, it's a constant struggle every day to fight the sins of flesh. For any man or woman to constantly fight off the temptations of flesh why dedicating their lives towards a god that they don't know truly existence but still have complete faith in him is beyond anything I've witness. The will power of humanity is stronger than any angels, we all have serve and walked the fields of heaven, seen god with our own eyes and yet at the Slightest taste of sins pleasures a third of heaven angels felt, you know this yourself for your brother Nataa was one among the many." "Enough! don't you dare say his angelic name in my presence!" Norwell slammed his fist on top of Valery's desk enraged by her commits and the use of his brother's birth name. Valery's legs uncrossed as she sat up straight in her chair, both of her hands laid calm on her desk as she stared down Norwell eyes. All it took was a glance in to Valery's eyes and he knew he made a great mistake, for she may look calm to most by he could feel the murdering aura of death emulating from her soul. like a caged beast whom haven't ate in a long time. Norwell began to understand why she is known as Valery the goddesses of death all throughout heaven and hell. "...please..forgive me sister Valery, when I hear my brother's name..his real name I feel such shame and anger, I was wrong to unleashed my grief and anger up on you. I am sorry." Norwell apologize his head down in shame for his outburst. Valery folds her hands together underneath her chin. "All is forgiven Norwell, but don't you ever smite my possession again. This material was around when one could simply walk to the garden of Eden, one could not go and simply replace such relics of gold and onyx, if you were to break anything here would put me in a very dark place indeed." Valery sights as she takes a deep breath of air calming her nerves. "Well to more important matters such as your brother the engineer, I'm assuming this is why you're here isn't it?" Valery questioned. "yes, our general Michael sent me here put an stop to him, which I wanted to do sense that day I failed, and he felled with Lucifer and the rest of the forbidden angels. Before this day he always was a salesman praying on humans lust and greed. there isn't nothing against the rules of conduct between human and demon so why now? Because he approach the angel of silence?" "No. as you already know both sides of heaven and hell are allowed to have agents among the living but they cannot force, attack or harm them in any way in their physical forms but you're brother found a way to bend the rules by resurrection one of his mark souls. A human known as Albert Houston, even as we speak he rampages slaughtering people. we believe once this murder finish killing the people he felt crossed him in his past life the engineer will send him after the other mark souls, kill them and resurrected them." "creating an army of hell spawns on earth and because they're aren't native of hell or heaven they can take human lives before there natural time. Harvesting massive amount of souls for hell before Armageddon even begun." a frightened looked cross Norwell's face. "Not only that Norwell but because of the amount of hell spawns roaming the earth heaven would have to break the rules sending an army of archangels to invade the earth." "jump starting Armageddon!" Norwell finished her sentence. "yes hearing you say it out load confirms to me this mission is of most importance. if you need of my assistance I am here." Valery offer her help. "No he is my brother, I and I alone will bring his soul to the pits of hell to regain our family honor." Norwell stood up from the chair and reach inside his robe and hands Valery a scroll. "Here is my seal of hunter ship. I shall start my hunt at dawn, I shall be in my quarters until then." Norwell started to walk towards the door. "Norwell my brother please I've seen this kind of hurt and rage before. do not let thy dislike for humanity or quest for honor to fill your heart of hatred, Don't allow the darkness to swallow thy soul." Valery warned Norwell, he stood still as he listened to her words then left her chambers without saying an single word. Valery said an prayer for her dear friend. Sixteen years ago South America, location classified. I hate this god damn jungle why the fuck a military specialist have to hunt down some foreign kingpin anyway what a fucking waste of time. Jessie thought to himself. "Hey tony bet you can't wait to get your ass back to the city?" Jessie asked Tony Abe clemente born in the Bronx, New York, Jessie's Brown best friend. Tony and Jessie stood next to each other in an nameless village on guard as they're fellow troops ask the locals some questions. "it's not that bad bro, I'm getting tired of the hustle and bustle life style you know what I mean. maybe I'll settle down and get a chicka down here feel me." tony smiled at his friend. "shit are you crazy, isn't enough meat on these girls. if you want a fly Spanish chick take your pick in the Bronx man." "Na. I had enough of those type of girls bro. I need a old fashion traditional girl that I can have a whole bunch of kids with living around nature in a house, Not all stuff up in some two bedroom apartment in the city know what am saying bro?" "shit man you can do that in Puerto Rico or the D.R man. Not in some nameless shit hole in south America some-where." Jessie shoved tony in the arm jokingly. "Yeah my mother sure would love if i brought a young old fashion Puerto Rican girl home." "That's what I'm talking man and when you go make sure you take me with you. Bet those girls won't know what to do with their selves once they laid eyes on this heresy chocolate." Tony and Jessie both laugh out loud enjoying each other's company. "cholite! cholite!" a little girl ran towards Jessie and tony in nothing but a dirty black t-shirt that ran down to her knees. "Damn tony man. no cholite! no cholite! scram kid!" Jessie shouted out. "chill bro. I got a chocolate candy bar for you little mommie" tony reach inside his utility pocket on his chest and pulled out a snicker bar. "come on man! if you feed one of them more are going to come this way man begging for shit!" "Jessie chill the hell out man she's like only three years old. They ain't stray animals in the street these are little children that can't help where and how they live. girl probity never had a candy bar before. so chill the hell out." tony told off his friend as he knelt down to rub the top of the little girl's head. "cholite! cholite pleases!" she asked showing a big smile that melt Tony's heart. "say cho-co-late, cho-co-late" tony pronounce to the little girl. "cho-o-late, chocolate please!" she smiled again. "close enough, here you go little princess." tony unwraps the candy bar and hands it to the girl, that's when he notices a lump in the back of her shirt as the girl bit in to the candy bar. "the hell is that?" tony said to himself as he open the back of the girl's collar in saw a flashing Red light. "Tony get outta of there! She's strap! The children are strap!" Jessie warns his unit as he ran for cover. " What kind of monster would strap an explosive to a three year old child!" tony grab the child and pulls out his combat knife to cut her free of the device while the little girl cries out for her mommy. "Tony what the fuck are you doing! Get the fuck away from her before she blows!" Jessie yelled out. "I got to cut her free man, she's a little girl! I can't let her die like this!" tony tries to cut off the c-four while Jessie sprints towards them hoping once he tackles them the momentum will clear them far enough from the c-four explosive. "I think I gtt....." Jessie brown felt a hard impact of hot air knocking him back off his feet. All he saw was red and black spots, his body felt wet ,thick and heavy, loud ringing sounds consumed his hearing. the taste of blood filled his mouth. "uuuhhh...tony...TONY!" Jessie called out as his eye vision starts to return back to normal. "Tony...tony where are you...tony cough..cough!" Jessie stumbles around the area where tony and the little girl were standing. All there was left was a crater full of smoke and fire ...and Chucks of blood. Jessie look's down at himself and saw a scene of horror of blood and gore. Jessie's brown entire uniform was drench in it. Oh god! Oh god! Tony is all over me! Oh god he's all over me! Jessie swaps at his clothing as chucks of flesh and blood spills on the ground. "Tony! Tonyyy! Oh god I'm sorry! I'm sorry!" Jessie screams out waking from his sleep. Jessie drench in cold sweat falls out of the king size bed inside one of Valery's guess chambers. "No, no I can't do this! I need to forget please god make me forget." Jessie pleads to god as he crawls across the floor, His entire body aches of pain like a thousand needles being stab throughout his body all at once. I have to get outta here, I need to numb the pain, I need my whiskey. "god I'm sorry I need my whiskey, I can't do this." "God has heard your prayers Jessie brown, Do not despair my child." Jessie looked up and saw the beautiful angel known as Natasha looking down at him but not of eyes of sorrow but of love. "Rise to your feet Jessie brown." Natasha asked. Jessie looks back down to the floor, slapping his hand on the ground in frustration as he weeps. "I can't I'm sorry! You pick the wrong person Natasha I'm nothing but a lonely drunk, I can't take the pain, the memories are too much please... please." Jessie felt a soft gentle hand underneath his chin, lifting his head up. "Rise your head Jessie brown for god have seen your pain and all is forgiven." Natasha said as she looked Jessie in the eyes as she knelt down on both knees to meet him. "please make the pain go away Natasha, please make it go away." Jessie reaches out and tightly Hugs Natasha, completely surprising her causing her wings to extend out of her back. Natasha felt a hot flash rise over her body, she never felt such raw emotion before. "please..Natasha..please" Jessie held her tighter. Natasha slowly and gently wraps her hands around Jessie's head and back as a mother would their child. "ssshhh Jessie god is here with you...I'm here with you." Natasha notices Jessie had heard her words and felled a sleep in her breast. All your pain, all your suffering was ease with just a simple hug of pure love. Natasha wrapped her wings around them both as they slept embracing each other in a hug.

CHAPTER FIVE

I t's happening all over again. A once precious innocent angel falling in to the pits of sin, I refuse to bare witness to another beloved angel descending to this endless trap of sin. A trap created by the angel of silence. Norwell decided to say goodnight to Natasha after his brief conversation with Valery but saw that she wasn't no longer in her bedroom, so he went to the angel of silence chambers and witness one of the horrific things he ever saw in his life time. An angel embracing a human as they sleep together, is something I thought I would never see Natasha do. It's one thing to pet one on their head or up lift there head's. All angels have some sort of feelings for their subjects, It's the same kind of love that a human have's for their pets but to physical embrace one like this to show this kind of emotion for a sinful human being... Natasha has already falling in to the angel of silence trap. He will drag her down in to the abyss of darkness because I've seen how this story play's out before. Eons ago in the kingdom of heaven. Norwell sharpens the edges of his sword. "why do you bother to sharpen a weapon you never use brother?" my young brother asks me standing in front me in our home palace as I Prepare my blade. "As a archangel one must always be ready to soil one hands against evil Nataa." "But it's only us angels that dwell throughout the universe Norwell, unleash you plan to soil thy hands on giant beast that dwells below in the earth brother?" "the beasts of the earth are strong and savage, I do not believe our father god have taught us the teachings of war to slay simple minded beast Nataa" Norwell explained to his younger brother as Nataa simply just nodes his shoulders. "well if you say so dear brother, are you still planning to come with me to brother Lucifer palace Norwell half of heaven will be there tonight. He said he'll show us things that no angel has never seen before in all of heaven. can you believe that Norwell. it's the talk of heaven right now." Nataa said excitingly. "Unfortunate I won't be able to attend this exciting show by Lucifer little brother. I must attend the meeting of archangels by general Michael today. I'll shall be back in three suns little brother and do not drank too much Spirit, I have heard of brother Lucifer love of the fine grapes in his gathering's." Norwell rubbed the top of Nataa head messing his hair. "Don't worry brother I'll tell you all about it in your returning day." what I didn't know that day is he wouldn't have to tell me anything I would bare witness to his horrific descend from grace. Once I've returned home from my journey's there wasn't no amount of training that would prepare me for what I've have foreseen before my eyes. thud! thud! thud! the sound of flesh being pounded on, being violated from behind as my little brother continues to intrude himself inside the anus of some unknown male angel from the second sphere. I couldn't believe it, right before my eyes Nataa were committing one of the greatest sins laying his semen with another male angel. "what... what have you done?" is all I could bring myself to say as my sword drops from my hands before my legs followed as I felled to my knees in complete shock. "Dear brother you have arrived, please join me, my friend will grant you pleasures that you've never image." Nataa continues to have intercourse with the male angel in front of his older brother Norwell. "Enough! stop this abomination before thy eyes before I smite you both where you stand!" Norwell stood up and shouted out in great rage which he haves never felt before this day. "be gone you, I'll beckon you when the time has come again." Nataa commands the angel to leave his brother and his palace. "this is what's happening in Lucifer's gatherings Nataa, this abomination of sin?" "sin! sin you say! why is it a sin to express your inner desires brother? why should we deny ourselves happiness? this is what our great brother Lucifer has taught us to express and we love him for it!" "you have lost your way brother, Don't let Lucifer temptation's control your actions Nataa...if you report Lucifer actions to the high council and plead for forgiveness it shall be given brother." "Dear brother you really don't understand what's happening, do you? this wasn't some mishap that went too far. we angels in all three spheres of heaven had these feelings balled up inside of us for centuries, and god wouldn't explain why accept for threating us with banishment if we disobey his word. If he felt so god damn strongly against sin then why he created it in the first place. No big brother there's a revolution that's begun and it will change everything that we know. when that time comes Norwell, you will be force to take sides, it has been foreseen." "leave here brother... leave here before I'll sin against my own flesh in blood. Leave now!" My brother left without saying another word, I didn't tell anyone about what happen that day hoping Nataa would find his way again but I was wrong and he was right. All of heaven was made to make a choice between god and Lucifer too my surprise a third of heaven sided with Lucifer way of thinking instead of god whom created them and build heaven for they can dwell in it for all eternally. the next and last time I saw my brother was in the final battle of heavens capital of Zion where he left me with this scar across my eye before his defeat and eternal banishment from heaven. No I would be able to just stand still and bare witness of Natasha fall from grace. Heaven has given me a chance to redeem myself by solely appointing me the task of reaping my falling brother. I can't sabotage my own mission by slaying the angel of silence because I'm afraid Natasha will fall from grace like my brother, No I must go. my god shied you from the sin he will try to befall on to you. Norwell grabs his sword and vanishes in to thin air. Stan Johnson finds himself wondering in the streets of Brooklyn New York, looking for a gun shop. I can't believe this is happing to me, I'm out here eleven o'clock in the morning looking for a gun shop in the middle of Brooklyn to kill some black man I've never met in my life. And for what?! just because I was born gay, I got this fucking mark on my wrist just because I didn't want to die like some fucking animal that needs to be put down, Now I have to burn in hell for all eternally if I don't kill this guy. I...I don't deserve this, I did everything I was supposed to do. I'm a good man I never try to hurt or harm anybody in anyway accept for liking men I guess? Is my sin so great I'll have to be dammed to hell for all eternally, Never ending pain and suffering over, over and over never stopping. Stan grabs his stomach bends over and throws up violently in the middle of the streets. "God oh' God please no, No." Stan said to himself as a few new Yorkers briefly looked on before going by their usual business. Stan can feel the heat in his body build up as the sweat on his forehead pours down his face. The fear of going to hell is starting to overwhelm Stan's body. I can't live like this, I can't be in fear every day of my life. Stan wipes his throw up from his lips with his back hand as he stares at the local gun shop in front of him. "I'm sorry angel of silence but better you then me." Stan said out loud to himself as he enters the shop. The gun shop was small inside, there were three glass counters connected as a half square. inside the counters were all types of hand guns which I had no knowledge of. the walls were all painted in blood red like most people did in seventies, there were shelves full of ammo packages I believe. There were no big weapons on display anywhere within the shop that I could see but I suppose that wouldn't be a big deal any way since I was planning to buy something more easy to handle for a novice like me. But where the hell is the employee at? "Hello, is anyone here? I'm looking to buy something!" Stan called out. "well I'm hoping I'm selling what you need friend. Sorry for the wait." A balled Caucasian man walked out a painted red door behind the counter made to blend in with the rest of the wall. "So how can I help you sir?" he said to me showing off his smile, my god he's so handsome with that beautiful sexy balled head and smile and those tattoos that covers his forearms wearing that button-down Hawaii shirt. Just the type of man I would love to be on top of me but that wouldn't happen, I haven't had a man for the last five years. Stan thought to himself. "Sir are you alright? It seems like you spaced out for a while there?" "what? uhmm.. yeah I was umm interest in a hand gun" Stan said nervously unable to look the store owner In his eyes. "All right so what are you interested in an desert eagle, colt forty five, smith and Wesson?" "o' no, no nothing like that, I don't know much about guns but those sound like those are too powerful for me..uhmm maybe something small like that one over there on your left." "what? the kolibri? I wouldn't think a nice strong man like yourself would be interested in something like that. I would have thought you be in to something big and strong with a lot of weight behind it that you could grip in those big strong hands of yours." What the hell? did he...did he just make a sex reference at me? Some kind of slick ass gay joke that isn't funny. well the hell with you then I'll just take my business elsewhere. "uhmm..you know what , I change my mind. Thank you for your help anyway." Stan said as he turned away from the counter and started to head towards the exit. "No wait don't go! Stan wait!" the gun shop owner shouted as he ran out behind the counter and grab Stan by his arm. "get the hell off of me! Who are you? How the hell you know my name?" Stan questioned the gun owner as he frantically tries to pull his arm free from his grip. "just calm down okay, the angel with the black wings told me that you would come today!" Stan stop trying to pull himself free but now there was a different type of fear that ran through his spine. "what the hell are you talking about? who are you?" Stan questioned him again. "my name is Alex Dondre, the angel he goes by the name of the engineer, he's one of the original two hundred fallen angels who help mankind advancement through life." Alex slowly lets Stan arm go, while holding both of his hands out to show no harm. "Here look at this, I bare the mark as well." Alex rolled up his left sleeve revealing the mark and symbol of the beast six hundred and sixty-six. "Look I'm sorry for what I said to you earlier, I was just really excited to see you. the engineer explains everything to me, you're like an fucking rock star in our community man." Alex said excitingly, it was like he was to talking to an celebrity it wasn't something Stan was use too. "really? so what he explained to you that all your people so excited about me huh?" "Are you kidding me man, you're our savior. you going to save the whole entire world man." "save the world? the fuck! I can't even save my own fucking soul and you think I'm going to save the whole fucking world!" Stan screamed out at Alex more in disbelief then anger at what Alex just explained to him. "look Stan I understand what you going through but you're selling yourself short. you are a very important man whom done nothing but try to please your creator god. but what has he done for you? Nothing but giving you a life full of grief and despair and now you have to burn in some fuck up eternal fire because of whom you chose to sleep with because of who you might fall in love with. No fuck that, god might have been our creator, but he isn't our father." Alex explained and started to head back towards the counter. "Come on Stan. I want to show you something in the backroom. There I can explain everything to you." "Before I'll follow you to the back Alex I need to know why. Why don't you acknowledge god as your Father but accept him as the creator?" Stan stood Still awaiting Alex's answer and if even for a moment He feels his answer is bullshit; he was going to walk right out this door regardless if he burns in hell or not. "Listen I'm not no history professor or some philosopher, but I do know one thing, and that's god created Adam and eve to live in peace and worship him in the Garden of Eden. But just because you give someone life doesn't make you a father. Adam and eve had the minds of children I doubt they would of ever had sex With each other, it took them to eat the forbidden fruit to realize they're were naked for Crying out loud. No everything that we know about life is thanks to Lucifer. He's the one who taught us about science, art, love, lust, war, self pride and self worth. God made us but Lucifer is the one who took care of us. Stan Johnson Lucifer is our true father, everything we are today is thanks to him." shit no one has never broke it down to me like that, now that I think about it, it all make sense now. from the beginning the word was that Lucifer was jealous of us and wanted to commit evil and harm to us. but that's isn't the truth at all if you really think about it he's always be trying to help us, to give us knowledge and power, to give us freedom to be who were meant to be. "yeah, you see it know don't you? I know because I had the same look on my face when I figure it out. you and me are very much the same Stan, a lot more the same then you think." Alex walks to the front door and locks it from the inside and puts the close sign on the door. "Now are you ready to follow me to the back room?" Alex key still inside the keyhole symbolizing that he would open the door and let Stan exit if he's feels differently. "yeah..let's go and see the back room." Stan said wiping the sweet off his pale forehead. "good to hear Stan. good to hear my man." Alex smile at Stan in such an way that cause Stan face to become flesh of embarrassment. man he has such an beautiful smile...no snap out of it Stan this isn't the place or time to thank about romance and with that joke he made earlier, it seems that Alex is a straight man anyway just my luck as usual. Stan fellows Alex behind the counter while he open's the backroom door and walks inside. "welcome to the Alex's den! Hee-Hee." Alex laugh. Stan was amazed to witness the backroom to be room to be twenty five to thirty feet larger than the main store lobby. it was an gunsmith wet dream come true in there. the walls were cover with rpg's, stingers-launchers, flame throwers, shotguns, assault rifle and all different types of grenades. the room was covered with red paint on the walls and red carpet and ground. There was also something strange in the center of the room. It was tall and reach to the sealing with a pointed top, I think it was some kind of pillar like those in ancient Egypt. there in the base of the pillar was a shape of an eight pointed wheel that the pillar was inserted through. "wow Alex! I have to a meant this room is pretty amazing. it's like a N.R.A fantasy or something." "yeah I know right. with the shit in here you can blow the angel of silence away without even stepping in to the front door man." Alex said feeling quit pride of his handy work. "listen Stan..about killing the angel of silence thing. I've never killed no one before, I've never even held a gun in my hand before. I'm just some overweight gay guy who's willing to do anything from burning in hell Alex, that's the truth." Stan looked down to floor afraid to see the rage or disappointment in Alex eyes. Alex lifts Stan head up with his index finger to look him in the face. "you're wrong Stan, you are a great man that can achieve great things and the weapon training is why I'm here. you're be more bad ass then Rambo when I'm done with you plus I like some extra meat on my bones." Alex kisses Stan passion tonguing him while fondling his penis through his pants. Oh my god what is he doing to me..I feel like I could explode any minute. "No you don't have to do this for the engineer...I don't need to be persuaded with sex to kill the angel of silence." Stan said as he reluctantly forces himself off of Alex. "you think I'm making out with you to goal you in to killing the angel of silence? Hell no man, I'm doing this because I fucking like you man, that's why I said what I said earlier. you understand me? right here right now I want to fuck you, so what do you want?" "I...I want you to thrust your fucking cock down my throat until my eyes water." I said. I can't believe I just fucking said that out loud. Alex helps Stan fall to his knees as he unzips Alex pants. Alex roughly shoves his penis in to Stan's mouth he imminently gags as he slurps and sucks Alex's rod like it was an oversize lollipop. for the first time in a long, long time Stan Johnson was a happy man and all he had to do was sell his soul.

Upstate, New York. David McDonald Residents.

Federal agent Andre Diaz has seen this type of handy work before, about seven years ago. Andre looks at the now lacerated body of David McDonald whom face been stab with enough force that his entire skull exploded. The amount of strength to do something like this is pretty much inhuman. this wasn't just a violent murder, this was pure rage incarnated inside a human being. whoever is this Albert Houston copycat obviously knowing that David McDonald was in charge of Albert's execution, even although that information wasn't release to the press. I also have to assume that this copycat knew Albert Houston last words of vengeance's. Especially the nurse who gave him the lethal injection herself. Rumor was that she said some inappropriate things in his ear before injecting him without the sodium thiopental that cause deep unconsciousness when a person won't feel that pain of the lethal injection before dying. Albert Houston was such a bastard the high ups just called it an botched execution and left as that. if this person really mimicking Albert Houston murders then nurse Jones will definitely be next. "Agent Li, I need you to find Mrs. Bridgett Jones who conducted the lethal injection on Albert Houston. Once you do find her send a team out there ASAP! I want to stop this asshole before he kills anyone else!" agent told his longtime friend and partner. I pray to god we'll find her before he does. Staten Island, New York city. the Jones residents. I love Wednesday's nights. It's the only time the whole family gets to spend time with each other. Every Wednesday is declared movie night, once every Wednesday me my husband Karl and my teenage daughter zukala pick out a movie we all have to watch, no matter how bad it is. My handsome beloved husband is a chief emergency room doctor, who works long hours almost every day except Wednesday nights. which he had to enforce by the way. He said to me one day if I'll leave it up to them I'll never have any time for my family, what's the point of being boss if you can't take any personal time off to be with your own family. Don't get me started on zukala. She's all personality that one. Got time for nothing I swear. but she's a great kid that works hard in school to keep up her grades. My husband and I don't pressure her too much knowing it's kind of hard to try to live up to standards of your father being a doctor and mother a nurse. that's why I've decided to work only part time to spend my time with my daughter when she come's home from school while being here when my husband comes home from work as well. God bless his heart he was fine with it as long I was happy. "Hey mom! Where's the hot Sauce!" zukala asked as she pulled the popcorn out of the microwave. "Really Zukala hot Sauce? really?" I can't believe this girl sometimes. where she learns these things from. "Look mom because you forgot about your African roots doesn't mean I have to depraved myself of urban popcorn." "O' never mind found it!" Zukala reach in to the top kitchen cabinet and grabs the hot Sauce. "Oh my god Zukala did you just say hot Sauce and popcorn are our African roots?" Bridgett Jones stare dumbfounded as she turns towards her husband sitting next to her in their Living room couch. "Karl did you hear what your daughter just said?" "uh,uh, no way I'm not getting in the middle of that." Karl smiled as Bridgett playfully smack him in the arm. Zukala flops down in the middle of the couch between her mother and father holding a large bucket of now hot sauce popcorn. "make way the Nubian princess has arrived!" Zukala laugh at her parents hurried out the way. "Zukala what I told you about flopping down on our couch like that!" Bridgett yelled. "Ah come on mom, I've been doing this since I was three. You thought it was the cutest thing in the world." "yeah that was when you were a hundred pounds smaller zukala." her mother smiled. "Daddy still loves it, don't you daddy?" zukala shoved a hand full of popcorn in her mouth. "that's right Zuzu. you're always be my little Nubian princess." Karl chuckle. "Daaad! I'm not three no more, stop calling me Zuzu." her face blushed red with embarrassment. "that's exactly what I just said Zuzu, and don't hog all the popcorn." she dip in the large bucket of popcorn. this is why we have movie nights to enjoy precious family moments like this. before you realize it your kids are now young adults on their way out, Exploring the world on their own. "what movie you pick this week Zuzu?" Karl asked. "you know nothing but the best realist movie in the world, Raising in the sun." A big sigh were heard from Zukala's mother and father as they really was hoping their daughter wouldn't be picking that movie. "Not again Zukala, please!" Karl beg his daughter for mercy. "Zukala what is it with you and this movie? it's depressing." Bridgett ask but Zukala didn't answer right away as her Goldie smile faded away. "really you don't know mom? I watch movies like these to understand the type of struggle you and father went through growing up and appreciate the hard work you and dad have done so I wouldn't have to experience such a hard life...that's why mom." tears came down her eyes, then we all startedto cry and hug each other. My little girl was growing up indeed but she's growing up to be the most humble Nubian queen that ever lived. "Aaww now look what you did, you got tears all in the popcorn."Zukala said wiping her tears away. "it's not our fault that your tears are contagious." "maybe I will have to stop calling you Zuzu with speeches like that." "that's okay dad, Zuzu is fine." everyone felt good, graceful for the time they all have with each other. Dang dong! Dang dong! the bell ranged. "Zukala you expecting someone princess?" Karl looked at his daughter puzzled. "of course, not dad, it's movie night." "it's properly just the neighbors honey." Bridgett charmed in. "Oh sorry I got it, be right back." Karl got off the living room couch and headed towards the front door. "who is it?" Karl answer the door while looking through the peek hole. Thud! a loud breaking sound is heard as the peephole part of the door exploded. Karl Jones head split right open as the tip of an axes slammed in to his skull through the front door. "KARRRL!" "Daddy! Daddy! Daddyyy!" Bridgett and zukala's screams were heard throughout the neighborhood as they watched there husband and father murdered in front of them. With the force of a tank the bolted front door is knocked down on top of the deceased father and husband. "Knock, knock honey I'm home!" Bridgett mind went in complete shock as she just witnesses her husband murdered by a man she killed during a execution five years ago in prison. "NO! NO! It can't be! It can't be! You're dead, you're fucking dead! I killed you!" Bridgett panicky screamed out. "Bitch I told you I'll be back! death won't stop me from giving you that fuck I own you!" Albert lick his lips. Albert Houston slowly enters Bridgett house by stepping over dead husband who he just murdered in cold blood. Bridget jones find herself completely horrified as her fear paralyzes her body. all see could do was watch the man who murder her husband walk in to her place and get ready to do the same to her. "Mom! who is that man? Why he killed daddy?" Bridget heard her fifth teen year old daughter called out to her and snap whatever trance she was in. No you monster! you won't get her, you won't fucking get her too! "Zukala run! go out the back window now!" Zukala looked on with wide teary eyes as she saw her mother rip the dvd player off the entertainment center while stepping in front of her daughter. "what are you waiting for? Go! Go! Gooo Zukala! Don't look back baby just like the bible said honey!" "I love you mom!" Zukala said as she turned and ran towards the back window without taking a final glace back at her mother. she understood what her mother was doing for her, the same thing she always done for her, made sacrifices. Now she's making the ultimate sacrifice. "oh no there wouldn't be a party without the kiddies!" Albert said as he turns his attention towards Zukala as he saw she had already started to lift up the back Living room window. "you don't fucking touch her!" Bridget charge at her husband murder who has now giving his full attention to her little Nubian princess Zukala. No you don't get her! you don't fucking get her too. Bridget peeks at Zukala, seeing her half way out the window. Bridget knew there was no way Albert would be able to run her down now but apparently Albert knew that as well, as he ripped the axes out of Bridget dead husband's head and arch's it back behind his head and throws it like an Tomma hawk axes. "NO!" Bridget leaps forward like she never done before in her life, arms stretch out like a scuba diver praying she could intercept Albert's axes in time. "Wwwaaahhh!" an terrible scream erupts from Bridget's mouth as both of her arms were cut off by the throwing axes. Bridget Jones howler and screamed in great pain then she began to laugh and cry in joy because what came after this didn't matter no more. All that matter now is that her little Nubian princess was safe and she was glad, she could die in peace knowing she could be in heaven with Karl knowing their little girl was OK. Albert Houston looks down at the dying nurse Jones with some confusion. "you at peace nurse Jones, you couldn't be that excited for me to fuck your pussy in to oblivion?" Bridget heard what the murder said but it didn't matter what he did to her physical body now. In an few minutes she will bleed out and die and she'll be at peace with it. "Oh we see you're at peace now huh? good, that's good. I've waited five long years for this. don't want you to bleed out before we start. No, No best to believe we can't have that can we." Albert grabs nurse Jones by the collar of her bloody night gale and drags her to the Living room wall by the windows. "Here let me take care of this first." Albert said as he reaches over and drop an limp body next to Bridget Jones. An screech of pain and horror emulated from Bridget mouth that will give her neighbors nightmares for the rest of their lives as they buckle down in their homes to frightened to even call the police for help. "Zukala god no no no please god no!" Bridget cried out as she watches the lifeless body of her only daughter dead on her stomach looking straight in to her eyes. Albert Houston drops his pants and starts stroking himself watching nurse Jones plead for the life of her dead daughter. "couldn't fuck you right without you saying proper goodbyes to your little princess. Best to believe we couldn't do that could we." Albert smiled. Albert lifts up Jones bloodied night gale and enters his abnormal penis, that literally rips Bridget Jones virginal open like she was giving birth to a newborn child. the pain of a twenty six inch object entering a woman's womb would cause severe pain and damage but Bridget Jones was beyond the pain of the psychical realm. "Zukala! Zukala!" the more she screamed her daughter's name the harder Albert would thrust. "yes scream out your daughter's name! Reach out and save her! she might still be alive!" Albert yelled out as he thrust inside of her harder and harder. "Zukala, Zukala I'm sorry! I'm sorry!" the mother yelled to her daughter's dead body trying to reach out to her, trying to comfort her one last time like she did when was an infant child. Bridget could never feel or touch her child ever again as she continued to reach to her child with no arms. This display of last affection Bridget Jones try's to show her dead daughter gave Albert Houston the ultimate climax. "yes grab her, grab uhhmmm.." Albert Houston came and Bridget Jones was no more as she bleed to death pleading for her daughter's forgiveness. All to the delight of man they call Albert Houston.

CHAPTER SIX

can't believe this shit. You fucking telling me, one fucking guy armed with only an axe. bust open these poor people doors down, start murdering and raping people in plain sight in a crowded neighborhood and nobody lifts a fucking finger to help them. Only reason the cops got here when they did is because I fucking called them from another murder scene. Mother fucking losers these people..they lived in this neighborhood for fucking twenty years. Now look at them because nobody couldn't at least pick up a fucking phone and call 9-1-1. Agent Diaz ranted to himself. Agent Diaz can't help to look at the dead corpse of Bridget Jones trying to reach out to comfort her already dead daughter while she was being rape. "agent li we got to get this mother fucker of the streets." Diaz said to his longtime partner. "I just spoke to the chief of police they're ordering a man hunt for this copycat but he's keeping a media blackout for right now." li reported to his partner. "Good I don't want this mother fucker to go underground because he knows were on to him, let him get comfortable and we can give him the same reward we gave his mentor five years ago." Jessie brown awoke feeling like a brand-new man. He couldn't remember a time in his adult life he felt so good waking up without the urge of drinking a half pint of whiskey in the morning. Jessie stretch his arms up feeling rested. "good morning Jessie brown. how do you feel this morning?" Natasha walk in to the room. "I feel like a young man again all thanks to you Natasha. I own everything to you." Jessie grinned. "thank god Jessie brown, he is the light that worked through me to help heal your pain." Jessie stood up straight and firm and walk straight up to Natasha about three inches from her face and held her hand. "yes I am grateful to god. grateful that he brought you in to my life Natasha." Natasha felt a unfamiliar jolt of nerves flashed through out her body which freighted and excited her all at once. Natasha quickly steps back to create some space and lifts up a leather book to show Jessie brown. "Jessie brown do you know what's this object I'm holding." Natasha asks. "yeah I thank so, is it the holy bible?" Jessie answered. "yes, it is but it isn't the one that the human council of Nicaea had put together. this is the word of god." Jessie brown was floored by this. if this is the real bible what the hell have people been studying centuries. All these religions all these wars and death for false information. "what? you telling me the bibles or the word spread around the world is wrong and you have this information here. why don't god give the world his true word?" Jessie argue puzzle and confused. "Because he has already Jessie, but man decided what they would use and what they wouldn't use as doctrine. this was the true nature of the first council of Nicaea. the Vatican has every doctrine in this book locked away from all of mankind to keep their power over the world. god has giving me the task to teach you all of his word." Natasha explained. "can I...can I touch it Natasha?" Natasha hands the book over to Jessie. Jessie slowly slide his hands over the cover of the holy book. "It's so thick and rough, what kind of leather is this? it looks ancient." Jessie asks in awe. "It was made from an unclean animal that roam the earth before god flooded it to be rid of all the unclean things up on the earth." "what!

are you telling me this a dinosaur skin!? the book is millions of years old!" the inner child sprung free from Jessie brown with pure excitement. "Heh dear Jessie the world is not that old." Natasha smile and Jessie saw her and he forgotten all about the ancient animals that were called dinosaurs. "Jessie open the book." she ask him and he reply but he couldn't read the words with in the book. "Natasha I can't understand any of this, what language is it?" "It's angelic Jessie. An ancient language taught and read by angels." she explained. "how am I supposed to be able to read and understand it then, I'm no angel." Natasha grabs the book back from Jessie as her other hand Is place on his forehead. "simple Jessie brown god has giving me the light to open your eyes for you can see the truth through new wonderful eyes. Angel of silence is more than just a name." "so are you ready to receive our lord god true teachings and word Jessie brown?" "yes, yes I am." Jessie answer as Natasha grabs his hand walks him towards his bed. "have a seat Jessie brown, god will help me unlock your inner power but it will be quite painful at first." Natasha explained. the hell is going on? What is she going to do to me? "yeah okay I'm ready when you are Natasha." Jessie said as he sat down on the bed. Natasha step on top of the bed and position herself behind Jessie than sat directly behind him. Jessie felt the warmth of her body as he sat between her legs. Jesus I can feel her whole body press on my back...she's so soft and warm. Natasha tightly wrapped both of her legs around Jessie's waist while both of her index fingers press against each side of his temple. "I don't mind your legs around me Natasha but it's pretty tight." "I'm sorry for the discomfort my dear Jessie but I must make sure your body don't shift. It's for your own protection. Are you ready to begin now?" Natasha said softy in to his left ear. jeez! I don't think she even realize what kind of sexual tension she's giving off by doing things like that. More importantly I must focus on the task at hand. "I'm ready Natasha do what you have to do." Jessie takes in a deep breath to prepare himself for whatever pain he might feel when Natasha does whatever it is she's doing. "Eeerrraahh!" Jessie yelled out as both of Natasha index fingers sank in to the temple of Jessie's skull. Blue and red lights flash before his eyes and then it was over. the pain was gone. "It is done Jessie brown by the great mercy of our lord and savior god, Yahweh the great El Shaddai all is good and well." Natasha praised god as she removes her legs from around Jessie waist but continued to sit behind him. Jessie turns towards her and touch his temple. There was the moist feeling of blood but there was no wound. "Natasha what did you do to me? I have blood on my head but there's no wound?" "I connected your mind and spirit as one. your wound healed as soon as my fingers left your mind, Jessie brown there won't be nothing that your eyes can't see." Natasha gently place her hand across Jessie's check and turn his face from her towards the holy bible. "Now Jessie take another look and tell me what it is that you see?" Jessie did what Natasha told him to do and he couldn't believe what he could see, what he could understand. "It's amazing Natasha! I can see it, I can understand it!" excited Jessie answer her. "Now read it to me. Tell me the word of our lord and savior Yahweh the almighty god." Natasha whisper in to Jessie's ear. Jessie's excitement and joy of learning the true word of god has spark emotions deep within her soul. It was something unfamiliar for her, she wasn't sure if it was something to be concern with. Jessie began to read the book and it started with the very beginning of creation. "In the beginning god created the heavens and the earth. The earth was without form and void(chaos) and darkness was up on the deep of the earth. god said let there be light. And there was light, and god saw that the light was good. God separated the light from the darkness. The light was called day and the darkness was called night. Then there was evening and there was morning. this was the first day of creation." Jessie read but it was something more. it was as if he was there as god started to create the heavens and the earth. "Did you see it, the miracle of life Jessie brown?" Natasha ask as she sat up and sat next to Jessie. "I couldn't quit see god himself, but I saw the earth, the light and the darkness but I couldn't see into the darkness." Jessie said. "you are not ready to see in to the abyss, the darkness is a void of chaos, only those with the complete light and grace of god could stare in to the abyss of darkness and even then, it is not an easy task. There is much to learn before you ascended that level of gracefulness my dear Jessie brown." Natasha explained. "It's amazing that god could create something so beautiful in seven days, I mean six days because god rested on the seventh day." Jessie smiled. "Also what did you mean earlier about this world isn't that old?" Jessie had to ask before he could continue to read on in the bible. "Yes dear Jessie brown for one day to god is one thousand years to man." "what! you telling me the earth is only seven thousand years old? what about the dinosaurs?" Jessie questioned, shock in complete awe at what he is being told. if this was anyone else besides the angel of god telling him this he would tell them to shut up and regard her as crazy and it still hard to believe. "well if you add up the years from then and now in human years the earths about twelve thousand years old now. and for the uncleaned beast of the earth. the time before the flood the falling angels that was task to watch mankind decided to teach man the forbidden arts of science, War craft, astronomy and witchcraft. with this forbidden knowledge that showed man how to mix clean animals with unclean animals and these animals grew and started to devour all living creatures upon the earth. These were the dinosaurs you speak of Jessie." "...so these things were nothing but sick experiment that went wrong." shit and I really thought the world was a fuck up place now, these time might be paradise compare to then. "All this is explained in the bible you hold in your hands, these events were also written in what you humans called the book of Enoch." Natasha told Jessie. Jessie sat silent for a couple of minutes after wards in deep thought, Natasha sat alongside him in silence she knew this kind of knowledge could be overwhelming. "On the second day..." Jessie continues to read the bible as Natasha smile on in joy. this would continue for the next twelve hours straight.

CHAPTER SEVEN

The pain and itching has become damn near unbearable. It's like someone took my wrist and buried it in a nest of red ants. Sherry shuford looks down at her left wrist which was heavily bandage with stains of blood from all the clawing and tearing she done to herself trying to stop the pain and itching that came from the mark of the beast. This damn mark been causing me physical pain and grief in the last five nights . since those murders in those private houses in upstate New York happened. something been telling me to keep watch of the Albert Houston murders...No this mark been telling me to watch out about these murders. Once that correction officer was killed by that murder the media haven't been reporting anything new about him. But I know he killed again some family in Staten island. someone uploaded a video to YouTube of audio of the people being murdered. the mother said his name, they think it's a copycat, but I know...this mark knows it's the real Albert Houston back from hell killing those who killed him in his past life and collecting the souls with the mark for the engineer. Jesus Christ help me, how..why is the mark telling me all of this? All I can think of is this is some kind of defense mechanism. it's telling me he's coming for me next. Every time he kills the pain in my mark worsen. I told Gabriella to spend the night at daisy house, to go straight there from school. the look she gave me, she knew something wasn't right with me, but she bought my lies anyway. She's such a good girl. I won't let nothing ever happen to her again. I'm not going to fucking burn in hell and have my little girl die anyway! No, No I won't allow that to happen, if he's comes he's going to come for me. Sherry boiled water to make spaghetti. cooking is a great outlet for sherry when she's stress out. I don't care what kind of psycho strength that bastard have's. I had the locksmith put two bolts on my front door, No axes is going to chop its way through that. Knock! Knock! sherry froze as she heard someone knock on her front door. Knock!Knock! someone knock on her door again. Sherry slowly and caution walks in to her hallway staring at the front door. "Who...who is it!" sherry shouted. sherry looked down and could see the shadow of the person knocking on her door. "OH, sorry wrong door." sherry heard the man say through the other side of the door as his shadow disappeared. He left, thank god it was a false alarm. sherry grab her heart and gasp a large breath of relief. O' thank you lord god. she thanked god again. sherry turn and headed back towards the kitchen to finish preparing her meal. Crash! a large exploding sound erupted behind sherry shuford as she fell to the ground. Everything was a blur, the entire hallway seemed it was spinning in circles. sherry couldn't hear a word, as her eardrums rang an uncomfortable ranging sound in her head. But even with a concussion sherry was aware enough to look behind her and saw the large man standing there pushing the rest of her metal bolted door that now resemble an expensive twisted piece of art. "Bitch did you really think some reinforce door would stop us! you best to fucking believe it wouldn't!" Albert mock sherry as he by passed the rest of her door. Sherry stumble to her feet and immensely sprinted towards the kitchen as fast as she could. "come the fuck here baby! we ain't have our fun yet! Best to believe it!" Sherry howled as her head jerk backwards from having her hair pulled while she felt an Sharpe piercing pain run through her shoulder blade. "Noooo!" sherry shouted in determination as she used all her strength and will power to break free from Albert's grip, ripping a chunk of hair from her scout. "The fuck?" Albert Houston smiled amuse by the woman's desperate attempt to get away from him. well look at that this one left me a patch of hair to keep. never had one do that before, she's a fighter we're going to have fun with this one. Albert Houston could barely control his excitement. since his return to this world his life been one long wet dream come true. Albert thought as he jogs around the kitchen counter after sherry shuford. For Albert Houston this is heaven. "WWaahhh!" Albert Houston scream out as he held his face as Sherry threw the boiling pot of water in to the murder's face. "Fuck you! why ain't you smiling now!" sherry tainted Albert as she grab one of her iron skillet's. "aahhh..bitch I'll kil..." SMASH! Sherry slams the iron firing pan in to Albert's already burned face. Albert falls down slump on the oven's door. "...gonna fu.." SMASH! sherry slams the pan in to his skull again. "Fuck you! Fuck the engineer! Fuck all you devil worshiping mother fuckers! you can't have my soul you heard me! my soul is for god! you hear me it's for god!" sherry smash the pan in to Albert's face again. SMASH! SMASH! SMASH! SMASH! SMASH! SMASH! SMASH! SMASH! Sherry smash the pan in to Albert's face until she couldn't feel his bones any longer, just smash broken flesh that use to be Albert Houston's face. Yet she couldn't let her self stop as she continued to strike the pan in to his deformed face until Albert's left eye pop out of his skull. "Oh' god!" sherry threw up all over her kitchen floor. "nnn..ki..u.bch..."Albert Houston mumble's through smash gums and broken teeth. Albert Houston's face was nothing but a burned smash sack of swollen flesh. the only thing that kept his head from falling from his shoulders were his spinal cord and yet he still lives. sherry stared at the now broken deform man known as Albert Houston and made a decision. No way. No way this thing is human, not after the beating I've gave him. I could run out the door now but then he could heal up and come after me again...No this murdering bastard don't get a chance at my daughter. He might not be human but he can bleed and feel pain which means he could die. Sherry thought. Sherry ran towards the bedroom and picked up the phone and called 9-1-1. "Hello this is sherry shuford, Albert Houston just broke in to my fucking house! I need the cops here now! Please hurry I don't know how long I can hold him off!" the dispatcher try to get more information from sherry but she hung up the phone anyway. sherry knew the cops will be able to trace her address through her phone call since all her information is public. sherry open's the small dresser door that the phone sat on top of. "you knew didn't you baby? You knew one day I would have to use this." sherry spoke to her decease husband as she pulled open the dresser door and took out the forty five caliber magnum revolver. you used to take me to the shooting range once a year for hours practicing how to use this weapon just in case you wouldn't be there to protect me and Gabriella. sherry opens revolver and starts to load up the gun. Bitch think she can fuck with us! she fucking think I'm going to die by some fucking willow stay at home mom. No way, no fucking way! An inferno of rage and adrenaline erupted inside of Albert's soul. Albert used every bit of his anger and pride to rise to his feet, still woozy from the head trauma. "Bitch!..u..thk..u.can..best meee!" sherry heard the raging demon make his war cry for her. sherry knelt down on one knee and calmly aim the barrel of her gun towards the entrance of her bedroom and patiently waits for the murderer to arrival. Albert Houston doesn't keep her waiting long as he stumbles in to sherry bedroom full of range and murderous intent. "there..u..are! ki..u!" even with a smash face his intentions are known and sherry is readily. Blam! Sherry pulled the trigger on one of the most powerful handguns that was ever made. A large splat sound echo throughout the apartment as half of the deformed face of Albert Houston face's was now blown completely off. Albert Houston lifeless body felt down between sherry's bed and large dresser. sherry with no hesitation walks over to the body of Albert Houston and points the barrel of forty five magnum revolver at the remaining thing that was his face. "I'm right here you murdering son of a bitch!" Blam!Blam! Blam!Blam!Blam! Sherry empties every bullet point blank range in to Albert's face's. Once sherry shuford was done all there was left of the once infamous serial killer was a limp body with no head or neck to be identified with. the serial killer known as Albert Houston was dead. Sherry exhausted slumps down at the foot of her bed. Thank you god I did it. I did it Gabriella. sherry thanked god as she could hear the police sirens outside and she knew this night-mare was finally over. SPLAT! Albert Houston corpse ex-plodes, sherry and the entire room is covered in blood and intestines. Something quick came out, something inhuman. All she saw was a blur then everything was upside down. Sherry could see it's gray long body now. it was about ten foot high, it's had two long blades that replace what should had been its hands. It was looking down at her and that's when she saw her headless body fall from the bed to the ground. Sherry knew then she would never see her precious Gabriella ever again, not even in the afterlife because she wouldn't be going where all the saints and angels go but she still was thankful to god for being able to keep her daughter Safe, Then there was darkness and Sherry shuford was gone, another soul collected by the Engineer.

CHAPTER EIGHT

Li has been a F.B.I. agent for the last five years while working with his partner and best friend agent Andrew Diaz. By far this is the most buzzard and brutal case I've ever worked on. I think the same can be said for my partner agent Diaz who have's fifth teen years under his belt. I think that sums it up right there how crazy this case is. Now I'm no rookie to this game nether, Before I became a federal agent I've worked the beat for the Los Angeles police department for eight years. Trust me you don't work the streets of L.A for eight whole years without seeing some fuck up crazy shit. But this case, this case takes the cake. While my partner been figuring out this copycat murdering patterns I've been doing background checks on every person who was in that room when Albert Houston was executed five years ago. Things ain't playing out as I hope they would. One of the witnesses that day was a fifty two year old father who only son was murdered in the New York slaughter house murders. After the old man saw Albert Houston executed went home and blew his brains out holding an old picture of him holding his son as a baby. Then There was Ms.Morris who was maimed by Albert Houston while he made her watch as he killed the baby father and the infant child. Her condition leaves her out as a suspect, Ms. Morris fifty year old mother attended with her eighteen year old sister and ten year old little brother. All whom been accounted for during the murder spree, while common sense would tell you none of them were physically fit to Carrie out those murders. Not in the fashion that this copycat had done it. That leaves the final two people left in that room on that day. Correction officer Sid Jamison and father Danielle Klum who was spit on by Albert Houston. Sid Jamison left the New York correction officer job and moved to Seattle Washington and join the police force for better pay. Father Klum three years ago had a stroke and has Parkinson's disease with arthritis and both legs. Which leaves me with no suspects and more disturbing the medical lab contacted me and told me the semen found inside and on Mrs. Jones head and body were 99.9% Albert Houston's dna. I've checked every sperm bank in the United States, there's no record of him donating semen. I had to go and see this guy and ask him how the fuck is that possible. I said to him. the look he gave me. That freighted spooked look I saw in his eyes before he said. 'Are you sure he's dead?' I'm not a religious or superstitious man but when he said that to me I swear a deep chill ran down my spine. Albert Houston body was cremated after his execution so how the fuck could he still be alive? The thought of something like that scared the shit out of me. Agent Li felt a cold shiver run through his upper body. "The hell I'm I doing?" this ain't me! damn horror movie shit. LI said loudly snapping himself out of his paranoid fears. Shit I sound like my parents with all that hocuspocus bullshit that their parents feed in to their brains when they were children in china. Agent Li opens the office door he shared with his partner agent Diaz. "shit li the shit you told me on the phone, was it true?" my partner asked me before I could get both my feet through the door. "You know I don't joke about shit like that Diaz." I answered him as I unbuttoned my coat and hanged it on the coat rack on the back of the door. "Fuck the how can that be? how is this mother fucker is doing this?" agent Diaz slammed his hand hard on their table. Ring, Ring our landline phone went off. "Hello agent Diaz speaking." he answered. "Where?" I heard the urgency in his voice as his brown skin became light red with anger, and I knew something was going down. Something big. "I want a fucking squat team there right fucking now! lock the whole fucking block down! No one gets in or out you understand me! No one!" He commanded the operator. In a blur his coat was half way on while his foot was already out the door. "Let's go li! we got this mother fucker you hear, we got this motherfucker Li!" Diaz repeated. I had to jog to keep pace with him, Diaz was already half way down the steps. "What's happening Diaz?" I finally could up. "there's a lady in queen's name sherry shuford is fighting off this motherfucker as we speak." "We got to get to her li, we got to save her." a look of sorrow was in his eyes. this case is personal to him now. Every death caused by this copycat, Diaz is blaming himself for it by not figuring out his murders pattern but like the original Albert Houston may be there is no method just chaos and mayhem. "we're get there Andrew. we're get there." I lie to give him some hope, but the reality is if swat don't there in time she'll be long dead before we're get there. Regardless the New York police department and swat will be there before he leaves that house. "He doesn't leave that house you understand?" Diaz said as we enter the parking lot. "yeah swat will be there having him surrounded before we get there." I answered. "No you ain't getting it. He doesn't make it out of that house alive, he die's...he fucking die's tonight." "Andrew theirs a good chance that news reporters and live camera's will be there. We can't do that on live television." I tried to talk sense to my partner. "The fuck

I can, and we will! this mother fucker die's tonight, nobody else die's because of this fucker you understand. We're making a public example of this bastard for all future want to be Albert Houston's in the world." that was it. The stage was set. we were on our way to murder the copycat known as Albert Houston for all the world to see. Gabriella knew she was supposed to spend the night at her best friend's house, daisy smith. Gabriella know something hasn't been right about her mother for the past week especially Earlier today. At the age of twelve you start picking up on little things like that. Things like the constant itching of her left wrist, the way her hand violently shakes when She tries to drink a cup of coffee. Teary red eyes from lack of sleep. My mother tells me there's nothing to worry about, but she's been on edge ever since the car accident seven years ago and these last five days she's been over the edge. When my mother held me tight before I left to go to school this morning something Felt wrong about it...like it was for the last time or something, but I went to school and caught up with daisy just like my mother asked. this bad feeling that washed over me, I couldn't shake it off. even my best friend knew something was eating at me. Real best friends can always tell when there's something wrong with you. So like any real best friend she prays the information out of me. I start telling daisy about my concerns about my mother's behavior and somehow that lead to us talking about that incident seven years ago, things that I thought were dreams and nightmares but deep down I knew they were real. I made myself forget because the fear my mother showed on her face when I approach her about the man with the goatee. She'll tell me it was just a bad dream, so I left it as that. Why The hell am I thinking about all of this now? why can't I stop discussing this with daisy? I tell daisy how I remember reaching out and grabbing my mother's hand Before feeling a very hard jerk, then everything went black for a little while. when I woke I saw something like a white man wearing a business suit and black goatee, There were giant black wings coming from his back, eyes were green..no his entire eyes Were green...then he was gone and I was staring at my mother holding and crying over me. I told daisy as she sat across from me on her full size bed. the color in her face seemed to disappeared with a blank expression on her face. I've seen that look before, usually that means she's terrified of something but trying to Hide it so she can be brave for her friends and herself. There was something else too? yeah, I remember now he said something to me. I think he said ' I'll see you again Gabriella. when you're responsible for your own sins.' I told her, what the hell! why did I remember that just now? Gabriella thought. Daisy reaches over and squeezed my hand as she looks me in my eyes. "Gabriella in the bible Jesus wasn't responsible for his sins until he was twelve years old." Daisy said to me. If I didn't know before i knew now how serious daisy took her religion. I mean how can she believe my story without the slightest hesitation or questions. "yeah..uhmm..Daisy thank you but how can you believe everything I've just told you without questioning it at all?" that's when she drops eye contact with me and I knew things weren't going to the same anymore. "I saw Gabriella...I saw your body being drag underneath that car. I saw your mother chasing after the rest of your body still holding your left arm in her hand Gabriella." Gabriella jolted off daisy's bed in disbelief as fear overwhelmed her mind. "No! No, No, No daisy just stop talking!" I pleaded to my friend to stop talking about it like I wasn't the one who open this Pandora box of horrors. Saying those things out loud to your best friend is one thing, you can always say it was the imagination of a young child trying to cope with a near death experience but having someone you know experience it with you...there's no going back no more, you can't just lie to yourself anymore and hope it all just go away. No matter how hard you try. "No Gabriella I won't stop. I've been holding this in for seven years! I..I was starting to wonder if I was imaging things but hearing you speak today, thank god, I know the truth and so do you Gabriella!" Daisy said with so much love and passion her eyes we're swelling up with tears as she fought hard not to break down and cry in front of me. "One second you were dead Gabriella! Dead! The next thing I know you were alive again without a scratch accept that scar on your left arm. The same area where your arm was severed at. I knew something magical happen, thought it was god but it was That demon wasn't It Gabriella?" Daisy asked me while she approaches me. She already knew the answer and she knew I knew the answer as well and for some reason my mother knew too, Didn't she. the thoughts flood through my mind, upsetting me with emotion and thoughts I couldn't handle it anymore as I hug daisy tightly and cried and sobbed on her chest. "I'm scared Daisy, I'm scared that thing is going to come for my mother and me." I confessed. "Gabriella I need to ask you something really important ok?" Daisy ran her fingers through my hair trying her best to give me comfort. She was scared too but like I said daisy hides it well so she can be strong for the both of us. "Ok." I answered as we both sat on her bed still holding each other's hands. "Gabriella has your mother ever talk to you about that day? Like how you survive the accident?" "No but I did ask her once that same summer. She told me it was the will of god that saved me that day and we shouldn't talk of it anymore while she kept squeezing her wrist." I told daisy. "This was before she burned her wrist, right?" daisy asked. "Yeah why?" "Don't you think it's a little weird that she's been covering or hiding that wrist since that day?" Gabriella rolled her eyes , To give Daisy a what the hell are you asking me stupid questions for. for In a time like this look. "Daisy you know my mother cut her hand back then. Remember I told you at the park?" "Yeah I remember Gabriella. First she cuts her wrist by accident, then burns it, and finally savagely scratches the flesh from the same wrist and none of that sounds strange to you Gabriella?" Daisy breaks down detail to Detail to her best friend that cause's Gabriella to look away. "I, I don't see where you getting at here daisy. You're being weird again." Gabriella said with a whisper with no conviction in her voice. "you see it haven't you Gabriella? Seven years since that tragic day. I know you had to see it at least once. I know you had to." Daisy voice got louder and the more she talked the more it makes sense. "Daisy stop you're too loud and seen what? I don't know..." "The symbol of the three sixes marked on your mother's left wrist that she keeps injuring Gabriella. I saw them myself one day when your mother was talking to my mom and accidentally spilled coffee on my mom's dining room table then attempted to clean it up. I..I thought I was hallucinating back then but now I know what I saw was real. "Once I heard daisy say that. The gig was up. Daisy was right I knew...I known For a few years now. I've never seen it, but I read it in my mother's dairy. "Daisy I read it...I read my mother's dairy how she made a deal with a devil in a black suit to restore my life, How it branded her with the mark...She's in trouble daisy I can feel it in my heart. I have to go back home." As I heard myself out loud I knew it was true. The troubling feeling I felt for my mother today. I knew it had something to do with that thing. "Then let's go Gabriella. Let's show your mother she's not alone in this." Daisy walked over to closet and grab both of our winter coats. "No daisy you can't come. you shouldn't get involved in this." I pleaded to my best friend. "Gabriella stop it okay. You're my best friend and you're in this predicament because I went for a stupid ball in the street. I own you for saving my life, so I'm not taking no for an answer." And that was that. like I said daisy was very brave, religious and when her mind was on something there's no changing it. Although she can be unbelievable stubborn I am truly bless to have her in my life. she is a true best friend. For daisy to have all those thoughts about me and my mother knowing how religious she is and yet still consider me as her sister and best friend. Daisy got her mother to drive us back to my house. She only told her that it was a medical emergency and I really needed to get home to my mother. "Oh god what happen here?" The shock I heard in daisy mother's voice snaps me out of my deep Thoughts In the backseat of the car. When I looked up to see what caused daisy mother to worry I'll realize that my night-mare was beginning to become true. There was a army of cops surrounding my house with emergency tape keeping people away. "Mom! Mommm!" I was screaming out as I ran out of Mrs. Smith car. One of the cops grabbed me by my waist Before I could cross the yellow tape. "Hold up little girl! You can't go pass the yellow tape honey." "That's my house! That's my mother's house! Let me in!" I yelled at the cop and fought desperately to get free of his grip. "Hey let go of my friend, that's her house!" Daisy tried to have my back. "Hush daisy. Officer what's going on here? this is her mother's house, she deserves to know what's going on here." Mrs. Smith questions the cop as she took over the situation. "Ms. I'm not at liberty to say but there's been a homicide..." that's all I heard the cop say as everything else became a hot blur once he said homicide. Everything else was an outer body experience. Next thing I knew my nails was hot and wet, the cop screamed something as he covered up his face. Daisy and Mrs. Smith was saying something as they tried to reach out to me but I was already gone. My body, my soul was already gone towards the house..my house. Everything seemed like slow motion. Dozens of police officers were reaching after me, stumbling and falling but none could touch me. It felt like there was a invisible wall shielding me, like when god Parted the red sea for Moses guiding him towards the promise land, God was guiding me to my mother as I ran through the front door of my house.

"What the fuck happened here!" Agent Diaz curse out loud in horror and discussed at the newest murder scene. The dead decapitated body of sherry shuford laying on the edge of the bed naked with her insides fucking hanging out of her virginal. Three feet from that on the floor is a headless rotten corpse with its entire back side Split open like a damn bomb went off. Its inside is all over the damn ceiling and walls. What the fuck is this shit! It's like some fuck up real life horror mystery. "I want this entire fucking zip code lock the fuck down! Nobody gets in or out until we get this murdering son of a bitch!" Diaz yelled over his walkies-talkie. How could this have happened so damn fast? How in fuck this bastard has time to do this shit before Swat fucking arrives? It's like he's a fucking phantom. How could I let this happen again...Another fucking death that I was too late to prevent. No, No this shit ain't making sense. She was fucking alive, Fighting this motherfucker when we got the call. The swat team was here in minutes after that call, minutes! No fucking way all this shit went down and had time to spare to write his calling card and escape in twelve fucking minutes. There's no fucking way! Agent Diaz tries to make sense of the current situation. "Andrew look at this! this body had to be dead for at least a year to show this kind of decay. Was this part of the original Albert Houston routine?" My best friend and partner ask me. Like I have the answers to this circus of fuck up shit. All I know once we get this bastard this Madness will be over. "I'm not sure Li...now he's carries rotten corpse around? It doesn't make sense, the original Albert Houston never done that." No this isn't making no sense at all, There must be something that we're missing here. "That corpse you're talking about is Albert Houston sir." the forensic expert said. All agent Li and myself could do was stare at the old man with disbelief, did we hear him right? "the hell you said old man?" I broke the silence. "Mr. Goodwin, Albert Houston been dead for five years now sir. his body been cremated so you see how impossible that could be sir." Agent Li interrupted me with a more professional approach. "Look I'm sorry I don't know anything about that, but I do know that the DNA we have at the lab, the DNA we have on file from his old murders match this decayed body and the semen found inside what use to be this poor's woman's virginal." Goodwin explained. Agent Diaz couldn't believe what he was hearing, is this real? is this god damn real! "The hell you saying to me Goodwin! you expect me to believe that this sick son of a bitch brought the rotten decease body of the original Albert Houston which by the way was Supposed to be cremated five fucking years ago. Then poor sherry shuford blows the head off the already dead body of Albert Houston instead of the copycat that doing All the fucking killing. And for whatever reason this corpse back explodes, Rotten gore and flesh splash all over the god damn bedroom walls, while the copycat use that as a distraction to chop off her head, undress her headless body, Rapes her with..god knows what! Ejaculate the original Albert Houston semen inside the woman's body, Fresh semen by the way writes Albert Houston was here on the bedroom wall in her blood, escapes somehow, Somewhere without anyone seeing a fucking thing! Is that what I'm supposed to believe?" Agent Diaz snaps, frantically weaving his arms around sarcastically like a crazy person. "Believe what you want Mr. Diaz but that's one hundred percent Albert Houston's body." The forensic officer said without blinking an eye but before agent Diaz could protest again he was interrupted by another police officer. "Agent Diaz, Agent Li we found a surveillance footage that recorded the entire house!" "What!. Jesus this is the break we needed to finally find out who this son of a bitch really is!" Diaz said excited by the discovery, smacks agent Li on the shoulder's. "Let us have that son, Hell of a job officer Anderson." Diaz gave his congrats. "Thank you sir." Both agents praise the officer before taking the evidence. "MOM! MOOMMM!" "No you can't go in there!" "Mom! Mom! Where are you? Mom!" Agent heard the commotion in the living room. "Oh god no...Nnoooo!" Gabriella screams in frightened horror as she witness the lacerated body that was her mother on the bed. "Jesus Christ! Some body hurry and cover up that girl's mother!" The federal agent said surprise that a little teenage girl got through a barricade of swat and police officers... Shit no wonder this murdering son of a bitch got away. Gabriella crumbles to her knees in tears as one of the police officers finally catches up to her. "Mom no god please no...please." Gabriella pleaded to god as her worst nightmare come true. "I'm sorry little girl but you have to come with me." the officer said as he put his hand on her shoulder. The entire crime scene became quiet with sadness and pity for the young girl. "Leave her. I got this." Agent Diaz told the officer before walking over and kneeling down in front of the little girl. "I'm sorry we couldn't get here in time to save your mother...please come with me in the Living room... you shouldn't have to see her like this." Diaz spoke to her with a very soft, low tone of voice while rubbing her left shoulder trying his best to comfort her. "Why? why?" Gabriella asks him barely uttering the words through crying sobs of tears. Agent Diaz helps her to her feet. "I wish I knew sweetie but there are just evil people who live in this world." he try's his best to comfort the child as he can feel the anger building up in his chest thinking about how this bastard is out there right now planning to make someone else an orphan. "She knew...my mother knew, that's why she didn't want me to be home. Oh god.aahh..ahha" Gabriella revealed as she broke down again as agent Diaz quickly grabs the girl around the waist as she collapses in his arms. protecting her from hitting the ground. She knew? What does she mean her mother knew? May be this little girl might know something about this killer after all. "I got you, don't you worry we're going to get your mother's killer. I swear it." "No you don't understand..I..I read my mother's diary! She cut a deal with him to save my life! Now he took hers and he's after me next! I don't know why but I can feel it!" Gabriella cried out. "Who's coming for you? Who? I finally asked her. "The man in the black suit! He's coming for me and there's nothing nobody can do about! Nothing!" The girl said to me with total conviction in her eyes that somebody was coming for her and there wasn't nothing anybody could do to help. Can't blame her because we haven't stop a damn thing yet, But I'll promise on my life I will protect her till my dying breathe. This copycat in the black suit won't touch her. "What's your name?" "Gab, Gabriella shuford." she said. "Well my name is Andrew Diaz and I promise on my life and honor as a federal agent I won't let the man in the black suit harm you. I am putting you in protective custody." Agent Diaz promises her. "No! I'm not going to some protective custody without you!" she warned him. "Listen Gabriella, there will be a team of professional..." "I don't care! I'll run away! How can you promise my safety when you aren't doing the Protecting yourself?" Shit Diaz thought. That's when he knew the little girl was right. How can I make Such a bold claim to protect her when I'm not there to do it. through? Guess I won't be going by the book but what's by the book in this fuck up case anyway. Agent Diaz looks down at the young teenage girl and could see she had a lot of fight in her just like her mother did but I'll make sure her ending is a happy one. "You're right Gabriella. you will stay with me until we know you're one hundred percent safe but I need to know one thing why me? I'm just a stranger?" That's when I saw her stop weeping and look me straight in to my eyes, like she could she my soul. "I can sense the good in you. I don't know why but I know I could trust you." Gabriella answers him then embraces him in a hug. A new union was made on that night that will last a life time. Agent Diaz failed to protect anyone from this mass murder. Now god has giving him another chance to correct his failures. He's going to protect this girl Gabriella the way he couldn't for her mother or die trying. Across the street from the highly guarded murder scene of sherry shuford's house. There in the deepest of the shadows of an alley way lie eight swat officers killed , Mutilated for crossing paths with the most notorious mass murder known in modern times Albert Houston. He stalks and watches from the darkness unseen by human eyes. He witness the federal Agent Diaz escorting a young black teenage girl from the scene where he just finished murdering And raping the girl's mother to a car. "Well look at what we found. Our good o'friend agent Diaz walking with a nice young tender meat. Yeah we should reintroduce ourselves yeah best to fucking believe it." Albert Houston licks his blistered lips. "She is not to be touch. I have great plans for the young ms.shuford." the smooth elegant voice is heard behind Albert Houston and he knew his master has return. "the girl was not to be harm Albert Houston this why I gave the girl's mother the ability to sense when danger was coming so she may send her child to safety." the engineer explained. "Why? why do all that for some little black bitch?" the engineer glairs at Albert Houston and he knew not to question his master on the matter anymore. "Ms. shuford serves a great purpose that will be dealt with in time. For now, I have another mission for you, a killing mission one that you will love Mr. Houston so that the undead ritual can begin." the engineer continues to explain to his servant looking past his poor matters and impulses. "Yeah best to believe it." Albert smiled. "Yes, believe it in deed Mr. Houston. Believe it indeed." Albert Houston and the engineer Vanishes in to the darkness of the night.

CHAPTER NINE

There are not many things in my life experience that has been good for me, It's so rare I can literally count them all on one hand. My late mother, god bless her soul was the only person who really cared about me. showed me real love not treat me like some piece of shit. Now here's Natasha a real life angel sent from heaven to save my soul. She's the only woman who treats me worth a damn in this whole forsaken world besides my late mother. Now she blesses me with a rare gift of teaching me the true words of our Lord and savior Yahweh with the bible of heaven itself. Why would god bless a pathetic drunk like me is beyond my comprehension but I know one thing I won't let him down, I won't let her down. "I'm very pleased how much you were able to get through in such a short time Jessie. Now you know the glory of god's word." Natasha see's Jessie tears of joy and gently Wipes them away as she stares at him like a mother proud of her children. "God is very pleased in your growth Jessie; I can feel his glorious light shine upon us." "What about you Natasha? Are you pleased with me? Jessie asks as he returns her gaze. Natasha gently caresses her index finger under Jessie chin. "Of course, Jessie I have witness you ascend from the darkness in to the light, this Pleases me greatly." Hearing Natasha express her words of gratitude while caressing his face gave him great pleasure but not the kind he was expecting, it was more spiritual. A deep feeling of peace and finally belonging to something that love's and adores him for who he is. For this he will always be grateful to Natasha. Jessie grabs Natasha hand and start's massage's, it with his thumb as he stairs deep in to her eyes. "Only if you knew how much that means to me, that you feel that way about me Natasha but I have to ask you something." Jessie said. "Yes what is troubling you Jessie?" Natasha answer using the opportunely to remove her hand from Jessie grip. Trying the hide the flesh in her cheeks as her dark skin became blossom red. "There might be something wrong with this bible Natasha because every time I try to read revelations I can't turn or read the pages, it's like the book is trying to lock me out." "That's because it is Jessie." Natasha said. "What! Why?" "Because god is not ready for you to witness the Armageddon. It is forbidden for most of us to read. I'm sorry Jessie but our bible study has reached its conclusion." Natasha revealed to him. Jessie stands before Natasha and grabs both of her hands and press it on his chest. "What am I supposed to do now then Natasha?" Jessie ask as Natasha pulled her hand A way from him taking a few steps back in order to make distance between them. I can't help to think since the night I help him conquer the darkness within and the strong drink things have become too physical between us. I've been comforting him a lot of late, May be too much...the way he touches me...I don't understand why it makes me feel... I just don't understand, As of now I shall guild Jessie brown towards the lord's light from A greater distance. "Jessie you..you must prepare yourself for the holy trails. This will be your ultimate task of being accepted in to the glorious lights of Zion or descending in to the darkness which is Babylon." "Holy trails, what is that?" Jessie looked puzzled. "The holy trails are the ultimate test against the light and darkness that dwells in the human soul. Thy true nature will be revealed... there is a chance one soul can be lost to darkness forever, Are you ready for such a trail Jessie?" She asks but Jessie doesn't response verbally. Instead he walks straight towards her as Natasha back paddles until she hits the bedroom wall, Uncertain what to do next. "what...Jessie what are you doing?" Natasha asks him as she felt the temperature in her body rise. "Tell me, do you think I'm ready for it Natasha?" "It's not for me to decide jes.." Jessie stretch out both arms against the wall, trapping Natasha between the wall and himself. "No, you tell me Natasha. You tell me if I'm ready... you tell me." Jessie tells her as he Lower his face towards hers, his lips close enough to touch hers. "Jessie. No don't.." Natasha barely utter the words from her mouth, her body paralyzed Unable to move a muscle. "Of course Natasha thinks you're ready but the question remains are you ready angel of silence?" Jessie slightly jumps as he turns towards the front door. "Valery!" Jessie utters her name in complete shock. "Yes, it is I young angel of silence but you have not answer my question." Valery repeated Herself while she stands at the entrance of the door with the presence of a goddesses. Natasha uses the opportunely to push past Jessie arms and stand between him and Valery. "Yes he is ready Varley. God has answered me this dear sister." Valery paused for an few seconds Before she decided to answer her old friend. "Good. For I have already prepared the ritual of the holy trails." Valery said as she stared at them Both. Valery turns her attention to Jessie brown with complete seriousness. "Know this angel of silence once the holy trails begin there's no turning back. You ether survival the trails and be bliss by heaven's glory or fail and descend in to the bowls of the pit of darkness." Valery warns Jessie what could happen to his soul if he's not mentally prepares to deal with the trails at hand. "God and Natasha have shown complete faith in me and I will do the same so to answer your question I've never been readier than I am now." Jessie stood with pride and full reinsurance in his voice. "Humph..we shall see angel of silence." Valery smirk as Jessie's warriors pride pleases her. "Now come I shall reveal the hidden path to the entrance of secrets." Valery leads the way as Natasha and Jessie fellows along. Valery makes a complete stop at the end of the hall in front of the wall. "Is this kind of hidden door like those old spy movies?" Jessie joked. "Hush now child if you are to survival you must be physically and mentally ready for this journey." Valery gave Jessie a final warning. "Don't worry about me Valery I'm a former soldier like you, I'm ready for anything." "Aye very well then angel of silence." Ancient sword of fire emerges from Valery's hand. A flaming sword that can only be weld by the cherubim that guards the tree of life, then she began to chant words, ancient words of the very first language of mankind before god and his Angels scatter man and gave them different languages so they wouldn't understand each Other to stop nimrod from completing the towel of Babylon. The walls and ground around them began to shake. Valery and Natasha were unmoved by these Events by Jessie began to have a hard time keeping his balance and fear of doubt started to creep in to his heart as everything began to dematerialize around him. "What, what the hell's going on? everything disappearing!" Jessie worried for all their lives. "Jessie, you must control yourself and have faith in god if you wish not to be swallow up by The darkness." Natasha explained to him, Not looking his way while sticking her hand out instead. Jessie understood what she was doing. This is a test of his faith and trust in god... His trust that he has for her. No he won't waver again Jessie grabs, holding her hand tightly While the entire sanctuary disappears in to the black void of space. Are, Are we in space Jessie thought to himself as he looks all around himself, He see's Billions of billions of stars shining bright in the deep darkness of space. As Jessie looks up on the sun and moon his hands begin to tremble. "Do not fear Jessie for god the mighty El Shaddai is guiding us." Natasha try's her best to Ease the fears and worries of Jessie brown. "I know...I'm not shaking from fear but from excitement. It's beautiful Natasha." He looks at Natasha and wondered how someone like him could be so bliss to witness all these wonders of god's world. Natasha gracefully smiles to herself knowing that Jessie is continuing to change for the better while not taking her eyes off of Valery as her chants begin to get louder. Bright blue lights of electricity surround them and all of space becomes a blue blur of light. Suddenly it was all over, and Jessie feet was touching the ground again. "Here where your journey in to the light or dark begins angel of silence." Valery said to Jessie. As she turns to face him only to find him knelt on both knees crying. "Jessie?" Natasha said his name in deep concern for his wellbeing. All of Jessie's senses are over-whelm with over joy of happiness trying to take in his new Surroundings. Only a handful of people have ever laid eyes on this ancient place of wonders and beauty, majestic ani-mals that was lost in time. It was a place that it's beauty ri-val heaven itself. "Is this..is this place what I think it is?" An emotional Jessie asks. "Yes it is angel of silence. you have read many stories about it now you are witnessing Its won-ders with your own eyes. Welcome to the garden of Eden." Valery reveals the name of the place that god once made for Adam and Eve before betraying his trust. Jessie still standing on both knees turns and looks up at Natasha with complete joy in his eyes. "Natasha, Natasha thank you...thank you so much. Is this my reward for passing the Holy trails, too live in this wonderful place for the rest of my life?" Shock and horror felled up on her face as she stood speechless, how could she explain to Jessie brown without breaking his spirit? Natasha knew that the garden of Eden can cause humans an overwhelming experience of happiness and fulfillment, to pull one out of the garden can cause them great depression that leads to suicide, But she never had to personally deal with such a situation before. "Natasha...Natasha what's going on? Why ain't you answering me? Natasha please... Tell me this is god's purpose for..." "No angel of silence you hadith not pass the holy trails. What you have experience is but a small test of faith which you would had failed if not for Natasha interference." Valery interrupted Jessie and Natasha displease at the sight she was force to witness. "Valery don't discourage him!" Natasha defended Jessie. "No Natasha we have no more time for baby steps. Angel of silence you hadith not been giving holy sanctuary in the garden of Eden to live throughout eternally. Here is where the holy trails will commence. This you shall do alone and if thy fails this test you shall Fall in the abyss for all eternally. Valery explained to Jessie harshly with no remorse. All was heard for the next two minutes was the sound of distant waterfalls and roaming animals all else was silent. Jessie finally looks up at both angels with bloodshot eyes, sweating feverishly. Jessie brown was sick, a sickness that ran through his soul. sick of all the pain and suffering throughout his life. Just tired...so tired of living sick and tired. But no matter how bad he is suffering, Jessie knows he can't quit, He's a soldier and true soldiers don't quit. "I see... I was never meant to stay here. this place is only here to host the holy trails." "Yes angel of silence no human or angel can live here in the forbidden paradise. Only in special occasions I am allow to enter a person to commence the holy trails." "Tell me Valery what would had happened if Natasha didn't give me her little vote of confidence back there?" Jessie asked his legs began to shake violently while trying to stand back on his feet. Natasha comes over to aid Jessie to his feet but he kindly wards her off. Valery notice his self pride and it pleases her so. "It isn't necessary now that..." "No Natasha everything's necessary now. Especially now that we're here. If you truly have faith in me like you say Natasha then you must have faith that I can handle all the truth." Jessie told the angel he holds so dear to his heart as he will himself to his feet and stood tall. For the first time sense meeting the angel of silence known as Jessie brown Valery really starts to feel that he might make a decent angel of the almighty god Yahweh, the El Shaddai. "You would had died angel of silence. You would had felled in to the black void and meet your death but your soul would had risen to the kingdoms of heaven. Now hear this young angel of silence if you shall fail thy holy trails you shall fall in to damnation for eternally." Valery explained to Jessie, so he may know the true consequences of failure. "So are you telling me if I fail this test I'm going to burn in hell forever?" He asked. "Yes that is correct angel of silence. Now are you ready to handle such a burden?" "Yes I am Valery. I will show god that his faith in me is just and Natasha trusting me won't be in vain. I will become the angel of silence." Natasha saw a brand new confidence and self pride reside inside himself. There was no more confusion or questions, He had complete faith that he will pass the holy trails and complete faith in our lord in savior Yahweh. thank you, my dear god, for blessing Jessie with thy strength. "Good Jessie brown you are truly ready to take the holy trails, god have complete faith in you." Natasha said as she approaches him. "Thank you." Jessie smiled at her as he looked in to her beautiful eyes with a brand new vote of confidence. within a blank of an eye all of Jessie's pain and sorrow was gone. "Then let us commence the holy trails." Valery lead the way through god's forbidden paradise until they reach a large lake with fire burning hot on top of the cool water. "we've have arrived on the site where you shall complete the holy trails, prepare yourself." Jessie looked at Valery then looked back at the lake of fire, confused. "I don't understand what's going on here? There's fire burning hot on top of water, Am I supposed to put it out or something?" Jessie asked. "This is heavens holy fire it can burn hot on any surfaces. Jessie you must cleanse your soul in god's holy fire." Natasha answer in her usually cryptic way leaving him uncertain How is he supposed to cleanse himself in a lake of fire? "Umm I hear you Natasha but I'm still not seeing how a lake of fire supposed to cleanse me?" "you must submerge your entire body in to the holy fire for god can cleanse the darkness from your soul." Jessie turned his head at Natasha with wide eyes as he finally understood what Natasha was replying to him. Jessie could feel all his self confidence slowly fading from his body. "And if it can't burn away my darkness?" Jessie asked Natasha. "you shall die angel of silence but this time your soul will be damned to hell for all eternally." Valery interrupted bluntly. "What the fuck!, listen sorry I swear but are you telling me if I fail this test I'm going to burn in hell for all of eternally!" "Yes angel of silence but if you succeed you shall become one of god's angels." Valery answered. "you will succeed Jessie have..god have faith in you to be the first." Natasha held both her hands together in started to pray. Jessie looks back at her and smiles. his confidence renew. "then let's not keep the all mighty waiting shall we." Jessie bravely walks towards the lake of fire as the two angels watch on as they prayed to their god. this is just a test Jessie. I mustn't wavier like I did before. This whole set up is about testing my faith and trust that I have for god. Jessie could feel the scorching heat of the fire as he approaches. like a man obsessed Jessie doesn't hesitate as he walks in to the lake of fire. Jessie felt no pain when his body submerge in to the lake of fire. i knew it! i knew it! god wanted to test my faith in him by seeing if i was willing to risk my life on his word. "Natasha I'm doing it! I'm doing it Natasha!" Jessie called out in excitement. Jessie slowly started to consume the holy blaze's around his entire body. this continues to happen until the holy fire was no more. Jessie stood in the middle of the lake, body smoking from the engulf flames of the holy fire, yet he stood unharmed, without a single burn throughout his body. Jessie chest stood out right, his hands out to his side, palms facing up. Jessie never felt such accomplishment, pride and joy before. he couldn't wait to walk out of this lake and hug and kiss Natasha beautiful face as Jessie celebrates not only his but her accomplishments too. "I did it! No we did it Natasha! We did it together! I am the angel of silence and it's all because you showed faith in me." Jessie spoke proudly as he walked out of the lake. Jessie notices that Natasha and Valery weren't paying attention to him. instead they continue to pray to their god showing no response to Jessie's victory. the hell? if there's more to the test they would tell me wouldn't they? with that thought Jessie stomach started to tightening as blinding bolts of pain shot through his entire body. sweat poured from every inch of his body, his skin burned hot like a furnace. Jessie insides felt like they were about to explode and he felt a great fear. it wasn't fear of death or even falling in to the pits of hell. all he could think of is how he wouldn't never see her beautiful face again. How he would never get to express his true feelings for her and never feel her gentle touch again. Holy fire exploded out of every opening in Jessie's body. There was no mercy, No relief just unimaginable pain. Bright beam of light shot out of Jessie's body, pointing towards the heaven's. Jessie's pain was over, His mind was blink as Jessie felt no more. "Now thy real test begins, Natasha pray that he succeeds." "All that is holy my dear sister Valery. I be leave he will succeed..He must." Natasha answer her dearest friend worried for her precious pupil. Valery watches her longtime friend continues her prayers for the angel of silence. Valery wonders does Natasha realize how much she change through her experience with the angel of silence and if this change is one that will damn her soul. white and black sparkles plague his sight of vision as his senses returned to him. Jessie blank his eyes hard for a long two seconds, when he reopens his eyes the sparkles were gone and so was the lake and the garden of Eden. There was nothing to be seen, Nothing but fog. Fog so thick Jessie couldn't see the ceiling nor the ground he stood on, it was like the entire world had vanished before his eyes. "Natasha! Valery are you there?" Jessie yelled out and all that was heard was the sound of his own voice echo. where the fuck is this place? One minute I'm busting open in flames the next I'm lost in some damn cosmic fog. The hell is going on? Jessie thought. "wow I've never knew we could look so pussy under distress. Man up soldier!" Jessie fanatically turns around looking all around to find out where that voice came from. there was something about his voice that frightened Jessie, something familiar and impossible that ran chill's down his spine. "Over here Jessie!" Jessie heard and fellow it's voice and saw a human figure appear out of the thick fog. It was a man, A black man but the fog was too thick to make out his face. Jessie did notice that the person wore official army camouflage bdu pants, A black t-shirt with a camouflage bandanna tied over his head. Jessie step forward to approach this man and stop frozen in his tracks. Jessie appeared to look pale and sickly and started to retreat backwards from the approaching man overwhelm in pure horror. "Jesus, Jessie you act like you seen a ghost?" the unknown soldier said as he smile at Jessie brown. Jessie couldn't be leave his eyes but he knew it was real. Ever since he encounter the demon known as the engineer, His life became a wild fantasy of bliss and horrors, But he couldn't had ever image this. "Who?...What the fuck are you? Because you sure ain't me?" Jessie said to the soldier who stood before him with every ounce of his body resemble Jessie brown. His build, the voice, his features even the militarily gear, Everything accept for his eyes. His eyes were pure black. "I am you Jessie, In some ways I'm more you then you are." the other Jessie responded. Jessie pause, size up his doppelganger and realize whatever it was, It wasn't out to hurt him. "Really, so what kind of test is this? You're supposed to be my Christmas ghost or some shit like that?" "yeah you can say I am something like that. You see I'm here to show you the truth about yourself. show you who you really are." the duplicate answer. "what you trying to say? that I'm like you some demonic soldier from hell. sorry I've seen how that story ends and I'm not burning in hell for nothing." the other Jessie didn't respond right away instead he smirk then reach in to his back pocket and pulled out a pint of jack Daniels. He then turns the bottle towards his lips and swallows it all down in one shot. "Aawwh! that's some good shit man. You want some? i got a whole lot more where that came from." the duplicate Jessie offer him. "....Na I'm good. trying to stay off that stuff." Jessie decline the doppelganger offer with a look of strain on his face. "well damn Jessie! Natasha really put some shit on you huh? Dying to do anything she says just to have a chance at getting some of that sweet angel pussy." "Fuck you! you don't know shit!" Jessie erupted at his counterpart. "No you don't know shit! I'm not some fucking demon who's taking your form! I am a part of your fucking soul! I'm your other half, so I know exactly how you feel and how you think!" The other Jessie lash back at his original self. "I know how fuck up other child hood was. I know that you feel like you're falling in love with that angel. I know everything about you man because I'm a part of you. Listen I'm here to help you man, you just have to be willing to hear me out." the other Jessie said, his voice soften with an edge of sorrow and pain that the main Jessie knows all too well. silence felt between the two Jessie's as they stood their ground. "...So what can you tell me that I don't already know?" Jessie said finally ready to hear his other self. There was something familiar about the pain in his voice. something that made me believe him enough to listen. "Good. Good man. First of I want to tell you straight up this whole test is about what side you're going to choose. heaven or Hell." "well shit man. If all this is about choosing a side then that's easy. I choose heaven for many reasons man." Jessie answer. "And what reasons are those?" the other Jessie asked seriously. "seriously man?... God wins. Natasha is a angel and on top of all of that. if I choose hell my soul is going to burn in hell soon as this test is over with. I think that's reason enough don't you?" Jessie said to his doppelganger with sarcasm. "yeah I hear you man but let me tell you this. Everything that Natasha and Valery told you wasn't completely true. There is a reason you're called the angel of silence." He revealed. "what the hell are you talking about! I've read god's original bible! Natasha reveal to me about what the angel of silence is and she wouldn't lie to me!" Jessie argue. "Heh first off angels do lie. Remember that Satan was an angel and so is the engineer, But you're right, Natasha would never willingly lie to you but she can be deceptive in her own way to pull you towards her side. For example saying if you fail this test your soul will be damn. Meaning when you die your soul won't be able to enter the kingdom of heaven and will descend to hell. Unlike Valery who straight up lied to you. so whatever choice you make, you won't die here. you understand?" He revealed. "yeah I hear you man but ain't it all the same in the end. Burn now or later in the end it's all the same, Satan loses and all his followers burns in the Pitt alongside him. it's already written man." Jessie said. "stop it man. What, you know all of this because you read the true book? tell me this bro where in the book of revelations you read that? the other Jessie question his other half while folding his arms together waiting for him answer. Jessie stood silent, he read the book but wasn't able to read revelations, he wasn't allowed to. "it's alright Jessie. don't feel bad man even your lovely Natasha hadn't read the true revelations and there's a reason for that." I don't know how he knows all these things but I'll go along right now Jessie thought to himself while he paid close attention to his other self. "the reason is the ending haven't been decided yet, this is why you have such a important role to play angel of silence." the other Jessie finish explaining as he open and drank another half pint of whiskey. "that still doesn't change my mind. I still chose heaven." Jessie claimed without the slightest hesitation. completely sure of his decision and faith in god Yahweh. "It's not that simple to just say what side you chose, you have to show it through your actions and what I'm about to show you might change your whole prospective of everything." "there won't be anything you can show me that will change my mind." Jessie responded. "Good because I'm not here to change your mind, only to reveal the truth to you." "...Fine! tell me whatever it is that you have to tell me." Jessie said irritated wanting to end this test quickly as possible. "good because I'm about to show you why our life been so fuck up. what really happen to mom and dad, the real truth why we were chosen to become the angel of silence." he explain as his arms raised up in the air like he was worshiping some idol god. the fog started to desperate underneath both of the Jessie feet, revealing a bright light glowing in a circle. before Jessie could utter a single sound all went white as Jessie brown lost his eye sight from the blinding bright light. "Aaahhh! mother fucker! my eyes! my eyes!" Jessie cursed staggering back in forth rubbing his eyes. "my bad man. should of told you to close your eyes first. it was necessary in order to get you too where everything started." he apologize as he place his hand over Jessie's forehead. "chill. let me heal you it's very important that you witness these events." Jessie's pain was gone. he slowly open his eyes as his vision returned better than ever. "What? Where the hell are we man?" Jessie was surprise to find himself back on earth. In front of a small Baptist church surrounded by large trees and thick bushes. All the church residents were African Americans. "This is Salisbury north Carolina 1973. June six, 6:00pm. This is where everything started." He answer the original Jessie's question then pointed towards a small group of christens Leaving the Baptist church. "There! Do you recognize her?" Jessie couldn't believe what his other self was showing him. His heart started to beat fast, his palm began to sweat, tears swelled up in his eyes. No longer could he control his emotions. "Mom? Oh god it is you. Mom! Mom! It's me Jessie your son!" Jessie yelled out to his Younger mother. "Jessie she can't hear or see you. None of them can. We are only here to witness certain events do you understand?" He asked his original self, Jessie wiped the tears from his face. "yeah, yeah, I'm ok, I'm good. She's so young." Jessie smiled. It's been nineteen years Since I last saw my mother alive. to see her here and now so young and happy. it's a true blessing from god. "I know what you're thinking Jessie. Let's see if you feel the same way after you watch this?" He smirks at his original self. Jessie saw his smirk and it really pissed him the fuck off. "What the fuck man! If you know something just tell me?" Jessie yell in anger. "No more questions. All your answers will be answered soon enough now watch and learn." Both Jessie kept silent to witness these past events. Events that will determine the past and future of the angel of silence.

CHAPTER TEN

1973 SALISBURY NORTH CAROLINA.

Jennies a.k.a Jennise Barnes is a happy eighteen years old, Dedicated Christian woman. Who loves to attend church with her fifthly three year old mother. A mother who raise her as a single mother since Jennies was the age Four, when her father left them to be with another woman in South Carolina. Jennies mother raise her to be independent and too always have faith in god. For that Jennies loves her more than anything. Every Sunday me and my mother serve the lord at this old Baptist church From 10am to 6pm at night for the past thirteen years, And I love every bit of it. Although I'm sure tired from all the praying and dancing I did, But That's how we praise the god almighty. Jennies helps her mother walk down the church steps. Lucida Barnes was a short heavy set woman known by many people to have a special gift from god. Word is that she can see things that yet to come. A gift of foresight from the all mighty above. "It sure was honey. any day that god allow us to wake and attend his service is a great day." "amend to that Ms. Barnes." a strong manly voice interrupted. "How are you both doing today?" jennies and lucida both turn their heads but jennies was the only one who felt a hot flash run through her body when she saw the young Christian man that came from new York city, Kenneth brown. "Were doing quit fine Mr. brown. how are you doing?" jennies ask as she finish helping her mother down the last few steps. "I'm doing just fine now that i got to see you Ms. Barnes and your lovely mother too." Kenneth took off his top hat, held jennies hand and kissed it. jennies fan herself while she pulled her hand away. trying to resist Mr. browns charm. "wow it sure is hot out here isn't it?" "to hot for a old woman like me to be out. come now jennies take me home." Lucida grabs hold of her daughter's hand and pulls her away. "Kenneth brown you have a good night now." Lucida said as they walked by him. "okay good night Ms. Barnes. I hope I get to see you in service again Ms. jennies." Kenneth said as he watch jennies walk away. "oh, you definite will Mr. Kenneth brown." jennies said peaking back. catching Mr. .brown looking at her ass. jennise love's that Kenneth watch her walk away every Sunday night. I'll give you something to watch. jennise switch her ass around so he could enjoy it better. "Good night Mr. brown." she said a final time before leaving for good. later when the Barnes women made it home Lucida stop and confronted her daughter. "jennise don't think because I'm old, I didn't notice what was going on back there. including you switching your little behind everywhere for Kenneth to see." jennise face turned red from embarrassment. my mother can she things that most people can't, sometimes I witch she would pretend she couldn't. "Mom. I'm eighteen years old. I think I'm old enough to like people now." jennies smile's but embarrassment that she's having this conversation with her mom. "jennise, honey listen to me okay. I know that you are a grown, smart Christian woman but you don't know everything." Lucida lecturer. "I want you to stay away from him." Lucida held on to jennise hands. "Mom! you're starting to scare me. if this about sex, you know I'm planning on waiting until I'm married." "jennise I know you're not that kind of girl. you're a better woman then I ever was." "Mom! No don't say that!" jennise protest. "No but it's true jennise. God as my witness it's true! I'm begging you please stay away from him! promise me you try okay?" Lucida pleaded again, this time she started to cry. I've never seen my mother like this before. why would she say something like this to me, unless... Jennise gasp as she covers mouth with her hand. "oh' god! you saw something! did you really see something in your vision's mom?" "Honey please, just stay away from him okay? promise me." Lucida beg her daughter while avoiding her questions. "...Okay mom, Okay I'll promise." jennise promise but there was a great depression that sank deep in to her heart. She began to wonder would her mother ever approved any man to be with her. Unknowing to the two Barnes women there are two visitors from the future watching them play out events from there past lives. your mother won't be able to keep that promise she made to your grandmother Jessie. Dark Jessie reveal to his other half. "hey man! so you telling me that young guy at the church was my god damn father?" Jessie asked but already knew the answer deep down in his heart. shit all these fucking feelings I'm feeling all at once. Jessie held his chest. this is the first time I've ever seen my grandmother a live. Before now the only thing I ever saw her was in the pictures hanging up in my mother's room. Then it was him.. The man named Kenneth brown, my bio-logical father. A father I've never seen before, never spoke to, Fuck I never seen a fucking picture of him before. Now I finally get to see him after all these years. why my grand-mother don't want my mother seeing my father? Is that why I never met my father? what..NO! why the fuck do I have to watch all this shit? what the hell does all of this have to do with me being the angel of silence? Jessie tortures himself with questions he knows he can't answer. "These events has everything with you being the Angel of silence." "what the fuck! How the fuck you knew what I was thinking? you reading my mind or some shit like that?" Jessie shout out as he step away from his darker half. "Calm down Jessie. I am not reading your mind but I know what you're thinking because I'm fucking you! Now shut the fuck up and witness these next events and all your questions will be answered." Jessie wanted to protest to argue but he knew his other side was right. it's just seeing all of this is bring up emotions I thought I buried long ago. All I really did was just mask my feelings under pints of whiskey every day. "This is six months later. Here is where your mother's life changed forever." The other Jessie said to me. Jennise struggles walking home holding two large paper bag of groceries in her arms. Damn it's so hot out here, I'm sweating out my press. Jennise huff and puff, Trying to keep the sweat out of her eyes. While she continues to struggle home a dark red fifth avenue slowly drove up beside her. " Jesus Jennise. What's you doing walking with those heavy bags in your hands?" Kenneth asked her. "Kenneth now you know better to use the lord's name in vain. And what does it look like I'm doing with them." Jennise rolled her eyes. "I'm sorry Jennise. that's was a stupid question to asks. let me drive you home, that's the least I can do." Kenneth apologize with a charming smile. why he got to be so damn hansom. Mom why you got to go and mess everything up. Jennise thought. Her face turned blossom red from Kenneth smile. "No thank you Romeo. I'll be just fine thank you very much." Jennise stumble, trying her best to act like nothing happen. "Ah come on Jennise. I can see you need help. And how come you been avoiding me after service on Sundays? I miss our talks."

"Because I can't OK! I'm sorry Keith you seem like a really nice guy but I can't be with you the way you want!" I said to him. The sad, broken look I saw in his eyes melted my heart but it had to be said sooner or later. "Why? I don't understand I like you and it seem like you like me too. Did I do something wrong Jennise? Because if I did I'm sorry." "No you didn't do anything wrong, it just isn't going to work OK!" Jennise said holding her head up high a voiding eye contact him. "Does this have something to do with your mother Jennise?" Kenneth ask but Jennise kept silent and continue to struggle along. "My god! It is because of your mother isn't it?" "Keith I told you don't say the lords name in vain!" she yelled at him. doing all she can to change the subject. Damn Kenneth why don't you just leave already! stop begging me, God please help me be strong. "jennise, please come on! you're a grown woman. Don't let your mother tell you who you can or can't see." Kenneth pulled over his car. Jennise stop and her tracks and turn to face Keith. "listen I'm only gonna tell you this once. Don't you ever speak ell of my mom you understand! you're new around here okay, so let me explain something to you. My mother's special, She can see things that nobody else can, So when my mother say don't do something people listen okay!" Jennise said sternly. Kenneth just sat there looking at me with water in his eyes. I could tell I was breaking his heart. "I'm sorry jennise. you're a good girl I had no right to tell you to go against your mother's wishes like that. listen just let me take you home and you won't ever hear from me again OK?" Kenneth said in a low depress voice as he slump down in the seat of his car. "Wait, wait a minute Keith. I've never said I didn't want..." "It's for the best jennise, plus that's what your mother want." Kenneth said as he step out of his car and held the door open. "so will you allow me to drive you home?" "okay, straight home." "sure, okay." jennise enters the driver side and scoots over the to the passenger's seat. jennise stairs at Kenneth expecting him to say something as he sat down. there was nothing but awkward silence between them. Kenneth start's the car and drove jennise towards her mother's house. Several blocks away Lucida sits in her living room, reading the holy bible waiting on her daughter to arrive home with the grocery's. Lucida felt a dark aura submerge all around her causing Sharpe pain in her chest. "who's there? this house is protected by god our lord and savior! Be gone in this house of the lord! Be gone!" Lucida shouted the lords name. "can you sense me woman?" Lucida heard the demonic voice in her living room. she held her chest trying to control her fears while she pray to god for protection. "yes I can demon and I rebuke you in the name of Jesus Christ, the holy spirit! I rebuke you in the name of Christ thy lord and savior!" Lucida grab her crucifix and continues to shout out holy prayers to protect her from the evil spirits that dwells in her house. "So you can hear me as well. you truly are gifted, How interesting I see why he chosen your daughter." the invisible demon said. "No demon! you cannot harm us! we are under the almighty gods protection! you cannot harm us demon!" "Yes you are right woman. There are rules that cannot be broken. But your child. your precious daughter shall give birth to a special child that will harvest souls for the true light bringer our lord and master Satan!" Lucida heard the demons voice closer now, it's dark presence weighting her down, the pain increase in her chest as he breathing became hard and heavy. "You devils won't have my daughter or any child she would have! Now be gone in the name of Jesus Christ!" Lucida announce. "Foolish child that name holds no power over me. Jesus is no different than any other prophet of god's but I shall obey your wishes and leave with a parting gift." "I don't want no gift of yours demon!" "child of god behold what a native of hell looks like!" A mass of darkness formed in the middle of Lucida living room. Arms and legs sprout from the darkness, It's eyes was the color of dried blood and its teeth were sharper than any creature of this world. the mere sight of such a horrifying creature can drive a man insane. image what effects that can have on an elderly woman who can not only see but feel the complete pure aura darkness of Satan's creatures. Lucida scream out in pure horror as her heart gave out. Lucida collapse hard in to her living room floor as she gasp her final breathe. A final vision appears before her eyes, showing a terrible fate that awaits her daughter. Lucida prayed to god to change her daughter's fate as tears ran from her eyes, Her vision became dark then she felt nothing.

CHAPTER ELEVEN

It's been a week since I been trailing the murders of this disgusting plague that my brother resurrected called Albert Houston. Since it's resurrection this abomination been murdering people whom crossed him in his past life. Normally I'll just be rid of the filth but I need it to lead me to My brother. God gave me the noble task of hunting down my demonic brother to regain my family's honor. If all it takes is to tolerate this demonic human filth killing other human filth, then I will gladly do so. Now this filth have taken a different course of action by killing this woman who bargain her soul to save her daughter's life. Once he murder's her then have his way with the human, it will return to my brother in order for him to perform the necromancy ritual. surprisingly the woman did not go down easy. she actually killed the filth in his human form..It was quite impressive. In the end it made no difference, she still died brutally. Once the beast leaves the apartment I'll have what I need. Norwell thought to himself as he patiently watch Albert Houston rape and lacerated sherry shuford corpse. When Albert Houston was done decorating the Livingroom with his calling card and left, Norwell reveal himself inside the apartment. Norwell approaches the empty hush that was Albert Houston's body. Such pathetic sinful creatures they are. I don't understand what god or Natasha see's in them. If it wasn't for Noah god would had wipe them all out of existence. All because of that one man I have to tolerate these abomination every day, that's why the very sight of Noah makes me sick. If it wasn't for him there wouldn't have been a Genghis Khan, Adolf Hitler or an Alert Houston... especially an Angel of silence. But whom am I to question thy lord and savior. Now that's everything in place I won't have to tolerate this hell on earth much longer. Once my brother is slayed by my hands I will gladly go back home in heaven with honors and put this place of human filth behind me. Norwell knelt down and placed his hand on the empty hush that was Albert's body. Norwell chants the first ancient languages of mankind before god sent his angels to change their languages for the fear of what man can do united. Norwell eyes became crystal blue beams of light. Norwell eye sight travel through new York city and found Albert Houston straggling a middle age woman in a back alley a few blocks from here. Norwell knows he can easy teleport there and be rid of this demon filth but he won't. he'll let his brother have his corpse for the ritual and when he does I'll be there waiting. Once the serial killer was done straggling the woman to death, Norwell release his hand of the empty hush and walked over to the dismember body of sherry shuford and repeated the same ritual on her body that he did Albert's. Norwell couldn't help himself and smiled knowing it won't be long before he put his falling brother to rest and be rid of this filthy world. I'm so thirsty, so tired...what? where am I? A confuse Lucida slowly starts to wake up. She surprise to see her daughter jennise standing over her. "Mom! Mom, Oh god I was so worried." jennise squeeze her mother's hand while she started to cry. "Why you crying baby? It's okay, mommy's OK .Lucida said as her eyes started to adjust to her surroundings. "What! Where? Jennise am I in a hospital? Why am I in a hospital jennise?" Her eyes were wild with panic as she realize where she was. "Oh god! Mom don't you remember? you had a heart attack. Kenneth and I found you on the living room floor and took you to the hospital." jennise explained. "That's right Ms. Barnes. I'm so glad I was around to drive you to the hospital in time." Kenneth agreed as he walk and stood next to jennise besides Lucida's bed. "No! Noooo!" Lucida scream out, grabbing her heart again. "Yes, yesss Lucida you can hear me can you? you can truly see me as I'm truly am can you my dear Lucida." A sinister smile rose across Kenneth's face. "you're the demon that did this to me! Jennise get away from him! Uuhh!" Lucida cliche's her heart tight. "Mom no calm down! Nurse! Nurse please hurry!" jennise yelled out for help as the emergency staff quickly rush inside to aide Ms. Barnes. "save your strength Lucida. No one can see or hear the things you can. Remember you're special and so will your grandchild. My son that I will have with your daughter will lead us all Lucida. He will lead us to a new era. He will help us win this eternal war against El shadda and his angels. It will be glorious Lucida! All thanks to you and your precious daughter, Now you can die with my gratitude." lucida could hear his demonic laugh while the doctors try their best to save her life. "Do not worry my child. God has heard your prayers." An elegant voice appear from a bright white light inside the room. Before Lucida could utter a word, The entire room was gone. Including the demon that started it all. It was only her now, standing tall and strong once again, in what she could tell was some kind of white void. "Am I in heaven? Is this heaven?" she spoke, hoping someone would answer. "No dear child. Heaven will come for you soon enough because you have been faithful to god's word Lucida." Lucida once again heard the elegant voice but this time from behind her and a lot closer. Lucida

quickly turns around and when she saw what has summoned her here. Lucida felt to her knees, crying thanking
god for his blessings while a tall angel stood before her, Her
skin was smooth like silk and black as night. Her hair was
tougher then wool that stretch down her back. Her wings
spread wide across the empty void that seemed endless.
the armor on her body was that of a warrior goddess. "Do
not bow my child fore I am not god. God has sent me to reveal a message for you." the beautiful angel help Lucida off
her feet, Holding on to both of her hands. "God, God sent
you for me?" Lucida said with disbelief that god would send
a real angel to speak to her. who was I to be blessed this
way. Lucida thought. "yes Lucida god has sent me to tell you
that your grandson Jessie brown will be protected by our
lord and savior no matter how much sin his father try's to
corrupt him with. Jessie will always have a free choice to
become the man he wish to be." she told Lucida. "Thank
you. Thank you god but what about my daughter she's still
with that monster?" "Our lord has already bless her with a
kingdom in heaven but she must marry the demon. It's gods
will, Jessie brown must be born." Lucida felt her heart sank
deep in to her chest but she understood the will of god. "He
must grow up to be a very important man. God always
knows best." "Yes he does Lucida. Now if you choose to use
the gifts that god has granted you. you will see your grandson watching us." the angel said as she turned and stared
straight at Jessie brown. "O' shit! she can see us!" Jessie
said as he turned to face his other half but there wasn't anyone there. Jessie brown was alone. "what the fuck!" where
did this mother fucker go? He thought. "There's no one but
us young Angel of silence. Don't fear child, come and embrace the mother of your mother." "Come honey. I don't
have much time left. look at you, your mother will be so

proud." Lucida said while placing her hand on his cheek. "No grandly, I'm a monster. There isn't a thing I've ever done right." Jessie turns his head away in shame. "No honey, you lift your head up high. you suffer and withstood pain more than most people have in their entire life but here you are, trying you're very best to serve the lord. when I touched you I was able to see everything in your past grandson and I can see you have become a man that have made me and your mother proud. You always remember that honey were all proud of you." Lucida manage to praise her grandchild before stepping in to the bright blue light with the angel. Jessie broke down in tears as he watch his grand mom disappear in to the light of afterlife. Once the light disappeared Jessie returned to Salisbury hospital in 1973. He watches his grandmother flat lines as the doctors try's their best to explain to his mother that they did all they could do to save Lucida's life. Jessie knew his grandmother was in heaven now but this didn't give him no peace. Jessie reach out to touch his dead grandmother's hand and phase right through her like a ghost. "I told you Jessie you can't intervene only observe man." he heard his voice speak out to him. Jessie didn't bother to look back or respond to his other self. His presence didn't surprise Jessie at all. whatever happen between him, his grandmother and that angel must of been hiding from him for some reason. I don't see no reason to reveal shit to him anyway. Obviously it was only meant for the eyes of the real Jessie brown, Me. "I wish you could watch me murder this demonic mother fucker that fucked up my life. Too bad that I wouldn't never get that chance." Jessie watch his mother collapse from sorrow in to the arms of the man who would become his father. "Tell me if you know so fucking much how can a demon walk around parading as a man and get away with all the shit he's doing? I thought there were rules for shit like this man?" Jessie asked still not looking back at his other self. "That's because he's not a demon." "what the fuck are you talking about! I see, we just seen this mother fuckers true form. He killed my fucking grandmother by a heart attack because she saw what he was!" Jessie finally turned around and faced him with enough rage in his eyes that can frightened a harden criminal. "Your father is a warlock who spent most of his years worshiping Lucifer, Learning the ancient arts of black magic. what your grandmother and us saw was a Astral projection of his soul. Your soul reflects what you really are. Your father was evil so his soul took on the form of evil." He explain. Jessie turns away from his other self as he calm down. "Why? Why my mother?" Jessie said in a shaken voice, fighting back his tears. " your mother was young, good nature and a god fearing woman, she was the Perfect choice. You understand more as we continue to watch." "... yeah, continue to show me." Jessie said as they both continues to watch his parents history from the shadows. Jennies sobs hard in to the chest of Kenneth brown while he comforts her. "I'm so sorry Jennies; I'm so sorry." He softy whisper in her ears as he rubs her. "Keith just take me home, I just want to go home." "Ok jennies I'll take you home. Everything will be okay, It'll be okay." "Keith just take me home please, I just want to go home." "Okay I'm taking you home, Everything's going to be ok." Keith said As he slowly walked Jennies back to his car and drove her home. "Well here we are, listen if you need anything and I mean anything Just call me. I'll be there for you in a heartbeat ok." Kenneth said as They park in front of Jennie's house. "Can you walk me inside? I don't want to go in there alone." "Sure jennies. Let me open up the door for you." Kenneth opened Up the car door for Jennies and walk here in to the

Livingroom of her house. "Are you going to be ok Jennies?" he said. "Yeah...I'm fine, thank you." "Ok then I'm getting ready to go but remember call me if you need anything. I'll check on you tomorrow. Good night Jennies." Before Kenneth could reach the Livingroom door Jennies reach over and pulled Him towards her and passionate kiss him on the lips. "No, don't go, stay with me Kenneth." Jennies asked as tears ran down her face. "Jennies wait; you don't know what you're doing. You're depressed." Jennies plant her index finger on Kenneth lips. "Don't tell me what I am or what I want...I need you here, I need you To need me." Kenneth couldn't believe what he was hearing but when He looked in to Jennies beautiful eyes he knew this is what he bargain for. "Yes this is everything you wanted isn't It Kenneth. The money, the power And finally the woman you always wanted. All we want is the child. You can raise him but his soul belongs to us." The demon voice spoke Inside Kenneth's mind, reminding him of the price he must pay for His bargains. "I've always wanted you Jennies, I'll always need you. I would even Give up my soul for you. I love you." Kenneth professes his love. Jennies and Kenneth passionately kisses each other. Kenneth lifts up Jennies up by her waist as she eagerly wraps her legs around him. Neither one of them willing to break for air while they continue to kiss each other as Kenneth carries her up the steps in to her bedroom. Kenneth gently lays jennies down on her bed, her legs still tightly wrapped around Kenneth's waist as he lays on top of her. "jennies wait, we don't have to do this now. we, we can wait." Kenneth said as he use all his strength to prey jennies off for a few seconds. "I know, I know I don't have to do this now but I want to do this now. I want to do you." Kenneth no longer could be the concern good guy as he gave in to his animal instinct and kisses her lustfully. Kenneth rips off jennies blouse with such veracity she wets herself through her panties and jeans. Kenneth pries jennies jeans and soaking panties off and slips right inside her moist virginal. jennies screamed and held on to Kenneth tightly as she felt a burst of hot pain pushed through her womb. "Are you ok? Do you need me to stop?" "No don't. Keep going don't stop moving." jennies pleaded and he did as she commanded. Once again they kiss passionately, Never letting up as Kenneth strokes deep inside jennies womb, Faster and faster as she holds on to him tightly receiving every inch of his manhood expanding deeper inside of her. "jennies I love you! I'm gonna, I'm going to..." "it's okay. it's okay. Do it, I want it, I want all of it!" "uuuaahhhh!" Kenneth released in a loud moan as his body shake hard in climax. jennies rubs Kenneth's back while he rest on top of her. "I need you to go again, Can you do that baby? I need you to do that?" jennies said in his ear before she swirled her tongue inside of it. Kenneth didn't say a word as he felt himself rise again and imminently stroke inside of her for the second time. All night long jennies and Kenneth made passionate love to each other until all of jennies pain and sorrow was gone. The following morning jennies finds herself snuggling in the chest of Kenneth brown while he held her in his arms. "Keith, my bed is, completely drenched in our stuff." "I know isn't great." Kenneth said as they both enjoyed a laugh together. "thank you Kenneth. I really needed to get away from the world for a while. I needed to feel physical compassion in order to handle all this pain I have inside. I won't hold you to nothing so don't feel obligated to stick around." "No jennies, this is a dream come true for me. I love you jennies." Kenneth confess. "How can you love Kenneth when you don't even know me?" Kenneth grabs hold of jennies hand then stairs in to her eyes. "No you're wrong jennies. I love you from the first time I laid eyes on you. I love that you care and respect the elderly, I love that you're a woman of god. The fact that you're pure as the snow that descended from the heaven's." "stop Kenneth! that was just to cheesy for me." jennies said as they both laughed. "That did sounded kind of cheesy huh? But the truth is I really feel that way about you jennies, I felt in love with you the first time I ever saw you. Kenneth kisses her. "well thank you Kenneth. can you help me to the bathroom, it's hard for me to move because of..you know." jennies asked. "yes of course jennies I'll do anything for you." Kenneth carries her from the bed into the bathroom. "listen while you freshen up, I'll go and get us something to eat." Kenneth told jennise He finished helping her in the bathroom before getting dress and driving off to the store. Kenneth returns to find jennise siting in the Livingroom and her mother's favorite chair. "you took a while? started to think you got what you wanted and decided to cut out." "No jennise I didn't get what I wanted, not yet." Kenneth said as he walk close to jennise then bent down on one knee while opening up a small black box with a twenty four carat diamond ring that's worth more than a quarter of a million dollars. "Oh my god! Oh my god!" jennise screamed out loud as she tries to muffle's her voice by covering her mouth. "Jennise Barnes I felt in love with you from the moment I laid eyes on you the first time I came to your church. I knew in that very moment I wanted to be with you for the rest of my life. Jennise Barnes will you marry me?" Kenneth proposed. "Yes! Yes I will marry you Kenneth brown." they hug and shared tears together as they kiss. "what the fuck is this shit!" Jessie said out disgusted. "your father heart and soul is darker then coal but what he felt for your mother was real. It's the reason he sold his soul to the devil in the first place." the other Jessie explained. Three months later. Hal lulu, Hawaii Kenneth brown and jennies Barnes stood on their wedding platform dressed in complete white. Surrounded by the beautiful island trees and fire sticks of Hawaii on a full moon night. the priest announce them husband and wife before they kissed each other on the alter. Later that night Kenneth and jennise made love on the very spot they were Pronounce husband and wife, still wearing their wedding clothes. two weeks later park ave, New York city. "Oh my god Kenneth it's beautiful! is it really ours?" she asked. "Of course it is beautiful. Remember you said you always wanted to know how it felt to live the fancy life of new York city, well there ain't nothing more fancy then the lower east side baby!" jennise started clapping her hands fanatically then jump in to her husband arms. "I love you so much Kenneth. I can't be leave were moving on up till the east side!" "Ha ha ha I love you too honey!" Kenneth spin's his newly Wed wife around as they laugh together in their new three floor reconstructed apartment in the lower east side of Manhattan new York. A year and six months later. Jennise brown been having a hard time sleeping in her deluxe bed next to her now alarm husband who sat up concern over his wife. "jennise what's wrong?" "I don't feel so good..wwwaaahhh!" Jennise threw up all over herself and their Egyptian cotton sheets. "Jesus Christ! jennise I'm calling the doctor." a worried Kenneth said. "No, No I'm fine I don't need no wwaahh!" the vomit exploded out of her mouth before she could finishing protesting. "No that's it jennise I'm taking you to the hospital right now!" Kenneth demanded. Twenty five minutes later at mount Sinai hospital. Kenneth wait's eagerly to know what's going on with his wife while he waits in the emergency wait room. what's taking so long I didn't fucking pay for a whole board of doctors at my bacon call to be waiting like this. "Mr. Brown?" One of his private doctors called out for him as he came out of the emergency room. "Yes! what's wrong with my wife doctor?" Kenneth rose up from his seat. "Everything's fine Mr. Brown. your wife just had a bad case of morning sickness." The doctor smiled. A baffled look ran across Kenneth face's. "morning sickness?" He said. "Wait I'll let your wife tell you." The doctor used all his will power to keep himself from laughing at his high paying client cluelessness. "Hi honey." jennise smiled holding a ginger ale can as she arrived from the emergency room. Kenneth ran and hug his wife hard and kisses her on the forehead. "you ok baby? what's morning sickness?" "It means you're going to be a father." she said. "A father?" "I'm pregnant fool! You really telling me you didn't know what I was talking about?" "No I didn't but I know now. I know now! I'm going to be a daddy!" Kenneth yelled out in excitement as he picks up his wife and spin her around in a circle. "No! You fool! put me down I have morning sickness! put me down!" jennise yelled at him while he gently puts her back down. "Huh?" Kenneth was confused. "You could make me sick Keith. Morning sickness is another form of nausea." jennise explained to him as she rubbed his cheek, letting him know she wasn't mad. "Oh, I'm sorry jennise I didn't know. let's go home for I can take care of you and the baby." "Uumm, Mr. Brown I need to speak with you in private for a second" The chief doctor spoke out to Kenneth. "yeah sure doc. Here babe, wait for me in the car." Kenneth hands jennise the car keys. "okay. Don't keep me waiting too long alright?" "Never. I love you too much." "I love you too." Kenneth watches his wife walk out to their car, Then he approaches the doctor in the emergency room. "what's going on doc?" Kenneth asked. what was once a friendly smile turned in to a unwelcome scrawl. "Don't forget the deal you made with our lord Lucifer. that child she's carrying belongs to the cause, Don't forget that." The doctor said. All the lights in the emergency waiting room started to flicker off and on. Kenneth eyes turned to crimson red and the doctor took a long step back, knowing he might of made a fatal mistake. "Who the fuck do you think you're talking to? you think you have the fucking right to approach me about my fucking son's destiny! My son will inherit this fucking world with Satan! I will be one of his generals to reap this world while you be lucky to be my fucking servant!" "please forgive me. I.." "Choke" Kenneth demanded the pleading doctor. the doctor imminently starts violently choking on his own tongue. Kenneth turns and walks away leaving the doctor trying to gasp for air while his fellow colleges runs out trying to do their best from keeping the doctor from suffocating to death. Kenneth opens the car door and sits in the driver's seat. "is everything okay Kenneth?" "yeah honey. things are better than okay." He place his hand on his wife's belly. Mount Sinai hospital, June 6, 1975 at 6:00pm. Jennies brown legs are spread open across the hospital bed while she in the worst physical pain she ever felt in her life, But knowing she's giving birth to the most precious gift that god and her husband can ever give her. this will be the best night of her life. jennise thought. "Come on baby I know you can do it! Just one push away, One push away from being the best mother in the planted!" Kenneth screamed out trying to motivate his wife. "Shut up with those chesssy ass lin..Aaahhhh!" jennise scream out as a big jolt of pain shot through her while she push out hard, One last time but not before she could squeeze the life out of her husband's hand first. Jennise heard the most beautiful sound as she felt something slip out of her and to the doctors hands. "Mr. and Mrs. Brown it's a handsome baby boy." the doctors announce. "Oh god, thank you. Kenneth he's so beautiful." Jennise glowed like never before. "I know he is because he looks just like you." he kiss jennise on the forehead. they hug each other in celebration of their first born baby. "Dad do you wish to cut the biblical cord?" the doctor asked. "what I've been waiting for this moment all my life!" Kenneth cuts the cord and the doctor place the new born on the mother's chest. "Kenneth. I'm going to call him Jessie. you hear that my little angel, you're Jessie brown, oh yes you are." Jennies kisses Jessie's cheeks as two doctors approaches the first time parents. "excuse us, I'm sorry to interrupt but the nurse needs you to step outside the room while she stitch up your wife. I'll take the baby to the infirmary for a moment." the doctor explained to them. "Don't belong with our baby doctor." Jennies told the doctor. "Don't worry jennies I'll make sure they won't." Kenneth promise jennies before kissing her forehead and walking out the room with the doctor and baby Jessie. Kenneth and the doctor walks down the hall and make a short turn in to a hidden door away from praying eyes. "How's your hand Mr. Brown?" "I think she broke it. is everything's prepared?" "yes. their all there waiting for us." The doctor answer. "Good. let's get this over with I don't want my wife to worry." Kenneth shared his concern with the doctor as they enter a secret double door. Inside stood three people dress in all black cloaks. the room was empty and devoid of light. The center of the floor was the Star of David drawn in lamb's blood. The doctor that came with Kenneth and two others dress themselves In black cloaks. Kenneth picks up little Jessie and proceeds by stepping in to the middle of the Star of David while the six people dressed in black surrounds them in an form of a circle. "The cobra's blood." The father commanded as one of the priest hands Kenneth A jar of its blood. Kenneth writes the number of the beast in the cobra's blood On his son's forehead. Kenneth drops some cobra's blood in to Jessie's mouth As he finishes the rest by drinking the serpents blood. Baby Jessie starts to cry while the star of David starts to glow bright red, That surrounds around Kenneth and his son. Kenneth eyes turns crimson red as they all begin to chant rituals. "It is I my lord and savior the general to your great army of servants! I offer you the soul of my son whom destiny is to conquer in your name o' great Lucifer. As it is written he will grant us the souls that will lead us to victory in this war that begun before time. grant him the essence of your power to lead us to victory o' great lord and savior thy Lucifer!" Kenneth prayed out to his lord. the ground beneath them began to shake. the star of David cracked open. A black and red colored mist rose from the cracked ritual ground. the mist enter quickly in to little Jessie's nose and mouth until it disappeared from sight. Jessie cried out in pain. the ritual was done. Twenty minutes later the doctor return Jessie back to his mother. jennise notice since little Jessie's return from the doctor he's been crying nonstop. "Kenneth what's going on? Jessie been crying ever since he return from That doctor?" jennies complained. "Maybe he's hungry jennies." Kenneth said pretending he doesn't know what's wrong with their son. Knowing it's going to take a couple of hours before little Jessie's body will accept the hidden power and the mark of the beast that was branded in to his soul. There's no medicine or love that could take away Jessie's pain right now, I'm sorry jennies and little Jessie but what's done had to be done. Kenneth thought to himself. Jennies try's to feed him and comfort Jessie with no prevail. "Nothing's working Kenneth! Why is he still crying?" she pleaded with her husband. "I don't know baby? But I'll find out, let me take him to the doctor." "No! Jessie wasn't acting like this until he left with that damn doctor." Jennies held her son tight in her arms, Kenneth began to protest. Jessie notice's that everyone and everything is frozen in place accept for little Jessie who continues to cries. "What the hell?" Jessie said to himself. A bright yellow light appeared inside the hospital room. A tall black beautiful angel appeared from the shining light. "It's you again. Who are you?" Jessie asked the angel who Appeared to him before with his late grandmother. The angel didn't respond to Jessie's question instead she reach out Her hand and place it on his younger self's head. The mark of the beast reappeared on little Jessie's head and the angel Begun to chant a ritual in the language that was during the time before The tower of Babylon. A blue light emulated from little Jessie's forehead then the mark of the Beast was destroyed. Little Jessie stopped crying and felt to sleep. "What are you doing to me? Why am I the only one who can see this?" Jessie yelled out to her hoping to get some kind of answer from her. "This is our lord and saviors parting gift to you so you can always Protect the soul of your child." The angel whisper into the now sleeping Jennies ear. The yellow light flash again in the hospital room. This time Jessie Had to protect his eyes, when he looked again the angel was gone. Everything was normal again accept for Jennies and little Jessie who Was now asleep together peacefully. Kenneth had his suspicion that something unnatural might had occurred But seeing his wife and son at peace, pleased him and whatever put them At rest he was graceful for it. Kenneth bend over and kissed them both on their foreheads. Seven years later 1980, Downtown Manhattan, the browns residents. The last seven years has been great for the brown family. Little Jessie was always happy. Even as a child he knew he was loved And there wasn't anything better then what he had. Every Thursday was bible studies day were daddy will tell him and mom the great Adventures of god's prophets. Saturday and Sunday was church services, I really liked those days with all The singing and dancing and miss Mary makes a great Marconi and cheese meal. Then there's Friday. Father's mystery day. It takes place once a month on Fridays. We been doing this for since I was one Years old. Mystery Fridays were my favorite day of the month but I Don't know why I have to always keep it a secret from mommy? Daddy said it was my and his secret. Today is that special day. Dad said he had a surprise for me today, a surprise that will turn me In to a man. Father said it will be scary at first but if I'll be brave and Indore I will become a real man. There's no way I'll be scare to become a real man. I'll become a real man just like you daddy you see. Little Jessie thought. "Honey I'm getting ready to go the meeting at my salons. You sure you Don't want to come?" Jennies asked her husband as she approaches the Penthouse elevators. "Sorry not this time honey bunny! Me and Jessie is going to have man time today while you're gone." Kenneth said. "Yeah!" the seven year old Jessie shouted out in pride. "jeezz! Ok! Ok! Already I'll let you boys have your fun but not before I get my kiss and hug from my little stinker butt." Jennies smiled. Jennies put both of her hands on her waist showing she's not moving Until she gets that hug and kiss. "What? Mommy!" Jessie pouted. " First lesson as a man son never keep mommy waiting?" Kenneth pad Their son on his head. "Okay dad!" little Jessie ran in to the arms of his mother as she hug and Kissed Jessie on the cheeks. "Ok, ok mom!" Jessie manages to wiggle out of his mother's grip. "I love you Jessie!" "I love you too mom!" little Jessie and Kenneth waved bye to jennies As she left inside the penthouse elevator. A few minutes after Jennies left the building. "So son, are you ready to become a man yet?" Kenneth looked down at his son. "Yeah, I mean yes sir." Little Jessie replied. "Okay then. Now fellow daddy in to the mystic room." Kenneth and little Jessie walked in side their library room. "Now Jessie before we enter this room do you remember our secret oath?" Kenneth asks his son. "Sure daddy. I will always remember to have fun and this room is a men's only secret club." Jessie said remembering the oath. "Good! That's my little boy." Kenneth said as he pressed hard on a hollow spot on his library wall. A loud clicking sound erupt from behind the library walls as the wall started to split apart revealing an hiding room. "Wow how you do that dad?" Jessie said in amazement. "A magician never reveals his tricks but I'll teach them to you one day anyway." "Yeah maybe one day after I become a man today right?" "Yep! Now let's get started son." the father said as he walked in to the room first. Jessie quickly follows behind his father wondering what cool game they could Play today that would make him a man. Little Jessie was frozen in place when he saw what was waiting for him inside the Secret room today and he wasn't sure he wanted to become a man anymore. "What's wrong son? You don't like what you see? Kenneth said with a smile. little Jessie shakes his head from side to side displaying his displeasure. Jessie stands freighted as he looks at a grown African American woman naked on her knees in the middle of the star of David surrounded by six people dress in black cloaks. "Jessie don't you like me? Ain't you ready for me to turn you in to a man?" she crawled towards him and unzips his pants. "No, Noo, daddy tell her to stop, daddy!" little Jessie cried out to his father who was no longer smiling. Jessie looked at his father put his index finger on his lips and his eyes became like blood. "Hush now child today is the day you'll become the savior of Lucifer and all of mankind." Kenneth said as his son felt under his power. "Now undress yourself and walk in to the middle of the hexagram." Kenneth commanded his now brainwash son as Jessie undress and did what his father commanded. The grown woman begins fondling little Jessie. "Wow! You pretty big for a little boy. it must run in your blood." the whore said. Kenneth began to chant an ancient ritual holding the top of little Jessie's head. Jessie's eyes became black as the void of space. "So son, Do you like your gift?" Kenneth ask Jessie. But Jessie wasn't the same scared little boy anymore. He was now something more sinister, A spawn from hell. "She's perfect dad. I can't wait to fuck her." Jessie said in a possess voice that was years ahead of his age. Jessie grab the back of the woman's head with unnatural strength and shoves his penis in to her mouth causing her to gag. "Suck it! Suck your master off you fucking cunt!" "Master Kenneth did you hypnotize him because if you did the ritual won't work. He have to do this willingly." one of the servants said to his master. "I know this already. I had to unleash his darker personally. Somehow the ritual inside the hospital didn't fully work but with this ritual done there won't be able to stop his full transformation in to hells greatest warrior and savior." Kenneth explain himself. "Interfere? what possibly could of interfere that night we were the only ones.." "Enough! There are things in play that's beyond your understanding. Now form the circle around the hexagram to complete the ritual." Kenneth puts his servant in their place. "Kenneth, Honey I forgot my car keys! Do you know where th..." jennise stood in absolute horror as she walk through her Livingroom to witness the man she loves, the only one she gave her body too standing in a secret room in their library with devil worshippers. Jennise saw the shock and fear in her husband's face, then we both looked down at little Jessie. I saw his pitch black eyes look at me. "Mommy?" little Jessie said as he returned back to normal, His father's spell was broken. "Jessie! get the hell off my son!" jennies scream out while she ran towards her son. "Jennise no!" Kenneth try's to ward off his wife but it was already too late. jennise had already picked her son up as she kick the woman who was molesting her son in the face breaking her nose causing the back of her head to hit hard against the floor knocking her unconscienced. The frightened jennise ran out of the library carrying little Jessie in her arms as the six hooded devil worshippers gave chase after her. "No! leave her alone I have this!" Kenneth commanded. Kenneth extended his hand out, completely stopping his wife with unseen power. "Master Kenneth she knows to much! you have to kill her!" the hooded servant said. "She's my wife!" "If you would of killed her after she gave birth, None of this would be happening. you put some god loving bitch before our lord and savior Lucifer!" "you dare!" Kenneth eyes turn crimson red. "I warned you about talking about my fucking family!" the devil worshipper yells out in painful shriek as he grabs his head. blood starts to pour from his eyes, nose, ears and mouth. His head swells three times its normal size then splat. blood and brain matter exploded throughout the Livingroom halls as the devil worshiper headless body falls to the ground. "Aahhh! oh god!" Jennise cried out in horror along with little Jessie. From the murder they just witness their father and husband committed. "Anyone else interferes with my family I will fucking kill you all!" Kenneth threaten, The rest of the devil worshipers step back in silence not daring to provoke their master's rage. "so that's your plan Kenneth, kill me and take our son and turn him in to some kind of demon?" Jennise said. "No! No i would never hurt you our little Jessie, please it's not what you think. I love you." Kenneth walked up to his family slowly with caution not wanting to cause anymore fear then he already had. tears of blood flowed from Kenneth eyes as his heart was filled with sorrow. "Mommy no! keep him away from me mommy! keep him away!" Jessie cried out to his mother to protect him from his very own father. "sshhh! child everything's alright." Kenneth place his index finger on Jessie's lips and he felt in to a deep sleep. "Jessie no! oh'god! Kenneth what did you do? what did you do?" "He's a sleep! He's a sleep Jennise. you know I would never do anything to hurt our baby or you" Kenneth pleads with his wife for her forgiveness. "you say you love us! you don't love us! you devil worshipping monster! How could you have that whore molest our son? what's next use him as a sacrifice!" Jennise said as Kenneth paused. searching for something to say that would ease his wife's pain. Jennise watch how Kenneth look at Jessie then at her. And she knew he was lost, Even with those crimson bloody eyes seè could see that he was hurting inside and she felt his pain because deep down she still loved him and knew he still loved her and she hated him for making her love him. "I'm sorry jennies. I'm so sorry. I didn't want any of this to happen. I sold my soul to Lucifer for you, because I love you jennies!" Kenneth confessed. "Are you crazy! I love god Kenneth and I always will! Damn you! you stupid idiot I was already in to you, from the very beginning I liked you. you didn't have to sell your soul to get me Kenneth because I was already there for you!" An emotional Jennise revealed to him. "h\How could you do this to us? Too us Kenneth! You're family! Just please let us go now Kenneth, let us go." Jennies pleas hoping his love for her will overcome the evil in his heart. "I was poor when I first saw you Jennies. I had nothing to offer you. One night Lucifer the fallen angel visit me in my dreams and offer me a choice

I couldn't, No I wouldn't refuse. He showed me the truth about Jehovah and this world. god is not what you think he is jennies. He's not this all merciful, peaceful god you think him to be. Jehovah created the archangels and taught them the art of war before there were any wars to fight. He committed genocide in the days of Noah. He had Joshua slaughter innocent women and children for land. For land!" "No. No I don't want to hear this from you." Jennies tries to avoid her husband words. "No jennise you need to hear the truth about me about your god and this world. Because I know the real truth about you're god Jennise but the real heart of the matter is I just wanted a perfect life for us and I'm going to do just that. I'll make it right by you even if you keep on worshipping that egotistic thing you call a god." Kenneth vowed as he wiped the blood tears from his eyes. "Don't you understand Kenneth there's no making it right! We won't never forget what you done. I could never be with you Kenneth. I feel so sorry for you, The devil is the ultimate liar and you felt under his spell but Jessie and I never will Kenneth." jennise told. "I promise you will baby. I'll show you the truth slowly, Revealing the true nature of this world before your eyes but first I have to make you forget this day ever happened. I'm sorry jennise I never wanted to use my powers on you but there's no choice now. I love you." "Don't do this Kenneth! Don't do it! If you love us you won't do this!" jennise pleas as Kenneth place his hand on her forehead. "I'm doing this because I love you." Kenneth chants the spell that would erase this horrific day from jennise memory forever as he starts to feel a burning hot sensation ran through his arm that's place on his wife's forehead. "uuuahhh!" Kenneth grunts out in pain as he pulls his hand away from jennise forehead. "No this can't be right? something wrong." Kenneth held his burned hand. "yes this is wrong Kenneth. this is god giving you a second chance to do the right thing." Kenneth eyes looked wild with fear as heavy beads of sweat ran down his face like a dear in head lights. "God?...No it can't be, can it?" Kenneth questioned himself out loud. Kenneth step exactly three feet away from his wife and son and extended his palms out towards his wife. Kenneth started to see a blue light emulate from jennise body. the light started to grow and grow like a hot blue inferno. "No! No this can't be!" Kenneth stumbles to his knees, hands shielding his face from the burning light that's rising from jennise body. The light slowly turned to a tall black angel that wings extended to each end of the penthouse wall. "No! No! you can't be here! you don't have the right to do this to my family, you can't interfere in human affairs!" Kenneth protested. "Once you decided to use your soul through the astral plane to murder Lucida the one with sight. God no longer view you as human. Kenneth the general of hells army." The angel said. "No! you kill her! you killed my mother to get to me!" jennise rage boils over with the realization of how deep Kenneth betrayal lies. it all makes sense now why my mother didn't want me near him, How he needed her out the way in order to have me. you devil worshiping bastard. "Damn you Kenneth! Damn you!" jennise erupts. "Jennise no I love you!" He pleas as Kenneth sees the angel turns back in to blue flames absorbing in to the body of jennise. "I hate you!" jennise screamed as the entire apartment was destroyed by a extreme blue flames that burst through jennise body like a shooting star descending from the heavens. Once the blue light was gone the remaining devil worshippers was all dead. All that remain of them was black ash. Everything was laid to waste by the angels blue light, Everything but Kenneth brown. Kenneth masterly of chaos magic is the only reason he's still breathing barley, weakened with second degree burns all-over his body. jennise with the help of the unknown angel is able to move freely again. jessie was still asleep as jennise pick him up and held him tightly in her arms. the thought that she murdered all these people..Even in self defense was all too much for her. jennies began running away. "Jennise...please don't leave me, please I need you both." Jennise stop as she heard the pleads of her wounded hus-band. "you deceived me Kenneth. you worship the devil, you killed my mother and you had some pedophilia molest our son in some kind of Satan ritual. still after all of that I find myself loving you but you're evil Kenneth and you won't ever see us again. Before the angel left she taught me how I could keep us hidden from you and any other devil worship-er or demon that's out to find us." "No don't jennise, you can't trust her...The strain of that kind of spell will kill you." "I know Kenneth the angel told me it would but I'm willy to die in order to keep our son away from monsters like you. Good bye Kenneth." "No! No don't do this. Don't leave me jennise I love you! jennise! jennise!" Kenneth beg his wife but his words felt on deaf ears as jennise walk out on him with little jessie. Kenneth never saw them again as jennise kept her word by casting the spell the angel gave her to keep them hidden from all devil worshipers and demons until her death in 1991 when Jessie brown turned eighteen and join the united states army. This is the origins story of Jessie brown the angel of silence. the adult Jessie reappeared in-side the white void again next to his other self. "I never had a chance did I?" Jessie look at his other self. "you're mother died trying to give you that chance at life and so she did. Now it's time for you to make your final choice Jessie." two large doors appear in the middle of the void. One on the left was an ivory colored door, the one on the right was crimson red. "what is this?" Jessie ask. "This is the final part of your test Jessie. the door to your right will lead back to the garden of Eden where Valery and Natasha awaits for you." "I choose that door then." Jessie quickly answer just wanting the test to be over with. "you have the right to choose which ever door you like but you cannot choose until I reveal both doors to you." the other Jessie said. "Fine. Say what you have to say for I can pick the red door and get the hell out of this depressing place already." A irritated Jessie said. "The door of ivory will lead you to new York city inside the residents of Kenneth brown." Jessie brown hesitated and looked back at his other self. "The fuck you mean the residents of Kenneth brown? Are you telling me that my father's going to be there?" He asked. "yes Jessie brown. Now you can choose." Since this test started Jessie knew what was the right decisions to make and deep down in his soul he still knows. But all he could think about is what his father did to him, Did to his grandmother and what he did to his mother. Jessie stood there thinking for what could of been fifty minutes. Fangs grew from his mouth as Jessie's eyes turned blacker then night. Jessie rage grew like a tumor, Unaware of his body and soul transformation. "I'm sorry Natasha but my father has to die." Jessie said as he walked through the ivory door to revenge his mother and grandmothers death, To get pay back for the fuck up life his father gave him. Both doors vanished just like they first appeared leaving the other Jessie alone. There are many mysteries in the dimension of the void. Like how can the other Jessie still exist without his original self. How come his other self could never see the angel that kept appearing throughout his past? or how could he know and show him things before Jessie was born? How the other Jessie stop saying us and ours and started to say you and yours. All the answer to questions was next to

133

Jessie the whole time if he would had notice the small changes. The other half of Jessie browns soul was never his soul at all. the figure that we thought was Jessie brown change to a tall black angel with long woven hair. Her wings expanded as long as a city block. Heaven knows her as Zinobiah the angel of prophecy.

CHAPTER TWELVE

Morningstar hasn't been on earth since she departed more than three thousand years ago in ancient Egypt. Morningstar hasn't been this excited since she first witness the wonders Moses done against the pharaoh sieges in palace courts when she was a child. I couldn't believe when general Michael came to me and said I will be returning to earth again. Everything is so different now. But I do love those flat black boxes where you can watch people do amusing things. Morningstar thought as she watched Gabriella laying on her stomach watching television on the Livingroom couch. such a precious little girl. she's been through so much having her mother killed in such a foul way. It was on that day that general Michael came to me and told me that god wanted me to protect this child from harm. Now she resides in this man's house but I do not feel I will have to protect her from him. "I love Lucy is on." Gabriella said while she turns up the T.V volume and ate chocolate cookies that the F.B.I agent left her. "Wow her performance is so great, this Lucy woman is very amusing." Morningstar said to herself enjoying the show that she been watching with Gabriella secretly since she was a signed to her. Morningstar was sent from heaven to protect Gabriella from harm but see can't be seen or heard by anyone including the one she here to protect. "This isn't really my kind of thing but I put it on anyway since it makes you laugh so much." Gabriella said staring at the T.V screen. Who is she talking to? There's no one else in this house, I made sure of it. "Come sit next to me. Don't be shy." Gabriella spoke again still looking at the T.V screen. "may god the all mighty El shaddai bless you child. Have you lost your mind?" Morningstar said as she wonders what she could do to help the poor child. "Don't be silly. Stop standing in the hallway like you can't understand me. sit down and watch I love Lucy with me." Gabriella stared right at her. A small dose of fear ran through Morningstar's heart as she realize what could be happening here. "You...No,No you can't see me? No one supposed to be able to see me." The ancient African Egyptian archangel said to herself. "well I can. I've seen you since the night my mother died. I was sitting on this very couch crying my eyes out when you just appeared out no-where and wrapped your arms around me, And I felt safe again." Gabriella said now siting straight up looking Morningstar straight in her eyes. Morningstar slowly walks up to Gabriella and kneels down to her level so they can be face to face. "You can really hear and see me, And you're not afraid?" "No. why would I fear something as beautiful as you." Gabriella reach and touch the side of Morningstar's face. Morningstar leaps away from Gabriella in shock. "By the grace of god you can touch me as well!" Morningstar yelled. Gabriella just smiled unafraid of the sudden move-ments of the angel. "what's your name? I'm Gabriella shu-ford." she introduce herself. "I am Morningstar of the archangels. I see now why god sent me to protect you. God has grace you with many gifts Gabriella." Morningstar said. Gabriella tried her best to stay happy but she felt a hard rush of sorrow wash over her as she succumbed to tears. "Why, why are you here to protect me but not my mother? The reason she died was all my fault Morningstar!" she cried. Morningstar walk over and place her hand on Gabriella's cheek. "Child no, No nothing is your fault. What happened to your mother wasn't of your doing. Your mother loved you so much that she Sacrifice her eternal soul for you to live again." "And now she's going to burn in hell forever because she loved me Too much. Now the psycho killer That murdered my mother probably out there trying to do the same to me." Gabriella confuse her fears To the beautiful angel that decided to sit next to her. Morningstar placed her hand over Gabriella's. "I'm sorry Gabriella there's nothing I can do about that because your mother Gave her soul Willy but I'm here to protect you from all harm even if I have to sacrificing my life to do so." Morningstar vowed. "is that why you're here? God has some kind of divine plan for me or something?" Gabriella asked. "No one knows for sure what god have in plan for us accept may be Michael, Enoch and Moses but I can see why he has such interest in a beautiful young woman like yourself." she explained. "Morningstar can I ask you a question?" Gabriella's mood suddenly changed. "Yes please, you can ask me anything you like as long as I can taste one of those round brown treats." Morningstar looked down at Gabriella's cookies box. "my grandma cookies?" "yes those things you said. I would like to have one." "Ok. I was going to offer you some anyway, so..uummm. where are your wings? I thought angels have wings?" Gabriella ask Morningstar as she ate an handful of grandma cookies. "yes Gabriella we have wings but we only spread them when we fly, get excited or prepare to shed blood." Morningstar explained as she stuff a handful of chocolate cookies in her mouth. "Mmmmm! these are so delightful Gabriella." Morningstar mumbles while she grabs another batch of grandma cookies. "Hehe! your face is so adorable when it's stuff full of cookies." Gabriella laugh.

"ummm. yes adorable they are." she ate more. "can I see them?" Gabriella ask. "see what?" "you know. can I see your wings?" "Gabriella I explained to you that angels only spread thy wings for special occasions." "well this is a special occasion. please! please! let me see them, I won't stop asking until you say yes." Gabriella pleaded with the archangel. "...ok but only if we can watch more of that Lucy woman in the black box with more of these grandma cookies." the angel propose a deal. "ok! I'll promise it's a deal." Her face was beaming red with excitement as Morningstar sat up and walk in to the middle of the Livingroom. "Now prepare your pretty eyes to be amazed!" two large wings slowly expanded out of Morningstar's back. Morningstar flap her wings once, creating a small gust of wind that knock Gabriella back down in to her seat. "Wow!" A amazed Gabriella shouted as she brush back some of her hair that was laid in her face from the gust of wind. "what do you think Gabriella?" Morningstar ask the young girl as her wings resends back in. "I think you're a beautiful goddess!" Gabriella said in excitement. "No I'm just a angel Gabriella, just a angel." "No you're my guardian angel." they both smiled at each other. while sitting down watching reruns of I love Lucy, eating grandma cookies. For Gabriella and Morningstar this night is a blessing from god as a brand new friendship is born. Kenneth brown sat down in his deluxe black leather couch. His luxury penthouse remodel after his dead ex-wife burned The apartment up with holy fire that killed everyone in the Place accept him and little Jessie. Maybe it would have been for the best if he would have died On that day. Better then siting here remembering the worst fucking Day of my life for the past twenty three years. Kenneth stares at the large portrait of his departed wife jennies. "you don't deserve to have that picture." Kenneth jumps up Off of his couch looking towards the entrance door of his penthouse where the voice Came from. Kenneth see's what looks like a man standing in front of his elevator door With pure black eyes, breathing hard and heavy like a mad dog that's about to Attack it's pray. "how the hell you get in here demon without my permission?" The demon stood there and smiled showing his murderous fangs to taunt me. "Heh! Demon huh. Well isn't that what you always wanted For me dad?." Kenneth stood frozen in shock, overwhelm By fear and joy. It felt like his heart was going to explode out Of his chest. "J...little Jessie?" the surprised father said. "Don't ever call me that!" Kenneth saw a black blur run at him And the thing that was his son was on top of him. "You don't have the right to call me that! Not after what you done To me!" Jessie smashes his fist in to his father's face Breaking his nose and splitting his lip at the same time. "What you did to grandma Lucida!" Jessie cracks open Kenneth's Cheek bone as his father's blood splash across his face. "For what you did to my mother! Your own wife!" Jessie opened up His fist as his finger nails became long talons that could peel up the Strongest of steel. The very claws he plans on ripping open his father's flesh ending his life. "Do it. end it, it couldn't have been anyone better." his father manage to say through a mouth filled with blood and smash teeth. Jessie for unknown reasons started to hesitate. Ever since Jessie found out what his father did to his family all he wanted was to murder him. why the hell am I hesitating, I killed plenty before as a army ranger. why in hell am I having a hard time murdering this selfish bastard? "I was hoping one day you will return to me and finish what I was to coward to do many years ago. So do it and become the man you was meant to be." His father said as Jessie hand started to shake. "Fucking kill me!" Kenneth yelled and spit blood in his son's face. Jessie saw his reflection in his father's eyes and knew for the first time what this test was really about, when he saw what he was becoming. "No father I won't kill you. I won't become what you always wanted me to become." Jessie stood up off his father allowing him to get up. "why? I killed your grandmother, I made you and your mother go through hell. she died just to protect you away from me, so why?" "Because I forgive you. I forgive you for everything you done to me, my grandma and my mother. I don't hate you Kenneth, I pity you. deep down I know you really loved my mother, that's why you felt like you had to sell your soul to get the finer things in life for her. truth be told if you never barging your soul to the devil you two would still be together today and you know it. that's why your guilt is eating you alive." Kenneth felled to his knees no longer able to withstand his guilt and anguish after hearing his son words. "This isn't the life I've wanted for you, for us." Kenneth admitted to himself and his son. Jessie knelt down and place his hand on his father's shoulder. "I can tell now that you're not the same person from the past and hell knows it too. that's why you was surprise to see a demon inside your apartment because of all the spell barriers to keep them out." Jessie said. "when you and your mother left me. I broke. those powers that angel gave your mother kept you hidden from all of hell's sight until her death. hell was furious. They sent hell spawns after me, I barely survived the first encounter so I had to barrage this apartment with anti demon spells to keep them away." Kenneth explained to Jessie. Jessie eyes and features returned to normal as he look at his father one last time. "Now that I cleared the hatred from my heart. I'm glad I've chose the door to come to see you because I wouldn't had known what kind of man you change to become." "It's too late for me to be redeem son but I can finally do something right by you." Kenneth leaned closer to Jessie's ear. "There is a ultimate lie that cloaks this world son. this is something that will add you in the time of Armageddon." Kenneth whisper secrets in to his son's ear that sadden Jessie's heart while tears ran from his eyes. "No it can't be?" Jessie ask sadden. "yes it is son. it is one of many things that will happened in the end of days. you have to Save who you can son, save who you can." Kenneth repeated. they both stared at each other without saying a word for two minutes. "It's time for me to go dad." Jessie said to his father as the crimson door appear inside Kenneth penthouse. "I'm glad you became a better man then me, I love you son." Jessie paused at the entrance of the crimson door and turn back to look at his father. "...I still love you too. I'm glad I was able to see you again." my son looked me in the eyes and said those words back to me and I knew there was no lying in his words. After everything I've done to him to still have that kind of love for me inside his heart. jennise. your mother was the same way. Even on the day she found out about me she still had love for me in her heart. Jessie is a good man, He's going to do great things for this world but for me it's time I've pay my debt. thank you god the El shaddai for finally allowing me to see my son one last time. Kenneth puts his gun inside his mouth and turn off the safety. "I love you jennise! I love you little Jessie!" Kenneth said before pulling the trigger, blowing his brains out. Satan hell spawns collects Kenneth soul for all of eternally before his body could hit the floor.

CHAPTER THIRTEEN

All Jessie could see was white, What felt like hours sense he left his father's apartment. A small beam of light appear in front of him. each second that went by the light grew bigger and bigger until the light was large enough that Jessie could walk through it. Jessie walks through the light without the slightest hesitation. the light was consuming, Jessie had to close and shield his eyes to avoid becoming blind. Slowly the bright lights starts to fade away and Jessie began to hear familiar voices. "Jessie is waking sister Valery!" Jessie heard a beautiful voice yelled out. "Natasha calm thy self, Remember what we might have to do" Jessie heard the two angels talk among themselves as his eye sight returned to normal again. Jessie opens his eyes to find himself in the very spot on his knees before his body burst in to light. Aint that a bitch my body never left the garden of Eden. "Jessie have you return with all the darkness cast from your soul?" Jessie looked up at Natasha then Varley standing a few feet from him with a smile. "I don't know if I could ever cast all the darkness from my soul Natasha but I know I've never felt so holy in my life." Jessie said as he step out the lake and stretch his arms out towards Natasha. "Now tell me am I worthy of that hug now that I pass the test Natasha?" Both Jessie and Valery were surprise to see Natasha run full tilt at Jessie, wings fully extended out as she hug and squeezed Jessie tightly wrapping her wings around his body as well. "Natasha calm thy self!" Valery shouted out what seemed to be on deaf ears as Natasha continued to embrace Jessie in a hug. "Wow. Natasha you must of really been worried about me." Jessie said as he stared deep in to Natasha eyes. Jessie heart skip a beat once he realized Natasha wasn't shying away but met his eyes head on. "I had faith that El shaddai will guild you through but, when I saw your eyes turn in to the blackest of the night, I..I began.." "sshh! It's okay I'm here now because of your faith and prayers Natasha. Jessie said softy silencing her fears as their lips grew closer together. "Natasha, Jessie stop!" Valery shouts as none yield to her words. Jessie continues to go in for the kiss while Natasha welcomes it. "Natasha no! In the name of god stop!" Valery scream was heard throughout all of the garden of Eden. Natasha heard the cries' of her fellow sister Valery and quickly jerks back while pushing Jessie off to the ground. "Natasha?" A confuse and startled Jessie brown said as he help himself up from the ground. "I am sorry Jessie brown. I didn't mean to throw you down, I just wanted to get away." Natasha apologize to Jessie while not making eye contact with him. looking down in shame. "No but thy meant to do other things to the angel of silence did she." "No, I...Valery it wasn't..." "Don't lie to me Natasha! have thy lost her way?" Valery ask. Natasha shame hits hard causing her wings to descend back in as she fall's to her knees. praying to god to forgive her sins. "My god Yahweh the all mighty El shaddai who is above all else please forgive thy for thy sins." Natasha prayed to her god. Wait a damn minute here. I can't let Valery shame Natasha like this. And for what? A kiss that never happen. "Hold on just a second here Valery. How could you say something like that to her. I was the one who was coming on to her. She's innocent yell at me!" Jessie came to

Natasha defense. "Don't you compare thy self with the likes of an angel. you are made of sin and flesh, whereas she is made of divine light. you are a angel only in name, Angel of silence." Valery said as she approach Jessie. "listen you're right Valery. Natasha is divine and I'm nothing but a man but there's nothing stronger then the love I have for her." Jessie turn his head to look at Natasha as he spoke those words. "Natasha can't hear your pledge of love and loyalty while she prays to god. Her thoughts are only focused on god, The almighty El shaddai but if what you say is true, If you truly love her you would let her be. Don't corrupt her any more then what you already done angel of silence." "corrupt!? how is telling her I love her corrupting her in any way? I'm not the same person you meet that rainy night in your chapel Varley!" Jessie stood his ground not backing down from the former archangel. I don't give a damn what Valery thinks about me. I love Natasha and I think she has deep feeling for me as well. Jessie thought. A small smirk creeps on the edge of Varley's mouth, A smirk that made Jessie brown very uneasy. "your courage has surprise me angel of silence, I can respect that. Now do you remember the story of the four fallen ones angel of silence?" "Yeah I remember them why do you ask?" Jessie answered. "Remember as they soar down from the heaven's lusting for the flesh of the human woman's of this world. How they lost themselves inside their wombs, impregnating them with their corrupted seeds creating the Nephilim. How god had to banish them deep in the mountains of mount Hermon till this very day." "What! Are you kidding me! You can't possibility compare Natasha to those bastards. They done a hell a lot more then in pregnant human woman that gave birth to evil giants Valery!" Jessie made his point trying to defend Natasha actions. "Yes angel of silence they had done many sins against our lord and savior Yahweh, just to have thy feel of woman's flesh. thy shall not forget their sins only begun with the lust of the flesh. Jessie angels ain't meant to breed with mankind, Even one as special as you angel of silence." Valery place her hand on Jessie shoulder's and lean over to whisper something in his ear's. "I believe you angel of silence when you said you love her but if you both decides to cross that line god will punish her and only her angel of silence. If you truly love her as you claim, you will stay away from Natasha in order to protect her from such judgment." Jessie was silent with heart break as he stood in place, speechless. "It would seem that you finally understand...I'm sorry that I had to put such a burden on you angel of silence." Varley sensory apologize to Jessie brown for crushing whatever hopes of him and Natasha ever being with each other but she had no choice. She couldn't just stand by and watch another angel fall from grace again, No not on her watch, Not if she could stop it. "I have received word from heaven that we must leave the garden of Eden and for I to continues to teach Jessie brown the ways towards our lord's light of grace." Natasha spoke to them after completion her prayers to god. "Then it shall be done." Valery clap her hands together and begun the ancient chants that will open the gateway back to her sanctuary. There stood is the most beautiful woman I ever laid eyes on in my life. I can't never be with her romantic because she's a angel and I'm just a man. I could of damned her in the eyes of god because of my feelings. I can at least apologize to her. "Natasha I'm so sorry. I would never knowingly jeopardize your wellbeing. Natasha I lov.., I care for you a lot. will you forgive me?" Jessie ask for forgiveness while looking down avoiding eye contact from shame but once again Natasha uses her finger to lift Jessie's head up high to meet her eyes. "Dear Jessie there is nothing for me to forgive you for. you have passed the ultimate test that our lord and savior had set before you. In time your light will shin brighter than any angel in all of heaven, you must have faith in yourself just like you have faith in our great lord and savior Yahweh the great El Shaddai." "Heh, this is exactly why you're the best thing that ever happened to me Natasha." Jessie couldn't help himself from rising a bright wide smile on his face. "God is the bliss of all our souls dear Jessie. I am just his loyal servant that he works his miracles through, Now prepare yourself as we return back to the sanctuary." "Then what happens next Natasha?" I asked and she turn and looked me straight in my eyes while she held her hand out for me to grab. "Then Jessie brown I will teach you to become the most glorious angel that god created on earth." Natasha smiled at me as her beauty made my heart beat a hundred times faster while we enter the portal, leaving behind the most beautiful land that god had ever created the garden of Eden. But I don't weep because I get to leave this ancient place with the most beautiful woman god had created holding my hand. Natasha would never know how much I truly love her such is the burden of the angel of silence. These last couple of nights has been the best experience in my life. specially the night that falling angel, the engineer approach me and recruited me for the most important mission in the world. Killing god's new prophet the angel of silence. Somehow murdering him will prevent the end of the world and help Satan win this war between heaven and hell. To be honest I don't know how killing one man prophet or not is going to keep me from burning up in that lake of fire called hell. All my life I've been doing the right thing. All the things a good model citizen would do I would do and what do I get for all my good deeds, An eternal one trip to hell. Not because my some kind of sick pedophilia, Rapist or murder, No I'm burning in hell because I was born gay. So I said fuck god and serve Satan and these last couple of days serving under him my life hasn't been better. I'm famous all over Satan websites of true believers. Once I kill the angel of silence they going to make me a reality tv star and do an auto biography about my life. I been getting fuck and sucking dick like I was back in Woodstock. My life is better than I ever had it and I'm going to do everything in my power to keep it that way. Stan thought to himself as he loaded his twelve gauge shotgun. Dress for war with a top of the art ballistic bullet and stab proof vest on. A utility belt with over hundred shotgun shells and fourteen inch hunting knife hosted on his hips, wearing a black leather trench coat. "Damn Stan the matrix don't have shit on you!" Alex the gun shop owner said as he lustfully check Stan out in his assassination outfit on. "You damn right after today you can call me Stan the angel killer." Stan said to his lover as he pumped his shotgun loading a bullet in its chamber. "Damn Stan the angel killer that shit is catchy as hell. My dick just got hard thinking about how you going to lay waste to all those god worshiping mother fuckers." "Don't worry Alex when I get back I'll welcome that stiff rod nice and hard with cherry's on top." they both enjoyed a good laugh on that together. "Now to the serious stuff do you remember the plan Stan?" Alex question with deep concern. "Yes after I kill the prophet and that Valery bitch for good measure, Drop the gun step outside and surrender myself to the cops." Stan explained. "That's right. Everything is already in place. Once inside the prison the league of Satan will fake your death in a prison fight. The nurse and doctors will declare you dead as your body will be smuggle through a black van that will escort you to one of our safe houses in west Chester county." "Shit it's still hard to be leave you have inmates, correction officers and doctors in your pocket for this mission. I can't believe it." Stan said in disbelief. "Well you better believe Stan! It's not as hard as you think. just think about it, nobody wants to die and we all want better things in life. You can see for yourself Satan provides it all." Stan hoisted his shotgun inside a hidden compartment in his leather coat. Walks over to Alex and kisses him passionately. "I promise on my soul that I will kill all those ratchet god serving bastards and rid the world of the angel of silence so we can fuck each other and live like kings for all of eternally on earth." Stan vow to his lover one last time as Alex knelt down on his knees to blow off some steam for Stan's departure to kill the prophet known as the Angel of silence.

CHAPTER FOURTEEN

These last few nights been very different for me. comforting that poor little girl Gabriella, these last few days has been very hard. I never had any children nor siblings while I grew up, this was unmarked territory for me. I thank god that she stop weeping but now she talks to herself while watching old reruns of I love Lucy. I can't blame her who in hell can stay sane after watching their mother get mutilated like that.. Agent Diaz thought to himself. shit I still have nightmares remembering that shit, Image what she feels like and that's her fucking mother for crying out loud. Gabriela is a strong, smart girl although I wouldn't have to worry about her doing anything stupid like committing suicide or anything else dumb like that. Agent Diaz lights up his cigarettes as he makes his way to the F.B.I federal building in new York city to meet up with his partner Li. this case is so fucked up I started smoking again...sight... right when you finally done with something, Here it goes dragging you back down. More importantly the recent actions of my partner and best friend has me very concern. A hour ago he called me at my place. His voice, shit his voice man. I've never heard Li so spooked before, never. that scared the living shit out of me the most. I couldn't get a straight answer out of him. Only thing he would say to me was. "it's the tape Andrew, it's the tape. You have to get down here now." Li repeated three straight times. "Li calm down and tell me what the hell is going on?" Diaz said. "Damn it Andrew! You just have to see it for yourself, just hurry and get the fuck down here! Jesus, dear Jesus." Li said just before he hung the phone up on me. I don't know what the hell could spook Li on that tape but whatever fear he's feeling is spreading through me like a damn plague. I finally made it to the office door and when I open it, that's when I see Li just sitting there with a half pint of vodka in his hand, deep bags under his eyes. He almost jump out of his chair when he notice me coming in. Every inch of his body radiated fear and stress and I knew when I look deep in to his eyes that whatever was on this tape was going to change my life forever. "Agent Diaz you're here!" Li said out loud with a look of relief on his face. The burden of knowing what happen on that tape was too much for him to deal with on his own. Jesus Christ this is the totally opposite of Li's personality. Li can handle anything, that's what I thought until tonight...Christ! "yeah I'm here Li now can you tell me what the fuck is going on here?" I asked trying to conceal the fear in my voice. "It's not something that I can just explain, it's best that you see for yourself. You're going to have need to sit for this Diaz." Li said. Before I could ask what the hell he meant by that, Li already turned on the TV monitor so it's going have to wait. The room was completely silent accept for the static of the TV monitor as it began to play out the last moments of sherry shuford's life and the true identity of the Albert Houston's murders. The video captures sherry running in to her bedroom pulling a butcher knife out of her shoulder. Jesus the adrenaline this woman had felt must had been at its max because pulling that knife out her back barely slow her down at all. Sherry got to her cell phone and called 9-1-1 while pulling out a military service box where she pulled out a colt action revolver. I read in her file that her late husband was a war hero. He must of taught her how to use that gun pretty good because she loaded that revolver like she was Doc Holiday it was so fast. Sherry aim's her revolver at the entrance of the bedroom with a marksman stance waiting patiently for her murder to arrive. "what? What the fuck!" Agent Diaz shouted as he witness Albert Houston stagger in the bedroom. His face was all mash and broken but he could recognizes that lunatic face from anywhere and in any condition. Once you mat that evil bastard in person you could never forget that face. "shut up you'll miss it!" Li said with urgency. I sat my Latin ass back down in my chair, letting that slid for right now and that's when I see it. BLAM! The right side of Albert Houston's neck exploded in chucks of meat and blood as sherry revolver hit's the mark. The recoil of the revolver slams her back in to the dresser draw. Sherry saw her would be murder siting there on the floor trying to stop the bleeding in what is a huge hole in what was his neck. Then she walks up to him. BLAM! BLAM! BLAM! BLAM! BLAM! All five shots connected blowing off more the a third of Albert Houston's face. Wait! what the hell is going on here? That's not how I thought things turned out. I thought that Albert Houston corpse was planted there, but if sherry killed Houston how did she die? "I know what you thinking, just keep watching. Li said never taking his eyes off the monitor. Li must of thought the same thing that I did. But I wouldn't ask no questions until this footage was over and then I saw it. Something that was going to give me nightmares for the rest of my fucking life. Even with my own two eyes my mind still couldn't be leave what I was seeing. The dead body of Albert Houston's back exploded wide open. I was shock in horror as a blur of shadow rose out of Albert's back and instinct sherry's head was decapitated on the floor. Jesus

Christ! Jesus fucking Christ! What the fuck was that?" I jumped out of my chair terrified but Li didn't respond he was completely focus on the TV monitor. I looked back at the monitor to see what had the attention of my partner so bad, I wished I never did because...because there was no words of the horror I was feeling when I saw the decapitated body of sherry shuford clothes was being rip off by the shadow black blur. Something goes inside of her, something that went between her legs so hard and vicious that sherry vagina literal splits open in to her lower stomach. The black blur kept moving in a back and forth motion on top of sherry's body. Jesus he was, he was raping sherry's decapitated corpse. I wouldn't had be leave this shit if Li had told me this, shit I see it with my own damn eyes and still I can barely be leave it. Andrew thought. The thing or Albert Houston, whatever the fuck it is just ejaculated all over sherry's dead body and her decapitated head spelling out Albert Houston was here. It then drags the lifeless body of sherry shuford off the bed by her lift leg in to the living room out of sight of the bedroom camera's. The rest of the video turn in to static. Agent young and I just sat there in shock completely speechless. I finally find the courage to speak my mind. "we show this to director Anderson. He'll know what to do. This is beyond just you and me now." I said. "Andrew... you do realize if Anderson take this tape seriously this becomes covert operations. No press or any other kind of coverage. This case doesn't exist it's ghost. They have some cover up story for the Albert Houston murders. They could never go public with this. You do understand this right?" Li explained. Li is right the government could never officially acknowledge something like this especially to the public but I already knew this. "Don't matter anymore Li, As long as they get that thing off the streets." "Then let's not waste any more time." Li gets out of his chair to retrieve the tape from the monitor. Once Li pushed the ejection button on the VCR it caught fire "Damn it!" Li shouted out as he pulled his hand away from the burning VCR. I imminent ran and grab the fire extinguisher off the wall but it was to late. Whatever this was it wasn't no electrical fire because before I was able to pull out the safety pin in order to take out the fire. Three numbers appeared on the television screen and it was the numbers of the beast. "what the!" BOOM! Everything went white hot for a moment as the TV monitor and VCR exploded right in front of us knocking Li and me off our feet, destroying all our evidence leavening us no way to prove our case. "uuahh, Li are you alright? "yeah, just a little dizzy. Guess that's it then huh Andrew?" my partner asked me as I help him on his feet. "No agent Li we still have sherry dairies and I be leave that Gabriella might be the key to our answers." the real question is how can I protect her from something that's not even human? Hundreds of thousands was laid to waste by her holy scythe. Their fallen blood drench the golden roads with a sea of blood that would take centuries to clean. The archangel who wield the scythe was known throughout the battle field of heaven as Valkyrie the goddesses of death. Her name was infamous among Lucifer rebellion army, Even as she slayed three angels with one masterful stroke. One of the fallen angels held on to her ankle in utter his final words. "To die by the hands of the goddesses of death is a honor." he gasp then died by her feet. Once more god's archangels paved a road to victory against Lucifer army, preparing their self's for the final battle for the throne in the capital of heaven, Zion. "very good my fellow brothers and sisters, god would be pleased with our victory here today. Now we must reunite with general Michael to protect the gates of Zion." Gabriel said. One of the inner circle of seven who commands the military decisions of archangels army throughout heaven and earth. "Does he truly feel pleased with the destruction of our brother and sisters high archangel Gabriel? You are one of the core seven. God speaks to you more than most angels, Is he truly proud of this destruction?" Valery asked as all the remaining archangels in Gabriel group felt silent as they all a waited his answer. "I can see Valery questions are share by everyone here with all thou stares and silence, am I right?" all remained silent as they stood and waited to hear Gabriel answer Valery's question. "Yes god is very proud that you all chose not to abandon your faith and stood by your lord and savior but he is also deeply sadden that so many of his children had to perish because of Lucifer rebellion against our lord Yahweh. Of course you all knew this but had to hear me utter the words. Am I right Valery?" "yes it is true what you say Gabriel. Now look at me as I stand before you. I am covered so thick in blood of our brothers and sisters that I can barely lift up thy wings because it's weighted down by their spilled blood." "I've had murdered hundreds of thousands of our kin that now they see me as some kind of goddesses of death. I cannot shed any more of my brother and sisters blood, No matter how traitorous they are." Valery announce. "Valery...what exactly are you saying to me?" the shock Gabriel asked the disheartening Valery, knowing deep down in his soul he knows exactly what she's trying to say but he needs her to truly utter the words out loud. "I cannot continue to murder anymore of my brother and sisters. For centuries I slaughtered them all without mercy throughout this war but now this war is over for me as I stand up on this field." Valery said. "I'm sorry I won't advance towards the battle of Zion, my soul isn't strong enough to fight off the darkness that I feel creeping deep in thy heart with every kill

I make. I won't allow thy self to be consume with darkness like our fallen brother Lucifer. I pray that you all will forgive me." Valery said no longer able to look her fellow angels in their eyes as her once great pride whether away until dust. Gabriel place his hand up on Valery's slump shoulders. "There is nothing to forgive my sister but I will admit brother Michael and Ralph will be greatly disappointed. They had big plans in voting you into the council of seven. No matter they will respect your decision." Valery stood speechless in shock. She knew that she was liked by the core seven archangels of heavens throne but she never considered they would embrace her among them as equals. "Don't look so shock my glorious sister. You are one of the best archangels we have in all of heaven. Now stay here and defend this place, I'll leave a few angels with you as the rest of us go to defend the gates of Zion." Gabriel left with the remaining archangels to regroup with other six members of the core seven and the rest of heavens army for the final battle in heaven. The battle of Zion and god's throne lasted over centuries. In the end El shaddai archangels won the holy war and cast out Lucifer and his rebellious angels which took up a third of heavens populace. To think that so many of us betrayed our father to just fulfill their lust of sinful pleasures. Shameful scum got what they deserved, All of them. It took centuries to clean up all the blood that filled the oceans and soak the land. So many of our brothers and sisters gone forever because of this useless war. Now that heaven was returned back to the glorious place that she was. It was my time to see the council of seven. I am to be judge by the council of seven for my actions during the holy war. There they were, Archangels Michael, Gabriel, Raphael, Uriel, Selaphiel, Raguel and Saraqael all stood before me. I stood firm and prideful as I prepared myself for my punishment as the council of seven stopped talking among their selves. Their focus was solely on me now. As our leader and general Michael step from the group and approach me. "sister Valery are you ready for this meeting to begin?" Michael asked. Valery clenched her fist hard to stop her hands from shaken from fear of judgment. By all that is holy am I truly ready for judgment? I Had centuries to prepare myself for this since I made the decision to abandon the holy war. No I must not falter now, I must take my punishment even if they cast me from heaven like Lucifer or something worst. "yes general Michael sir I am ready for thy judgment." I manage to say out loud with conviction. "Do not fear Valery such behavior does not fit your stature. You are not here for judgment." Michael said to me. I couldn't be leave what I was hearing if I wasn't here for judgment then why am I here? "sir I don't understand if I'm not here for my war crimes then why have you all summoned me?" I asked the council confuse but relived all the same. The council of seven began to laugh at me like what I said was so amusing. "Dear sister Valery theirs no crime you committed. Quite the opposite actually you are a war hero, Even Azura approve the name Valkyrie the goddess of death." "It is a great burden to cast out your brothers and sisters for all eternally we all understand why you choose the path you taken and we will not punish you for such judgment sister Valery." Michael explained. "general Michael not to sound ungrateful but if I'm not here to face judgment then why have thy summoned me here?" I asked bewilder by all that has happened. A few seconds after my question the council became very quiet and there were no more smiles among them. This left me feeling very uneasy. The next words the council would say would me of great importance. This drove more fear in to me then when I thought I was going to be banish from heaven for treason. Now this time Gabriel step forward. I'm guessing the council want me to hear the news from Gabriel since he was my field commander. "Valery as one who fought by your side in the holy war I witness your bravery and astonishing skills first hand. It is one of many reasons why I recommended you to the council." Gabriel praised. Valery suddenly felt her back straighten up her chest poke out a little more, Even a small smile started to creek across her face but Valery knew better than that. "Varley we want you to know that even the best of us can be worn down from the effects of war, the death of former comrades, friends and family is sometimes a burden that one cannot bare for so long, But as the archangels of god's throne we must. It is why god created us, To protect heaven and the word of god. No matter the burden or the cost it might have on our lives this is the reason why we must strip you of your title archangel." So this is the true meaning of this meeting with the council. They say this isn't a punishment but to be a archangel is a birthright. If I don't have that, then what am I? But no matter Gabriel is right. A archangel must fight and protect the throne of god until their dying breathe no matter of the cost and I wasn't willing to pay that cost. I've failed the punishment is justify. Even now the council treats me gentle and sensitive to my feelings. The council didn't need to show up themselves and explain why they needed to strip me of my birthright of archangel but they do so because of the respect they have for me. They were going to make part of the council, the first female angel and I destroyed that reality. I do not deserve such honorable treatment. "Yes I understand sir. I shall return my uniform and scythe imminently." Valery bends down on one knee un host her scythe then hands it over her head. "no that won't be necessary sister Valery. You might still have use of those." Gabriel responded. "....I don't understand sir Gabriel if I'm not to a archangel anymore what use are these to me?" Valery asked confused of the council decision. "Valery do you remember when we casted out Lucifer and his followers out of the gates of heaven two centuries ago?" Michael asked. "...yes Lucifer and a third of heaven felled from the heavens like a shooting star destroying all animal life, imprisoning their souls on earth for all of eternally. Why do you ask general Michael?" "Because Valery god created a unique creatures called humans but since their creation Lucifer has corrupted them with the fruits of forbidden knowledge. These fallen angels or demons which ever one they call themselves now can't just roam free on earth interfering with these humans as they please. Our lord and savior created rules of engagement. We all agree that you were best choice to go earth and enforce god's will as a watcher." Michael explained. I had to give this some serious thought. They were asking me to arrive in earth to be a babysitter and make sure that these demons and our angels don't break the rules then report it back to heaven. Once again the council was depending on me I couldn't fail them a second time. It's been centuries since I've said yes and been on this world preaching and teaching the true word of our lord and savior Yahweh the great El shaddai to mankind and never regretted it since. Valery finished her thoughts about that day so many centuries ago as she change in to her church service clothes. Now I must watch the path of Natasha and the Angel of silence. "Varley my dear sister I am very excited to hear you preach the true word of god to mankind for the very first time." Natasha said with a bright smile. "Don't expect too much Natasha, service here isn't the same as the divine in heaven." Natasha and Valery shares a hug as Valery returns Natasha smile. "Valery seeing you preach the word of god is divine." Natasha said then turns to her right to see Jessie brown dress in a very fancy grey suit. "Jessie are you joining us on stage as we worship the word of the lord?" Natasha asked. "yeah of course why else would I be wearing this expensive suit." Jessie turned completely around to show off his clothes to the two angels. "yes you do look very delightful Jessie brown, How did you get such clothes?" "That would be from me Natasha. If he's going to stand on my stage there is a standard that must be obtained." Valery said as she open the double doors that lead them to her church followers to hear her spread the true message of the lord. Once the sanctuary fells up Valery starts to introduce Natasha and Jessie to her followers while they stood by her side on stage. Valery preaches the word of god to her followers when a sudden dread washed over her as one of her most faithful god worshiper walks in to the sanctuary. Valery couldn't understand why she felt such a demonic presence and bloodlust from such a kind soul until she saw a shotgun pulled from his trench coat. BLAM! Valery heard a loud scream behind her when she realize the shot wasn't for her. Valery looked back and saw Natasha upper body covered in blood, She was drench in it. I saw Jessie brown in her arms, that when I knew it wasn't her as she cried out desperately trying to stop the bleeding that oozed from his body as she held him close to her chest. The Angel of silence been shot. I shot him! I really killed that motherfucker Stan thought to himself as he watch the beautiful young woman cried out in grief while she held the dead prophet. Bitch must be his girlfriend with all that howling she doing. Better kill her off to make sure she ain't carrying any of his offspring. People in the sanctuary started running towards the exit in fear, So Stan reach back in to his trench coat and pulls out a auto full semi machine gun and spray bullets through the panic crowd in front of him, paving a way towards the stage. Killing three men, two women and a child. "Stan I know you! Why are you doing this? Stop it now!" Stan heard his old priest yelling out to him. Bitch I'm here to kill you too. You want to judge people and punish them because they don't fit a description in a fucking book. Well fuck you we have our own book and soon were rid the world of all you god serving son of bitches! "Valery that's you girl! Because I know all about what you are too and your precious angel of silence who I just blew back to heaven over there." Stan sprayed his machine gun at Valery but she ducked under her polonium. "Hide all you want that won't keep you sa...." No somethings wrong. Stan gets a clear look at the stage again as he sees the beautiful girlfriend of the angel of silence on stage alone but where the fuck is the angel of silence? "Hey tell me where your boyfriend crawl to and I promise I won't kill you." "you like killing innocent people you fat fuck!" Stan heard a deep inhuman voice behind him. Stan quickly turn around machine gun ready to fire. "should of killed me when you had the chance!" Stan yell as he pulled the trigger of his semi auto machine gun. Nothing happening. What the hell's going on? How the fuck this black bastard still standing. Stan pulls the trigger again. "Die! Die! Why ain't you fucking dying?" Jessie just stood there in front of a frantic blood lust Stan seemingly waiting patiently for his rant to be done as blood still ooze from the six bullet holes in his chest. "may be because you don't have these asshole." Jessie answer. Jessie showed Stan the machine gun he once held with his bloody hand still attached to it. Stan eyes looks down in disbelief as he sees his right arm missing from his elbow down. "Jesus, Jesus fucking Christ my arm..you cut off my fucking arm." Stan said in shock. Jessie instinctively grabs Stan's neck almost crushing his windpipe. Slamming him down to ground splitting the back of his head open. "Tell me who sent you! How the hell you know who I am? Answer me before I spill your guts all over this fucking floor!" Jessie demanded. Stan saw death stare down on him with pitch black eyes and talons ripping in to the flesh off his neck and he knew right there and now his mission was just."...ugh..so this is who you truly are. What kind of god would make something like you a prophet, Heh I guess the same kind of god that would make a man gay then punish him to hell for it." Stan manage to say. "that's what's this all about! You kill a bunch of innocent people because you feel that god gave you a unfair life!" "fuck you! Die angel of silence!" His war cry was made as he reach in to his belt and pulled out a combat knife with his one remaining hand. "No!" Jessie involuntary rips out Stan's throat avoiding his knife attack. Stan chokes on his own blood reflecting back on his choices of accepting Lucifer deal, killing all those innocent people here just a few minutes ago, Not being able to live his life with Alex. After everything I done..I'm going to die and burn in hell anyway. "Forgive me..." Stan chokes out his apology through his shredded throat as he looks up to the ceiling and die's. Another poor soul collected for Lucifer by fallen angel the Engineer.

CHAPTER FIFTEEN

Necromancy is an ancient ritual that been around for centuries. The most infamous tales of this can be found in the book of Enoch when the witch Edor summoned the spirit of Samuel with necromancy. There are three types of necromancers in the world. First is those that can summon the souls of the dead for brief time period. The second kind is to reanimate the soulless body of the dead who can control the reanimated corpse to do physical deeds. The third type of necromancer is the rarest and the most powerful kind of spell caster. You can return the soul of the dead in to the body of the animated dead. Who can feel and thank but have no power to free themselves from the control of the necromancer that summoned them back among the living. Even In ancient biblical times such kind of necromancer masters was almost unheard of. The engineer is one of these few masters of the dark ancient arts of true necromancy. Now once again he will use these forbidden skills to summoning the dead to bid his will. The engineer stand's on top of a stage inside an old catholic church that surrounded by lid candles, the walls and stage floor is covered in an ancient Latin language written in lambs blood. In the center of the stage is a blonde dead woman that Albert Houston straggle to death a few hours ago inside of a back alley, Wrapped in loft covered in lambs blood. The engineer starts chanting the ancient languages of man that was lost during the days of babel to complete his ritual. Albert Houston watches his master finish the last of the dark ritual of the dead, un impress. "why all this drama? Just summon her up the same way you prong me back from hell." Albert asked frustrated hating that he have to stay and watch this crap instead of going out killing ,Hunting down souls for his amusement. "Because you volunteer your soul to serve hell completely and willingly Mr. Albert Houston while with her I only have possession of her soul. It takes a few years for those in hell to return to earth but with necromancy I can bring back the dead within a few hours." the engineer patently explains to his hitch man. "yeah but why a church? Don't you demons hate church or something? Wouldn't a back alley had been better?" Albert Houston interrupted the engineer ritual with his meaningless conduct. For the first time since the engineer started his necromancy ritual his eyes diverted from the dead corpse and turned his attention on albert Houston. His stare wasn't one that was welcome as Albert Houston step three steps back from the aggressive look in his master's eyes towards him. "Hear me boy for this will be the only time I will explain myself without dare consensus for your own wellbeing you understand?" Albert Houston reply by nodding his head up and down like a child does when responding to their parent. "like you Mr. Houston most people thank that a church have's some great power over us. That these churches have some sanctuary from all the evil in the world but the truth is that's the world's greatest lie." a wicked smile ran deep across the engineer's face that ran chills down Albert's spine. "Judaism, Christians, Muslims, Buda, Hinduism, all of them use symbols of old pagan religions. Looking down, shaming there women, wars of mass murders in the name of their gods. Idolize and worshipping false gods and those who claims to be the reputation of God on earth. There are very few places in this world that have true fellowship and because of this. These items and idols that they worship gives us power and dominion over them. The engineer explained as he turned his attention back to the corpse. The engineer raised his hands high to the shy and chant ancient words once again fire exploded up from the candles like fireworks on the fourth of July. The blood on dead corpse turned in to words as the blood boils in to her flesh, smoldering all that she was like a phantom on its prey. Her skin turn rotten gray covered by deep lacerations across her entire body. The necromancy corpse opens up her eyes no longer the woman who was straggle to death by undead killer Albert Houston but the eyes of another who felt under his murderous onslaught. "oh shit! It's really her!" Albert shouted out surprise by his own surprised. "welcome back among the living mrs.shuford." the engineer welcome back the recently departed sherry shuford from the dead by giving sherry a helping hand to her feet. In amazement albert walk's to the necrophobe sherry to admire his handiwork by caressing the scars he left her. "I've done a hell of a job on you haven't we. Yeah you best to believe we did." Arouse by seeing his handiwork on the necrophobe sherry Albert stop's caressing and shove his fist deep inside sherry's virginal. "yeah that pussy just as tight as before." Albert taunts. Sherry doesn't react just stare in to space as if Albert Houston was never there. What was once a gloat of pride quickly turns to anger and shame for the resurrected serial killer. "what you think you're to bigtime to notice me? Best to believe Albert Houston always gets notice!" He threating sherry. "your threat goes on empty ears Mr. Houston. Sherry only reacts and moves on my command, for example mrs. shuford please show Mr. Houston what you think of him."

less than a blank of an eye sherry choke slams Albert hard in to the floor shattering the ground. Blood gash out of albert's mouth from his crush throat. "Die you murdering bastard!" sherry screamed out in a blinding rage. Her left hand turned in to a long metal spear as she raised it high to deliver the killing blow. "Now I'll send you back to hell where you belong!" "Enough." the engineer said in a calm matter. The slightest sound of her master's voice froze her in place. Like the famous statue of archangel Michael about to deliver the finishing strike up on Lucifer, sherry stood over Albert's body frozen in time. Imminently Albert jump off the floor back to his feet, pissed off ready to deal some serious damage. "Bitch you think that I've fucked you up before best to believe this will be worst!" The engineer steps in between them his hand place on Albert's chest. "you will do no such thing Mr. Houston. I have other means for you to attend." "the fuck I do!" Houston bark at his master. "Enough don't make me repeat myself Mr. Houston!" Albert heard his master's voice become stern and he knew he had to back down if he was to survive this night. While in hell Albert saw the limits of the engineer's patience with other servants. It's something he would never want to experience, especially when he's about to send me out to do what I love doing best. Raping, killing there's nothing better than that in this entire fucking world. "Pssh..you can have that bitch, I had my fun with her anyway." Albert spits an out rotten blood. "Good choice Mr. Houston I would hate for something unfortunate to happen before the most important task I have for you." Albert cross his arms together clearly still pissed but wouldn't dare speak out against his master again. "who you want me to kill now." "good Mr. Houston good. I want you bring me back sherry's little girl Gabriella. It's time for a family reunion and understand this you shall not harm in any way Mr. Houston." Albert Houston frowns in disappointment. He thought he might at least get a little pink time in. that was his feelings before he looked in to the face of the undead sherry. The way she reacted once the engineer let her express herself shows that she can still feel, hear and understand everything around her but can't do shit about it unless the engineer's allows it. Albert's disappointment quickly became excitement knowing that sherry is well aware that I'm about to ruin her daughter's life and there ain't shit that could be done about it. Hell maybe the engineer planning on making sherry do some fuck up shit to her own daughter. Albert laugh out hard until tears ran down his eyes. He couldn't wait to kidnap the little black bitch now as he exit the church to hunt down sherry's daughter Gabriella shuford. Valery's sanctuary. Inside Jessie's room. For the last couple of hours all Jessie brown could do was stare at his blood stain hands in despair. What am I? What was I doing? Was that all I could think of. Why was my first reaction was to rip his throat out? With all the power I have, that was the only thing I could think of ? There had to be another way. God did I become the angel of silence just to murder my enemy's? Killing..is that all I'm good for. Wasn't my purpose to save people souls, isn't it? Jessie tortures himself with self doubt and questioning the reason of his life actions. "God what am I supposed to do, what am I supposed to do dear god please?" Jessie pleads to god as he buries his face in the palms of his bloodied hands. "God wants you to keep doing what you're doing Jessie brown." Jessie looks up from his hands and see the beautiful Natasha standing over him. "Natasha, you still have faith in me?" "Of course my dear Jessie brown. What you done, You had no other choice. You could had killed him once you had position behind him but you did not slay him do you know why that is ?" Natasha held both his hands. "Because I wanted him to fear me." Jessie answer. "No Jessie brown killing wasn't your first instinct because you have a good soul. Do not weep any longer dear Jessie for his soul was already corrupted by the falling one named Lucifer and he was here to do his bidding. His soul could not be saved Jessie brown." Natasha continues to hold on to his hands as she kneels down on both knees to meet Jessie eyes, face to face. "Thank you Natasha. Thank you so much. ...do you know what's so sad about this moment Natasha?" "No, I do not know dear Jessie." "you the only person who ever showed me any kind of praise since my mother died but the real truth is you're an angel so in reality there's no living human being that ever gave two shits about me." Jessie confessed breaking down in front of Natasha. Jessie began to cry from loneness, grief and sorrow. All he felt was great shame swelling in his heart. Natasha place Jessie right hand on her heart and place his other on the soft cheek of her face. "Am I not real. Don't my heart beat. Am I not warm to touch? Am I not a living soul?" Natasha asked him and he knew that very moment that there wouldn't ever be any woman, Human or Angel that he would love other than Natasha. "I'm sorry of course you're a real person. You're the most beautiful soul I've ever seen in my life and always will." Jessie said with pure love in his heart. "...Thank you now Come there is much that I have to teach you. I am afraid our time might not be as long as I would like." she explain. "Wait, Natasha.. I love you." Jessie final reveal his true feelings for the angel. "Yes I love you too Jessie brown. Now come we must..." Jessie stood firm holding Natasha hand tightly looking straight in to her glorious eyes. "No Natasha. I'm in love with you and I want to be with you." Jessie announce his love for the heavenly angel, Now it was Natasha turn to look away. She knew for some time now that Jessie feelings for her was more on the romantic side but she never image it will reach the level where he would openly confess his love for me and now it would seem I to have deep love for him as well. I promise to my great lord and savior Yahweh that I would never cross the line like my fellow angels did so many centuries ago. Natasha remembers her covenant to god, lord and savior. "Jessie I am sorry this cannot be for it is a sin before our father's eyes." Jessie turns Natasha head towards him and passion kisses her on the lips. Natasha try's to pull away from Jessie but the more she resists him the more he presses himself against her body relentlessly kissing her , Not allowing an ounce of separation between them. They both stumbles as Natasha continues trying to break free as they crash in to the bedroom wall. Jessie can feel the heat in her body rise, Hear her heart pound hard in her chest as Natasha breathing became hot and heavy. Natasha flesh became flush. Jessie felt moister on his pants from between her legs. "No..don't do this Jessie..please stop.." Natasha pleaded in a low heavy breathing voice. "Stop denying your feelings Natasha..I can see it, I can feel that you feel the same as me." Jessie starts kissing slow passionate kisses on Natasha neck pressing her against the wall. "No don't do this! God don't want this please!" Natasha beg him to stop not wanting to physically move Jessie off her, Afraid of seriously harming him. "I think this is why god send you to me. This is why were so attractive to each other." Jessie kisses Natasha in the mouth again parting her legs open with his own, sliding in between them. "No..don't..you don't know what you're doing..I..can kill you." she warned Jessie. Natasha breathing became hard and frantic, sweat run down her entire body. Her skin became torching hot that it burned Jessie skin. Instead of making him yield Jessie became more aggressive. "If that's what it takes, I'll die for you Natasha..I'll die to be with you." Jessie continues to kiss Natasha again this time she returns his kiss back with a more aggressive approach. With Natasha will completely broken she gives in to her temptations for Jessie brown. Jessie started to feel like a beast was unleashed from its chains as Natasha nails digs deep in to the flesh of Jessie shoulder's. Jessie made a slight moan of pain as the smell of his blood made Natasha more excited, Her wings exploded out from her back, Ripping off all her clothes. Her wings ark high in to the ceiling and drops down cutting Jessie clothes off of him. This surprise Jessie for a moment. It's almost as if Natasha was a different person. It's like all her pin up emotions and lust that she had suppressed for millions of centuries was unleashed. Natasha wraps her angelic wings around their naked bodies. "Unlike my fallen brothers Jessie if you truly in love with me, you must now and forever vow yourself to me before god, that we do not lay in sin." Natasha said. My god is proposing to me. Is this beautiful perfect angel asking me to marry her. "yes Natasha I will always be faithful and loyal to you. This I vow to you and god." I vow to her and the smile she showed me when I utter those words to her. Was a grace of beautiful unlike anything in this world that she filled my heart with joyfulness as tears came down my eyes. Jessie then inserts his penis inside Natasha vagina as a burst of painful pleasure erupts throughout her body. Blood pours down Natasha legs as her virginity was no more. For Jessie it was heaven in its own right. Natasha was so wet but unimaginable tight. Jessie penis would of been able to move more freely inside a vise. He knew when he broke through Natasha's vagina walls there were damage to his foreskin but a little pain wasn't going to prevent him from making love to the most beautiful woman in the universe. Jessie breathes deep squeezing Natasha tight in his arms as he manages to stroke deep inside of her pussy. Natasha yells out a roaring cries of moans, Jessie strokes deep inside her as he feels a unbearable gust of pleasure as Jessie explodes deep inside Natasha womb. Jessie moan out as he came. Only two strokes before he came, her body is so hot inside that it burns, Natasha walls tears his foreskin every time he penetrate her. This one of the reasons Natasha said she could kill him, it would be impossible for a normal man to even penetrate a female angel without severe tearing and blood loss but there isn't a thing on this universe that would stop Jessie from loving his wife. Natasha was overflowing with hot moister from her virginal causing Jessie penis erect harder than before he first enter her. His body starts to adapt to hers as he starts stroking her deeper and harder now. Speeding up inside of her as she moans out. Her moans gets louder and louder as she bits down in to Jessie's shoulder's tearing in to him. "Aaahhh Natasha!" Jessie yelled her name in a feel of pain and pleasure. Jessie pounds inside her up and down relentlessly stroking her hard and fast repeatedly. Natasha founds herself matching his moves grinding hard as she begins to lose control of herself. Moving back and forth fanatically. "Aaawwhhh! Devour me! Devour me!" she scream commanding her newlywed. Jessie pace became firmer and quicker as she felt him grow harder deep inside her. "Aaahhh natashaaaaa I love you." Jessie released deep in Natasha for the second time. "Jessie I..uuuaaahhh!..." Natasha body spasm hard as her nails racks deep across Jessie's back as they both climax together fulfilling their unity. Exhausted they both collapse to the ground Jessie on top of her, Still inside her as they both laid there embracing each other. Nether ever experience anything like this before. Natasha looks up at the man who she was send to train in to the ultimate angel for Armageddon who now turned in to my husband. She worries for the open bleeding wounds across his back. "Jessie.. you're wounds let me heal you." Natasha said as she realize the damage she done to him while she can taste his flesh in the corner of her mouth. Jessie's blood pours on top of her from his gaping wounds. "Ok. But leave the scars." Jessie said exhausted. "why when I can heal your wounds completely through?" A confuse Natasha asked. "Because I love you with all my heart and soul. You made me what I am today. These scars will remind me of the day we announce our love for each other for the first time." Jessie explain to her as he passed out while laying on top of her. Natasha held on to Jessie sleeping body tight healing all his wounds, Gently kissing his forehead and she began to speak to god. "Thank you god oh mighty, my lord and savior El shaddi for blessing me with these two gifts. Now I truly understand why it was I whom you trusted to deliver the Angel of silence from the darkness unto the holy light that is your grace Yahweh my lord and savior. Natasha smiles at god then towards her new be wedded husband then she felt in to a deep sleep, dreaming of their future to be.

CHAPTER SIXTEEN

I stood there like a freighted deer in headlights after Gabriella answer all our questions about her decease mother's diary. Gabriella told us about the man in the black suit, How he's the one responsible for Albert's Houston and even her own resurrection. How the man in the black suit is using Albert Houston to kill every living soul that made a deal with him and plans to resurrect them all from hell, Jump starting the god damn apocalypse. We asked her how would she know all of this? I couldn't believe what she said next. That her guardian angel told her so. A real life guardian fucking angel she says. The most freighted thing wasn't that I believe her or not but watching my partner and best friend drop down on both knees and started praying to god for forgiveness then to make things worst Gabriella stood over him placing her hand on top of his head like she was some kind of pope or some shit. "Li do you believe that Jesus the lamb of god was sent to die for your sins.?" She asked "Yes, Yes I do believe Jesus the son of god died for my sins." I couldn't believe what I was hearing, It was as if I was living in the god damn twilight zones. "Li do you ask our god lord and savior to forgive you for your sins and to accept his graceful mercy on your soul?" "Yes. Yes I do, dear lord god please forgive me for all my sins." Li prayed out as Gabriella now places her hand on his shoulders. "Now that god has heard your prayers, knowing you are true in thy heart and soul my guardian angel said that you are forgiven and your soul is saved. You may stand up now." Li raised up from his knees a brand new man as tears of joy ran down his eyes. It was a great burden that was finally lifted from his soul. He spent so many years denouncing god for allowing all the horror in the world but here and now... He changed before my eyes. All his despair was gone as I watch him give Gabriella a long hug, Even she began tearing up. "Gabriella do your angel Morningstar knows if my parents are in heaven?" Li asked. Gabriella looked over her shoulder at what was supposed to her guardian angel named Morningstar, then she back at li. "Morningstar said your parents were faithful followers of the lord. When heaven opens its gate your family will have a place among them." Gabriella answer. "Thank you god. Thank you Gabriella and your angel for opening up my eyes to the real truth." Li thank her and they hugged again. This seem like a good change for Li but I need to ask him why. Why now he believes. "Li what's going on man? You always explained to me that you didn't believe in God, That everything was a scam. Now you on your knees praying, thanking god. What the hell's happened to you Li?" I asked. I knew the shit we saw could break any man, God fearing or not but I would of never thought I would she a man like Li repent his sins because of it, Not him. "I've seen the light Andrew. For the first time since I was twelve years old I've seen the light. This special little girl and that demon we saw on that tape changed everything for me Andrew. The devil clouded my mind with so much shit of evil I couldn't believe there was anything good in this world. You remember the story I once told you about what happened to my family, How I was the only surviving person?" Li explained. "yeah I remember man but don't relive that shit man just forget about it." I tried to change the subject, Bad enough we're living through this shit now, I don't need him thinking about the most fuck up day of his entire fucking life. "No I want to tell it Li. I've never told nobody the full truth of that day and that's including you. It's been a cancer in my soul for way to long Andrew." I saw the look in his eyes and I knew there wasn't going to be anyway to talk him out of it now. "Do you think it's fair to burden a little girl with a ugly story li?" Diaz "No Mr. Diaz let him speak his peace. I know too well about the ugliness of this world personally plus Morningstar said it's part of cleansing his soul." This girl is really something huh. Well I can't argue with that know can I. "sight...Alright Li we're all ears." Agent Diaz said folding his arms. "I was twelve when my parents and I lived in san Francisco. My mother and father was devoted christens. My father hung Li was a preacher who preach at a small church in Chinatown every night from Thursday through Sunday. There were an organization of thieves and murders who forced businesses to pay a fee to operate in town. Even a place of worship wasn't exempt." Li explain. "most organize crime would leave churches off limits but these bastards had their hands in to everything including nursey schools. "One night my father and I prepare for Friday night church service. When these two assholes came busting in to our church. They had the nerve to demand protection money from my father. Like the true man that he was, my father told them no and didn't budge. The pussies had a fit when my father didn't apply by their rules and they started trashing the place breaking the windows and chairs, One of them even pissed on the statue of Mary. That's when my father lost his cool. Before we moved to the united states my father was a self defense instructor for the Hong Kong police department. My father hit one of the guys in the throat with a closed fist, he instantly felt to ground

174

gasping for air and for the one who piss on sister Mary my father broke his arm and made him mop up his piss with his face, Before kicking them both out on their assess. Could you imagine how proud I was in that moment knowing my father was a man of god that could kick anybody ass that disrespected our family." "yeah I could see how that could make any child proud." Gabriella said. Andrew didn't say a word because he knew this was leading too. "yeah Gabriella I was a proud kid for those following two weeks until that Sunday night. When those two thugs returned this time with a third member during our Sunday night service. They was strap with full automatics and a saw off shotgun and a house full of church followers praying to their lord. That's when I heard one of them shout out I'll give you something to pray about. Tata! Tata! That's all I heard next. My father had a small church there was only one exit in they were standing in front of it. There was nowhere to run to. They killed...they killed everyone even the fucking children. Accept... Accept my parents and I. Li voice started to break as he tried to keep composed. "Li I'm so sorry." Gabriella said. Andrew stood quite knowing things would get worst in Li story because he knew his parents died that night. "We quickly understood why we were spare during the killing spree when we saw them blow away both of my father's knees out with their shotgun." Li continued. "Li stop. Gabriella don't need to hear this, she just lost her family to a gruesome murder as well man." Diaz interrupted not wanting the young girl to endure anymore horrors that resemble her own. "No it's ok Mr. Diaz. Morningstar said for the gates of heaven to fully open to him let him confuse the demons of his soul." Gabriella smiled. "All is forgiven. Mr. Li" Once those words was utter I knew there was nothing that I could do to keep him fully sharing this story. "After they shot my father in the legs they pointed their guns to my father and my head and instructed my mother to strip her clothes off. My mother was a proud woman she said. she would die first before she would allow their filth to ever touch her. That's when the third guy took his gun and started to pistol whip me in the face with it. My parents beg him to stop and his only response was if you want your son to live get naked. Gabriella and agent Diaz couldn't no longer listen to Li story while looking at his face knowing full well where this story was heading. It was shameful knowing someone had to endure such horrors. That's when, that's when they forced her clothes off and took turns raping her while making my poor father watch as she pleads for them to stop, crying ,screaming she begged them. The more she begged and plead the more excited they became as they raped my mother. Gabriella gasp in horror, she covered her mouth with tears streaming down her eyes. All agent Diaz could do to ease her tension was to rub her shoulders knowing this was just the begging of Li's story. "After repeating raping my mother over and over again my father..my father just died. He died right there with a emotionless expression on his face. This of course really pissed them off, I guess they wanted him to suffer more so they decided to focused their attention towards me. The one that my father made wipe his piss up with his face decided that I should take off my underwear while shoving his shotgun behind my head." LI said as he closed his eyes as he remembered that painful night. "Oh' my god!" Gabriella shouted out. "Jesus Christ li! You never told me man Jesus!" Andrew said. "No, it's not what you think I didn't get rape...it's much worst then that." "what the hell could be worst then... Jesus Christ Li don't tell me you did that?" Andrew said disgusted with sick horror. "I didn't fucking have a choice man! I swear I resisted at first Andrew. When my father died I just didn't give a fuck anymore. I told them that you think I give a fuck about living after what they just did to my mother and father. Fuck them I said they was going to kill us anyway I'll welcome my father with open arms in heaven. I told those bastards. The one with the gun to my head said if I didn't do it he would blow my head all over the church like I gave a shit at that moment. I didn't want to die of course but I said to them why the hell would I do anything they say when they're going to kill us anyway so fuck you. I said. "Heh! I fucking like you kid. You got some real balls on you for a preacher's kid. I can tell from your eyes you aint fucking around. That's why I'm going to give you my word. If you fuck your mother and give us a good show I'LL give you my word that you both will live through this. The one that was violated by my father started to protest. "The fuck you say! That mother fucker made me clean my own piss with my fucking face. they all die for that you hear me!" He shouted at the third guy. "who the fuck are you to tell me shit! I'm always left cleaning up your shit Johnny! Because I'm your older brother but I'll give you my word that the next time I had to clean up your shit I'll shoot your ass didn't I." "Joseph what the hell are you..."Blam! Joseph shots his little brother Johnny in the left shoulder. Johnny felt to his knees holding his shoulder trying to stop the bleeding. "Joseph what the fuck man!" "Didn't I fucking tell you the next time you fuck up I'll shoot your stupid ass! I'll gave my word!." "I thought, I thought you was fucking joking man!" Johnny said. "I don't fucking joke around about my honor man." Joseph points his gun back at Li "Kevin knows that, my little brother and now you know it. I'll keep my word so what's it's going to be?" Joseph asked the young LI. "Li it's ok that worry everything will be alright." Li mother said. "Mom, No this isn't right." Li said. "It's okay honey god will forgive us just close your eyes and pull down your pants everything will be okay." Li's mother promise. You have to understand that I wasn't ready for something like this who the hell was. "Mom this is a sin!" "shut the hell up and pull down your pants okay... please I don't want you to die." my mother beg and pleaded with me. "put on a show boy and I'll give my word both you will live through this." I did what Joseph and my mother ask me to do. I...I enter inside of my mother's womb. "Li my so sorry man. Jesus Christ." Andrew said as Gabriella listen in disbelief. "you have to understand Joseph wanted a show, I was only a teenager, I was ... I was still a virgin before that moment. Jesus I was fucking my own mother! I only lasted a minute or so before I came. I broke down and started crying on top of my mother She padded me on my head and told me, And told me everything was okay and that I did well, That nothing was my fault. They blew her brains out, Jesus they blew out her brains while I was still, I was still inside of her. She was...She was all over me. After that the only thing I could remember was that he said to me was "To bad you were a virgin and couldn't give your mother a proper fuck to save her life but look at the Brightside how many people could say that they lost their virginally to their mother." the next thing I knew I was found by some local police officers and put in to foster care until I was eighteen years old. Gabriella felt in to Andrew arms crying uncontrollable in his arms from Li's story. "I joined the police force and graduated second of my class. Once I became a police officer I was able to track down Kevin and Johnny but they were already dead. Both seemed to die from a drug overdose. I found joseph inside some abandon crack house two years later. Once I caught sight of him I aim my gun directly to his head, treating to blow out his brains. He just sat there and looked at me like I wasn't even fucking there. "kid you have to be more pacific, I'll killed a lot of mothers and fathers." Joseph said to me while he lit up his crack pipe. "I'm the kid you made fuck his own mother while you blew out her fucking brains out while I was still on top of her you son of a bitch!" I yelled at him. I could of just blew his brains out but I needed him to re-member, Remember who I was. To know my rage to know why I was going to kill him. "Heh! Damn I did some crazy shit back in the days but what the fuck you want now mommies boy." He laugh as he continues consuming crack. "I'm going to kill you! I'm going to blow out your fucking brains all over this fucking place! For what you did to me and my family!" "Then what are you doing? Do it already." Joseph said as he blew smoke in to my face. "you think I won't? I've waited a long time for this Joseph! Li shouted. So why ain't I dead yet? What things ain't going the way you imagine? Thought That I would plead and beg you for my life, That my life has change. That I'm a different person now. No fuck that I don't give a shit if I die or not. I'm not scare of death fuck you and your dead momie and papi!" Joseph scream out in my face, Daring me to pull the trigger. I stood there for a moment frozen, uncertain and that's when he took his crack pipe bust it open against the table and rammed it in to his throat. "pussy..that's how you..kill someone." Joseph said with a wicked smile as he stared me in the eyes bleeding out, fi-nally succumbing to his death. Leaving me standing in de-spair and shame. In the end he knew I didn't have what it takes to revenge my parents while showing me what it means to be a true killer by murdering himself robing me of my only chance of vengeance's. He truly reveal what a cow-ard I really was with his death." Li explained his story. Jesus Li you never told me. I'm truly sorry brother." Andrew said to his dearest friend and partner. Gabriella ran to Li's chest and hug him tight. "Don't feel ashamed mr.Li. Morningstar said you show that you have a pure soul for you did not fall in to the abyss of the sin that is vengeance's. You made god and your parents proud." Li shed heavy tears of joy from the blissful words of the young girl that he feels is a true gift from god. "Thank you, thank you Gabriella." Li thanked her. "No need to thank me or Morningstar mr.Li but thank god we're just his messengers." LI pad's Gabriella on top of the head. "Trust me on this, you are surely more than just a messenger Gabriella." Li answer but he and agent Diaz notice Gabriella wasn't paying attention anymore. Her body became stiff her face was frozen with deep fear and terror. "Gabriella what's wrong?" Agent Diaz said with concern, Trying to mask his own fear that had shot throughout his being. Gabriella eyes turned completely white as tears poured from them. "The darkness is coming, the spawn who murdered my mother has come for me now." Gabriella said as her eyes turned back to normal but I can still see the fear in her eyes. I don't know dick shit about guardian angels and hell spawns all I know I can't wait for some miracle from heaven to protect this little girl from the same fate her mother had. I won't let her die on my watch not while I'm still drawing breathe of life. "Li we got to get her the fuck out of here! Let's take her to the percent, then figure what else to do from there!." Andrew told his friend while he pulled out his gun and grab Gabriella by the wrist. Already thinking ahead Li un hoisted his automatic and secure the exit door. "I'll take point! Keep close!" Li commanded. Crash! Metal explodes across the Livingroom hall as a large blade rips through the door piercing through Li's throat. Blood splatters across agent Diaz face as he witness the blade rip's back out of his friends neck. Li sees his best friend screams out to him while pushing holding back the terrified little girl we swore to protect. Andrew, Gabriella I'm so sorry I couldn't protect you. I couldn't protect anybody. Li thought as his mind becomes dark with death at his door. A bright blue light appear before him and a dark beautiful black woman came from it. She looked like a Egyptian angel as I watched her walk up to me then place her hand on the side of my face. "You have not fail anyone Li young now go in peace knowing that god has sent me to protect them from the evil that waits. Your family awaits you in heaven. She blessed Li as he died knowing the gates of heaven was open awaiting his arrival.

CHAPTER SEVENTEEN

"**H**oney I'm hommeee!" the inhuman voice shouted through the solid metal door before Knocking the door of its hinges. Crushing the now lifeless body of agent young. What was more disturbing to agent Diaz then seeing a man that was dead five years ago knocking over a fully padded metal door over like it was made of paper was his hands. The hands that murdered his partner and best friend wasn't a knife but some kind of gray matter that look like something made straight from hell. "you son of a bitch! That's the last person you kill, you hear me mother fucker! That's the last!" Agent Diaz yelled as he unloaded his entire clip in to Albert Houston's head. Albert stood motionless for a brief second before a evil smile ran across his face. As the bullet holes in Albert's face closed up just as quickly as it appeared. Albert Houston was unharmed. "Heh..Heh..My master increase my power. Those things no longer have any effects on me now best to believe it. Me and that little girl is going to have a good o'time together. You remember how I love the kids don't you Andrew but don't cha worry I'll keep you alive long enough to enjoy the show." Albert said as he slowly advance forward. Fuck! There's nothing I could do but give my life and be a human shield for you Gabriella. God I hope my sacrifices will give you enough time to escape. "Gabriella when I grab him make a break for the door and keep going!" sorry Gabriella that's all I could do against this monster, god willing it will be enough. "Enough! You will not harm them!" A voice screamed out as a enormous blue light gulf the entire apartment. I've have seen many things in my life but I've never seen anything like this as a Egyptian goddess stood before him. A real angel, then she turned and looked at me. "Take her from here Mr. Diaz. I will deal with the hell spawn!" the guardian angel said to me. What was her name again? Morningstar it was Morningstar as she reach over and touch my forehead. Everything became black then I was standing in front of my building outside holding Gabriella's hand. Right in front of my car, this wasn't by chance. "Gabriella get in the car!" I pulled her towards the door. "No wait ! We can't leave Morningstar with that monster!" "Gabriella listen it's ok. She's your guardian angel, God sent her to protect you. She won't lose to something like that, let her do her job and let me do my and get you the hell out of here.. please." I pleaded with her. "Do it for Morningstar, Do it for Li Gabriella." I said. "...Ok let's go." she said as she looked up at the apartment where agent Li died protecting her and where Morningstar now fight's also protecting her. I won't just selflessly throw all that away. Gabriella thought as they got in to the car as agent Diaz drive us to safety...I hope. "Heh, A real life angel. Didn't know they came in black. I heard that angels pussy was the best in the universe best to believe I'm going to get a taste of that. Dead or alive." Albert Houston licks his savage blood lusted lip's. Disgusting cretin of hell thinks he can ever violate me with his loins. I will dissect it before I slay him and cast him back to his masters. "you foul hell spawn you will never touch anyone ever again! Come to me Agios Thanatos!" Morningstar calls out her holy weapon of destruction that was forged in heaven that was giving the name holy death. "yeah I'm cuming for you angel then I'm going to cum in the little girl!" Albert taunts as the flesh from his body starts to peel off revealing his grotesque demon form. With no hesitation Morningstar charges forward as she takes flight with the speed of a jets engine blowing every window in that building's floor. "Die! Hell spawn!" Morningstar's shouts her war cry as she whales Agios Thanatos to dislodge albert's head. Barley matching her speed albert manage to put up one of his hands to blocking her kill shot. To Albert's surprise Morningstar overwhelms him with pure power as she drives his own blade in to his face slicing open his forehead. In order from keeping Morningstar from splinting his head in half with his own blade, Albert reinforce his block with both arms as Morningstar out powers him, ramming him in to the apartment wall. "The fuck!" Houston utters using all his strength trying to keep Morningstar from splitting his head in half. How the fuck is she that strong only using one fucking hand. "Aaawwoo!" albert howls in deep pain as Morningstar slits a dagger across his lower ribs just missing disemboweling his insides. Since Albert's resurrection from the dead this was the worst pain he felt. It was the worst pain he ever felt living or dead and Albert knew he was in the fight of his life. Best to believe he didn't like that one bit, not one bit. Albert thought. "you pay for that you fucking black halo bitch!" albert shouted disappearing in to the shadows. "Best to believe it." Albert's voice echo throughout the shadows of the apartment. "Coward the darkness will not aid you in this battle demon." she yelled out prepare for his sneak attack. A large blade reach out from the shadows behind Morningstar. Morningstar quickly spun around completely avoiding the attack. "Demon I knew you would attack from behind like the coward you are!" Morningstar's Agios Thanatos cuts albert Houston down his shoulder. the pain was unbearable, it's as if death touch him his self. His right shoulder became dead flesh. Albert was no longer able to lift up his right arm. All that Agios thanatos cut becomes rotten flesh. this is why Morningstar is the most feared guardian angel in all of heaven. "Aahhh! Get the fuck away from me you bitch!" Albert shoots out a black mist from his mouth at Morningstar. Morningstar shields her mouth with one of her wings protecting her from his poison gas. "I thought you wanted to get close so you can violate me demon. Your poison won't work against me." Morningstar mocked. "It's not poison bitch. I'll get close once we get rid of those troublesome limbs of yours best to believe it." Albert's long grotesque tongue licks the bottom of his Sharpe teeth. The shadows in the apartment came alive as it submerge around Morningstar's arms and legs. "the shadows! What sorcery is this!?" panic creep in Morningstar's voice for the first time in this fight and the sound arouse the loins of albert Houston. "The darkness has come to feed my black angel but the worry the best parts are left for me. Best to believe it." Albert gloated as Morningstar screamed out in pain from the shadows. The shadows..the shadows are biting me it's eating me alive. with a clearer look in to the shadows, Morningstar realize that it wasn't shadows but creatures of the night. Roaches, maggots, fly's and rats where all around her, devouring her limbs. All so their master can have his way with her defenseless body. No! No I refuse die like this. I won't be consume by vermin and rape by a hell spawn. "I won't die like this!" Morningstar yelled out as a burning bright light that guilt the entire building evaporating every insect, rodents throughout the building. Years later this building will be one of the most sorted out. The only building in all of new York city that will be completely insect, rodent free. Albert goes in for the kill while

Morningstar is distracted. "Die bitch! I'll fuck you when you're dead!" Morningstar recovers in time from getting impale but not fast enough to avoid getting her back cut open slightly between her wings. "you won't get another chance hell spawn!" Now in close quarters with in Albert's guard Morningstar stabs her Agious Thanatos through Alberts right side of his chest so hard that the momentum cause them to bust through the building. Falling from the third floor of a sixth story building. "Die!" Morningstar shouted in rage as her Agious thanatos starts to rot albert Houston's chest that will spread to his heart causing instinct death. Morningstar was confuse to see a grin appear on the demons face as his body start's to die for good. "you're...to late..bitch!" Albert smirk as Morningstar realize it was night outside. The block was shrouded with darkness there wasn't a single working light pole. The shadows reach out and swallow Albert Houston whole. Escaping the killing strike of Morningstar's Agious Thanatos. No. God forgive me the demon avoided my holy death for now. Even as I speak the darkness is healing his wounds. It will take hours for him to recover from my blade but a demon doesn't need to be in full strength to kill a human man and little girl. Morningstar pulls out a cloth dip in holy water from a canister in her belt and wrap it around her wounds. Morningstar chats her native ancient Egyptian prayer to god. The cloth starts to sizzle on her skin as the flesh on her arms, legs and back began to heal. You're not the only one who can heal from wounds demon. The next time you seek out Gabriella I'll be there waiting demon to end your abomination on this earth forever. Morningstar vanishes in to a blur of light, praying to find Gabriella before Albert Houston does.

CHAPTER EIGHTEEN

"Tell me what is it that you see? What is it that you're feeling my beloved Jessie brown?" Natasha asked her newlywed husband. Sitting behind him while her legs wraps around his waist, her fingers press against Jessie's temple. "I see and feel myself about to make passionate love to my beloved wife any second now." Jessie smile hard leaning his head backwards to look at his beautiful wife's face. "Hush my love. You must focus on the task that god appointed you if you wish to be one with me again." Natasha said. "So in other words if I don't do what I'm supposed to do for god, I won't be bless with the loving of my beloved wife but when I do this I'll can have personal time again is that right beautiful?" Jessie continues to smile. "yes that's right my love only once you do what god has set in motion for you. Remember that our lord and savior Yahweh the great El shaddai is always first my beloved husband." she said as she kiss Jessie on his forehead. "ok let's bust through this training so we can have the real fun." Jessie clap his hands together in preparation. "Enough fun talk. Close your eyes and focus." Natasha demanded her husband. Jessie does what he is told and close his eyes. "Now Jessie tell me what is it that you're feeling?" Natasha ask once again. "It's strange. feels like something is moving around in my eyelids." "Good Jessie just focus on that feeling and tell me what you see." "my god! There's lights Natasha! I see lights, so many red and blue lights flashing before my eyes. It's beautiful Natasha." A amaze Jessie explain to his wife. "Jessie I need you to lock on to the red, blue lights. Can you do that for me my love?" Natasha gently strokes Jessie's temple to help his concentration. "of course I can beautiful." Jessie said but it wasn't easy, the lights were very fast to keep track but Jessie is a soldier, failure wasn't an answer. All he could think of was pleasing his wife , to keep her faith in him. This love empower him as he repeatedly told himself to concentrate. The lights began to slow then they all completely stop in place. Now that the lights was frozen in place he could see them all now. There was three of them. The one he focused on the red and blue mix together. Then there was pure blue and pure red lights. "The mixed color lights of blue and red is the one to touch." Natasha revealed. Jessie did what he was told as he touch the light he felt his body get pulled in what seem like a wormhole. Once the sensation was gone he was surrounded by billions of people submerge in blue and red light. "what is this?" A confuse Jessie asked his wife. "This is the astral projection of the human race Jessie brown. This is called the astral plane where you have the ability to connect to every human being on this planted." Natasha explanation was still confusing to the angel of silence. "what's the purpose of this? I'm still not understanding Natasha, why is everybody cover in lights?" A overwhelmed Jessie expressed. "don't be frustrated my love. God has granted you this rare gift. Let me explain it importance. You have the sight to see in the souls of mankind my beloved. The lights you see around the people are the aura of their souls. If you concentrate on a pacific person soul you can make contact with that person. Natasha explained. "amazing...I can't believe god gave me power like this Natasha. So all I have to do is concentrate on certain person color and contact them." Jessie said as he reach out and grab the red light. "what about this one?" "Jessie no don't!" Natasha warned Jessie but it was already too late as the red light pull him through another wormhole of light. This time as he exit the tunnel of light there was only red lights of people committing rape and murders but there was one that was different from all the rest. This person covered in complete red light seem to notice him. He keeps staring up at me, can he see me as well? Jessie wondered. "It's you, Indeed it is you Mr. Brown. I've been looking for you for a long time." the person of light spoke to him. "I know you. You're the guy from the bar." A surprise Jessie said. All the lights that once surrounded Jessie now was gone replace with avoid of darkness. Then the tall man with the black suit appear before him. "yes it is I Mr. Brown, The Engineer. There is much that we must discuss. The engineer reach to grab the angel of silence. Jessie tried to get away by concentrating on the lights but there wasn't any to focus on. There was no escape for the angel of silence. "No he is not yours to befoul demon!" A beam of light rips a hole through the darkness as Natasha came through, wings spread wrapping her arms around Jessie's body. Both vanishing back through the beam of light. Jessie and Natasha reappears back in their room. Jessie quickly jumps out of Natasha grip. "O'shit! What the fuck was that?" Jessie shouted out pissed off and scare about what had happened. "don't be afraid my beloved god has appointed me to always protect you." "what happened Natasha? Once I touch that red light the next thing I know I'm face to face with that guy from the strip club again." Jessie asked "Once you made contact with the red light you were connected with all the pure evil of this world." she explain. "so what the blue light is the opposite or something?" "yes. Blue is the pure of heart which appears in most children and angels that are station on this planted my beloved." "Natasha why didn't you explain all that at first! I wouldn't had touch the damn thing!" Jessie sass his wife. "watch thy tongue my beloved. We had spoken about this." Natasha soft spoken was sharpen with a harsher tone. Jessie knew that his wife wasn't pleased. "look...I'm sorry Natasha, I'm sorry ok. I don't get how was he able to see me?" Jessie ask while he held both of her hands with love. "It's because he's a fallen angel. All angels good or bad have the ability of sight in the astral plane." Valery interrupted them standing by the entrance of their door arms folded across her chest showing her disapproval. "Valery my sister. I did not sense your presence." Natasha smiled Valery didn't return the pleasure. "How can thy sense anything with thy mind filled with filth." "Hey you don't talk to her like that!" Jessie stood up for his wife. Natasha cuts in between Jessie and Natasha, and turns her attention briefly towards her husband. "It's okay my love. My sister and I must discuss this alone." "your love! Is there any shame in thy soul? The human I can understand. But you..you of all angels how could you commit such sin. Did thy forget what happened to our brothers whom felled in to the sin of lust? Did you forgotten everything Natasha!" Valery questioned in anger. "No my dear Valery I've haveth not forgotten about our fallen brothers who felled in lust nor haveth I've forgotten our talk in the garden of eden." "then why Natasha? Why have you committed such a sin? That the boy was able to survive this shame of the flesh is a miracle in itself. Natasha you must quickly repeat for your sins before god lay judgment on you please my sister." Valery pleaded something that is rare emotion with the former archangel. "No I shall not ask the lord for forgiveness because I've have not sin my dear Valery. For one to make love to one husband is not a sin among the lord and savior." Natasha reveal to her fellow angel. Valery felt her legs go numb and began to shake she quickly holds one hand on to the wall to keep herself from dropping to the ground in disbelief. "Dear sister please tell me in the name of our lord you have not done what you confess. Please in your name Yahweh the great El shaddai please not let this be so." Valery prayed to god. "I am truly sorry that this news bring you such grief my sister but I am in love with Jessie brown and he is in love with me. Our souls were meet to be together for all eternally Natasha place her left hand on her heart and her right on Jessie's heart. "it's true Valery I love her with all my soul and heart and would never hurt Natasha. I am who I am because of her." Jessie joined the conversation to explain his feeling was true for Natasha to Valery. Valery shakes her head and laughs. "you think I don't get it. That I don't understand love. Well you're wrong I understand it, I understand it all too well. Natasha did you even explain to the angel of silence what happens after you finished training him?" Valery exposed. "Natasha what she's talking about? What supposed to happen?" A confuse and worry Jessie brown asked his beloved. Natasha looked away avoiding contact with her husband with a look of sorrow buried in her eyes. "I'll tell you angel of silence. Once you are gone Natasha do you think he can be faithful to an absence wife who isn't there to hold him at night. Please his needs. With someone who can't produce him with children for the rest of his life. Your marriage is a shame. It will bare no fruit but pain and sorrow. Heed my words my sister." Valery foretells. Jessie looks at his wife and touches her cheek. "Does Valery speak the truth Natasha once you finish training me you're leaving back to heaven because if it's true then I want to go with you. There's nothing on this earth more important then you." Jessie's love for Natasha wash away all the shame she had of having to leave the angel of silence as tears of joy flow down her face. "you have such a good soul Jessie. This is why I'm in love with him Valery but you cannot follow me in to the gates of heaven my love, For god still have use for you up on this earth. However I do not for see god summoning me back to the gates of heaven once I'm done training you my beloved." Natasha said. "please my sister don't prolong it, It will only make the pain worst to bare. All angels that are station on earth, watchers, guardian, archangels once their mission is complete they are summoned back to heaven. Natasha you are no different." "what if I am different my sister for something has happened to me that no other female angel has ever experience. I am pregnant with the angel of silence child." Natasha placed both of her hands on her belly. "you're pregnant! We're pregnant!" A excited Jessie screamed out as he picks up his wife and spins her around the room in joy. Valery watches on in silence, stun, speechless from the news she heard. Valery was afraid for the first time since the rebellion in heaven first started. She doesn't knows what this means once again history will be change forever. A human man impregnating a female angel has never been done, Intercourse was virtual impossible. I'm barring witness to something new and only god knows if it's a sign of a new beginning or the end.

CHAPTER NINETEEN

He stood all alone dressed in a black suit inside of an old abandon church. One hand reach out towards a statue of Jesus Christ. "Ah..so close Mr. Brown. So close but one can see why you turned down my offer Mr. Brown. What is a legion of human whores compare to one beautiful female angel, Don't you agree?" the Engineer ask as his arms returned to his side watching the statue of Jesus Christ. "One female angel is worth more than every filthy human females on this entire planted but you already know this little brother." Norwell said as he step from the shadows of the church, sword ready in hand. The engineer looks over his shoulder to see his brother there watching. "that's not what your precious god thinks does he. Heh look at this statue of Jesus Christ, he looks nothing like that." The engineer said looking back at the statue. "Do you ever miss it brother? Do you ever miss him?" Norwell ask his little brother trying to find an ounce of good in him before he sends his soul back to the pits of hell. "who Jesus? Absolutely not, way to righteous for my taste. there are certain things in heaven that I do miss but earth is the true gateway of pleasure." The engineer said as he turned around to give his older brother his uninvited attention. "I had to see if there was any ounce of good left in your soul brother before I send you to the depths of hell." Norwell wings slowly expand from his back really for combat. "Tell me brother why did you come here. Heaven could of sent any archangel for this mission." The engineer asked his older brother. "yeah heaven could of sent any worthy angel to slay you but this was personal brother. I beg Michael for this chance to rid the shame from our family name." Norwell explain as he step in to his fighting stance. "Brother there is one thing in heaven I do miss, that is you Norwell. Stop this and join me brother there is nothing left for you in heaven anymore. Come with me so we can be a family again." The engineer open's up his arms willing to embrace his one and only brother back in to his life once again. "you break my heart little brother fore there can never be a union between as you serve hell." "very well brother before we start I would like for you to meet a friend of my." on cue a woman covered in scars from head till toe across her body walks from the shadows of the church to meet the two brothers. "Mrs.shuford I would like for you to introduces yourself to this nice angel." sherry nails grew in to long talons as she charge Norwell with a speed of a great beast. Norwell wings spread out across the space between him and the undead sherry with in a flash of light. Before Norwell wing returned to him sherry found herself split in half bleeding out on the church floor. "Sorry brother your undead puppets won't be able to help you in this battle." Norwell said as he walked over the detach body of sherry shuford. The blood that was oozing from sherry's detach body shot up from the floor slicing Norwell across his cheek, wasn't for his fast reflexives he surly would of died from being impale through the head. Sherry's blood pulls her rotten corpse together, completely healing her wound. Norwell look's on with great annoyance. "A regeneration necromancy, the worst kind." Norwell said to himself. "That is correct my brother. No matter how many times you kill her she will always come back better than before. My knowledge of the dark arts has grown over the centuries brother." The Engineer brag. "Have you forgotten little brother that sorcery runs throughout our family's bloodline." Norwell quickly clap his hands together. "I bind thee to the light of the lord. I bind thee to the light of the ether of god's grace. Thy shall be bind!" Norwell chanted. A white light wrapped around the undead sherry's body. Immobilizing her movement. "very well brother you will get the battle you graved for but it shall not go the way you pleased." The Engineer said as his voice turned from elegant in to a deep harsh demonic voice as his eyes turned green, His teeth became razors his nails became talons, His ears to pointed of a shape of a bat. The engineer former angelic wings burst out of his back. "witness my true power brother!" The engineer shouted as he flew towards his brother in gauging in what will be their final battle. Norwell swings his sword to decapitate his brothers head, The Engineer blocks the attack of his would be death and counters slashing Norwell across his chest. Drawing first blood. Without a moment of hesitation the engineer spits out green flames from his mouth. In great pain from the gashing wound across his chest Norwell manages to recover enough to shields himself with his wings. Norwell grunts out loud in pain as the green flames burns in to his angelic wings. Norwell explains his wings outward with enough speed and power that cause a gust of wind, extinguishing the green flames and slamming The Engineer through the statue of Jesus Christ. Norwell let out a war cry of rage that could be heard throughout heaven and hell. "Brother there won't be no mercy for the wrath I'm about to unleash up on thee!" Norwell digs his hand in to the wound of his chest, Soaking his hand of his own blood. "By the power of our lord and savior Yahweh the mighty El shaddai boil the blood of all that's wicked and spare all that is holy and righteous in your name!" Norwell chanted as he drew ancient marks on the church floor with his blood. "No you fool! You could destroy us both!" The Engineer scream out trying to stop his brother from chanting the ancient spell. "Only those who share thy blood and felled with wickedness will suffer by thy hand amend!" Norwell finished his spell before the engineer could stop him as Norwell blood writing on the ground to begin to glow white that brighten the entire church with light. "Aaahhh!" The Engineer scream out in great pain as the blood with in his body began to boil. But the Engineer screams wasn't the only heard that night throughout the abandon church. Norwell skin became a deep red as the blood with in him began to boil as well. A great confusing of emotion ran throughout the mind of the archangel. How could this be happen to me? Why would my spell backfire on me? Only those with true hatred or great sin could be harmed by this spell. Norwell thought to himself. The Engineer knew his brother would also be effected by that spell because he knew the darkness that dwell deep inside Norwell's heart. The hate that he held for all of humankind. For every man, woman and child that dwell up on the earth. The two brothers collapse to the ground weaken and wounded from the ancient heavenly spell that effected them both. "you foul...I told you not..to use that spell." The Engineer said. "My lord and savior why have you punish me? What..what sin have I committed that I face the wrath of such judgment?" Norwell ask god. "Heh... God won't tell you brother, But I will." Both brothers stands up on wobble legs, breathing deep breathes. "Your heart and soul is filled of hate for all of humankind brother. It has been buried deep in your soul but since your encounter with the angel of silence the darkness in your soul has burst through the surface of your being." "Shut your mouth! I won't have some demon preach to me about sin and hatred!" "This will be our final exchange in this battle brother." Norwell warned his little brother. "Norwell this unnecessary. We can still be a family again." The Engineer's pleads falls on deaf ears as Norwell begins to chant one of his most powerful spells. "God bless thee with thy heavenly light , Thy source of life and heavenly fire that dwells deep in thy soul up on thee." Norwell started chanting as his body began to glow a bright white light that would blind a normal human being. The Engineer shakes his head with such pity for his older brother. "you just don't get it do you Norwell but I shall you your true path." the darkness that the Norwell's light haven't touch surrounds the engineer feeding him enormous power and strength. "All that dwells in the darkness of thy earth, All that breathe lust, hate and despair up on thy world feed all through thy soul and body to be unleash up on thy creator's." The Engineer enchanted. One brother of light release all that is good with in to destroy the darkness of his younger brother. The younger brother summons all that is evil and dark with in and unleash it returning fire to destroy the light of his fellow brother. At first it would seem the light and shadows are a stalemate. Until the shadows slowly starts to consume the light until all of Norwell was engulf in darkness. All the light and righteousness within Norwell wasn't a match for all the hate and darkness within the Engineer's soul. "your soul isn't pure enough to defeat me brother!" The Engineer mock his brother as Norwell collapse to the ground defeated. "kill me Nataa.. send me the ether feld with the rest of my brothers and sisters. Do something honorable for once." The dying Norwell pleaded to his once little brother. The Engineer walks up to his dying brother but no longer wearing his true demonic face but the face of the falling angel Nataa. "I will grant you your wish of a honorable death brother but only if you hear what I have to say first." "very..well then just make it..quick." Norwell said grunting in pain. "I want you to join me brother and before you say no. I must show you something important. Something of great importance involving the angel of silence and Natasha." the Engineer explained. "keep her koff! Koff! Out of this." Norwell tried to yell. "No she is of great importance of what I must show you, then you can die if that is your wish." A dark mist appeared before the Engineer as it turned in to a visual. Images of the angel of silence spinning around Natasha celebrating their pregnancy together. "you see brother its worst then you ever feared. The human known as the angel of silence has married and in pregnant your dear Natasha." he revealed. "No! It's lies! Koff!koff! It's impossible!" Norwell somehow manage to yell out in grief and his dying heart sank down in to the depths of his chest. "you know I don't have the power to show you false images brother. When I made contact with Mr. Brown I was able to see parts of his near future somehow the angel of silence has done the impossible. For him to have intercourse with a female angel is unheard of but to in pregnant her...this never have been done before brother, Ever. A female angel giving birth. Billions of female angels will gladly fall from grace at a chance of giving birth to life, to have a child. This baby will change everything brother, Everything! Everything we knew about heaven and hell will change forever unless you join me brother and put an end to this abomination known as the angel of silence. Or you can die and watch heaven descend in to chaos once this child is born. What's your choice brother?" The Engineer ask his brother for the final time. Norwell laid in silence as he thought long and hard about his decision. In that moment the Engineer knew it was a new age up on him and everything indeed will change.

CHAPTER TWENTY

"**E**verything is tight in secure agent Diaz." A fully armed equip police officer confirm him. "I just pray it's enough officer Murry." Diaz said. "Are you fucking kidding me sir. I'm sorry about your partner sir but this is the new York finest here. A full squat team fully armed and ready to shoot on sight. There's no way nobody is getting through all of this, I don't care how psychopathic this motherfucker could be sir." police officer Murry brag. The police H.Q was on complete lockdown. There was no way no living soul was getting through all of this but we ain't dealing with the living aren't we Andrew. May Jesus Christ helps us all. The F.B.I agent thought to himself. "Mr. Diaz why didn't you tell them about that monster ?" Gabriella ask him as she pulled on the sleeve of his jacket. "sorry Gabriella there's no way I could tell them the truth about Albert Houston and still can't. they would dismiss me and say I'm suffering from some form of depression because my partner Li was just killed. No it was best to tell them that there is some psycho albert Houston copycat who had plastic surgery to make himself look like the original. Equip with full body armor and blades which resulted in him killing Li and surviving my gunshots. That sounds more realistic then saying a murdering psycho returned from hell as a hell spawn with blades as hands and killed my partner huh?" Diaz said. "...Do you really think they can stop him?" "...No.

No I don't but it's the best chance that we have at the moment." Diaz said honesty. "don't worry Mr. Diaz Morningstar is my guardian angel she won't lose to some stupid demon." Gabriella said as she pump her fist in the air. Agent Diaz couldn't help himself but to smile a little. "Heh. That's the sprit Gabriella. Good always triumph over evil." agent Diaz said to Gabriella just before everything turned pitch black. The precinct was completely dark. "Andrew I can't see!" Gabriella shouted out in fear. "It's ok Gabriella I have you. Don't let go of my hand understand?" "okay, okay." Gabriella claim herself. "what's the hell's going on guys?" agent Diaz asked. "don't worry agent LI the power just went out. The backup generators will kick in, in three minutes." one of the officers said. "that's more than enough to slaughter every single one of you, Best to believe it." the voice heard by all throughout the darkness. "It's him! Albert Houston is here!" agent Diaz warns the other officers. "Everyone night vison on now. Shoot to kill." The commanding officer ordered his people. "here take this and take the girl to the safe room. This won't take to long." the officer hand over a pair of night vison googles over to agent Diaz. Agent Diaz puts on the googles as he picks up Gabriella and makes a run for the safe room. "what is he doing here? What happened to Morningstar?" "I'm sorry Gabriella...there's just not enough time to think about that right now." I'm so sorry Gabriella I don't have the stomach to answer that question right now because if albert Houston is here that means your guardian angel is dead and she was the only thing keeping us both alive. "Everyone fan out. Cover all entry points boys were sending this son of a bitch back to hell tonight." the commander order his squad. "you think you're toys can save you from the darkness." The voice in the darkness was heard. "yeah keep talking so we can zero in on your ass." The commander whisper. "Best to think again!" albert voice erupted throughout the darkness. "Aaahhh!" multiple screams echo throughout the precinct. "what the fucks going on?" The commander radios his unit. "It's in the shadows. It's in the fucking shadows!" the officers screamed out in their radios. Tat tat tat tat! Burst of heavy ammunition was heard throughout the precinct halls. "Die! Die! Fucking die already!" "O' god the shadows are moving. It's moving!" "it's alive! Jesus Christ it's alive!" "calm the fuck down! It's just one fucking man hiding in the dark!" the commander said over the radio to calm his men down just before he saw one of his men shooting and yelling...At nothing. "what the hell are you doing William's?" "it's there sir! It's right th..." officer William's explanation was cut short when commander Shane saw what look like darkness impaling William through his head and heart and he knew in that moment that none of them would be leaving the precinct alive. The shadows then came for him and all he saw was darkness before his end. BLAM! BLAM! BLAM! BLAM! The remaining four squad members open fire in the shadows with no effect. "this is a losing battle man. This thing ain't even human!" "this is hell on earth! This is god's punishment for.." "shut up! I don't want to hear that bullshit!" the officers argue among themselves "listen! Fucking listen for a moment! If this thing is made of darkness what could stop darkness?" officer Murry asked. "I don't know man, light or something?" "Exactly! Use your flash grenades and blow this shadow monster back to hell!" "and if it doesn't work?" "then were dead anyway." officer Murry answer. All four officers pulled out their flash grenades and toss them in to the darkness. A burst of white light consumed the precinct halls evaporating every shadow in sight. "you're some smart pigs. You all just been promoted to die by my hands.

Congratulations." albert Houston said as he sprints through the blinding lights cutting one of the officers in half with his sphere hands. "Open fire!" Murry ordered. The three remaining officers shot multiple rounds in to the body of albert Houston. As soon as a wound would appeared it immediate closed up. "sorry boys you're little pee-shooters won't work on me but my blades sure as hell will work on you. Best to believe it." albert gloated. "best to believe you the one that's going to die tonight motherfucker!" Murry unstrap a grenade launcher from his shoulders and blast it in to albert Houston's chest. "O'shit!" Albert manages to say just before his upper body exploded in to hundreds of roasted rotten flesh all over the precinct halls. "John call in reinforcements. Anthony make a quick scan, see who's still alive. I'm going to get the F.B.I agent and the little girl and we can get the fuck out of here before some other shit start's to happen." Murry gave out his orders. "to late for that piggy! Best to believe it's way too late for that." the exploded body parts of albert Houston's starts to reassemble it's self together again. "No! Noooo! "Murry yelled as he reloaded his grenade launcher while Anthony and john open fire on the reassemble body parts. Murry hit albert Houston with the grenade launcher again with no effect this time. "fuck this! I'm out of here!" Anthony said as he ran for the rear exit. "Eeerrraahh!" Anthony screams were heard throughout the precinct as the darkness tore his body apart piece by piece. "No damn you to hell!" the two remaining officers continues to open fire as it held no effect. "Already been there. It's a very fun place if you have the taste for it. Here let me show you." albert's mouth open wide enough that could consume both officers whole. "Agent Diaz run! Get the girl out of here right now!" Murry yelled out in the radio in his final attempt to save the little girl's life as his partner and him is engulf inside a green inferno flame that consumed their bodies as they died. Blam! Blam! Blam! A burst of bullets smack in to the top of albert Houston's head. Albert Houston looked up to the second floor baloney where the Latin F.B.I agent stood pointing his Beretta as he opened fire again. This time ten bullets hit albert's face. All with the deadly accuracy of a true marksman. Albert's body absorb the bullets like water to a sponge. Albert Houston was now beyond the weapons of mankind. "Ah, there you are agent Diaz. And here we thought you wouldn't join the party." "you won't find her albert! You can torture me all you want but you will never find the girl." Diaz told. "Heh!Heh! You really think I don't know where the girl is boy? The shadows are my eyes and ears now. There is nowhere on this fucking planted that she can hide from me, Best to believe it!" Albert revealed. Blam! Blam! Agent Diaz continues shooting albert Houston hoping one bullet might slow him down somehow as he reloads his gun. Albert starts to walk his way towards the baloney. "God damn you! what the hell you want with this girl that you willing to go through this much trouble for." agent Diaz ask anything for a distraction, just to slow him down a little. Anything to keep Gabriella safe for as long as possible. Andrew prayers to god's ears it worked as albert stop advancing forward. "My master wants her for whatever the hell business that he have with her. More importantly he promise once he done with her I can have her, and you know how I love the kids. Best to believe it." Albert licks his lips. "You son of a bitch! I won't let you! You hear me I won't let you!" Agent Diaz yelled out in rage as he empty out his clip in to albert Houston with no effect. With a single leap albert landed on the second floor baloney two feet away from agent Diaz. "I'm going to enjoy her like I enjoyed her mother and there's not a fucking thing you can do about. You can't even hurt me." Albert smiled. "But I can demon!" Agent Diaz heard an angelic voice as he saw lighting burst through the precinct ceiling blasting albert Houston through the baloney, slamming him to the main floor. Agent Diaz was awe of amazement not because of the lighting that just saved his life but to witness the most beautiful and elegant thing he ever saw in his life as the Egyptian angel revealed herself and spoke un to him. "Go! Watch over Gabriella until I arrive. I will be rid of this demon for good. God will bless you, now go!" I heard the beautiful angel say to me. I didn't hesitate another moment as I sprinted towards Gabriella's hiding place. I think I was bless when you showed up to save my life and I sure in hell what waste it. "I'll watch over her with my life just make sure you send that murdering bastard back to hell!" I said as she sprinted to battle, I could of swear I just saw a smile on her face. the injuries this demon cause me was more serious then I original thought. This is why it took me so long to find Gabriella's grace. So many innocents lost while I was healing. He won't escape death a second time. Morningstar dives straight in to reap the soul of albert Houston with the Agious Thanatos. Albert use the shadows to pull him out of harm's way avoiding the fatal blow of Morningstar's Agious thanatos. "You ain't strong enough to kill me bitch! You Best to believe!" albert Houston mocks her but Morningstar pays no heed to his bickering as she perform ancient hand signs. "lord of all there is cast out of thy darkness that consumes thy holy lands!" Morningstar prayed as all the darkness with in the lobby floor was evaporated with pure white light. "Bitch you think I need the darkness to kill your ass!" Albert's shoots flames of green fire at the sprinting Morningstar who uses her wings to shied herself not stopping her advancement. Morningstar uses her wings to push off the flames creating a gap, allowing her an opening to decapitate albert's head. Albert quickly counters with a x-block with his two sphere hands protecting his neck. "Bitch you think you could jus..." the air was knock out of his lungs with a hard front kick to midsection. The impact of Morningstar's kick was so hard it cause albert Houston slide against floor splitting his back open. Morningstar leaps forward to deliver the finishing blow before Albert could make a grunt sound of pain. With a uncanny sense of survival albert manages to block the killing strike again . Unlike before the situation favors Morningstar as she has him pin down with his spheres protecting his throat against her Agious thanatos. Leaving her left hand free to do whatever she pleases. "I'm pretty sure you are enjoying yourself with me on top of you like this?" Morningstar said mockingly. "once I free my hands I'm going to fuck you in to the depths of hell bitch!" "yes I remember from our first encounter you said you was going to penetrate me. I will take you up on that offer but I will be doing the penetration." Morningstar smirks. "what? Wait! No! Aaahhh!" albert Houston beg and pleaded as he howl out in pain as Morningstar repeatedly stab him through his balls with her dagger. Further down the hall agent Diaz can hear the screams of albert Houston and couldn't help himself from smiling and laughing out loud thinking of him being tortured to death. "Good for you, you murdering son of a bitch hope you howler in pain until your dying breathe." Diaz said as he finally makes it the weapons storage room. "Gabriella it's me Andrew! Are you ok?" agent Diaz ask as he enter the storage room. "Gabriella! Gabriella! It's me Andrew. You can come out of hiding now." Diaz said as he continues to walk further in. Ka-chick! Andrew felt a hard barrel of a twelve gauge shotgun press against his spine. "I'm not hiding. If you're Andrew what's the password?"

Gabriella asked as she press the barrel of the shotgun harder against Andrew spine. "God is good. God is great, may god protect us from the evil that awaits...Gabriella it's me." Gabriella puts the shotgun down as Andrew turns towards her. Gabriella hugs him tightly. "I was so scared for you Andrew. I heard a lot of gunshots and screaming, then I felt the ground rumble underneath my feet. What happen? Is the demon dead?" Gabriella looked up at him for answers. "Morningstar is alive Gabriella and right now she's handing that demon a can of whoop ass but more importantly I have to get you out of here. Morningstar catch up when she's done with him." Agent Diaz answer. "she's alive! Morningstar alive! Thank you god! Thank you!" Gabriella shouted out in joy and excitement that her guardian angel is still alive and able to protect them. "she's not the only one who came back for you Gabriella." Gabriella and agent Diaz both turned around to the familiar voice. "Mom?" Gabriella couldn't believe her eyes but there she was standing right before her eyes. Gabriella's mother was wearing a white silk gown with gold trimmings. She was beautiful. "Andrew you see her too right?" she ask making sure she wasn't delusional. "yeah I'm seeing it but I'm not be leaving it." Andrew responded. "I understand your suspicion but it's really me Gabriella. It was Morningstar. She spoke to god and explain how the demon in the black suit trick me and god sent me back down to you so I can say goodbye before I return to heaven forever honey." sherry explained. "Is it really you mom? Have you really come back from heaven just to see me?" Gabriella ask as she step closer towards her mother. "yes it's really is me honey. Come to me so I can hold you for one last time." Sherry reach out her arms for her approaching daughter. Agent Diaz quickly steps between Gabriella and her mother, shielding her with his body. "Andrew no!

She's my mother." "Last time I checked your mother bare the mark of the beast. If she is really a descendent of god she could announce to us that god is her lord and savior." "that's ridiculous Andrew of course she can. Go ahead mom announce that god is your lord and savior so he can see you're telling the truth mom." she asked sherry. "Of course I am honey. That's why I'm here." sherry reach out for Gabriella again. "Okay I believe you mom but we still need to hear you say the words." Gabriella said with a hint of annoyance in her voice. Sherry stare at Gabriella and the F.B.I agent that felt like minutes. "Mom just say the damn words already!" Gabriella yelled out in anger. "Gabriella know that I am truly your mother." sherry spoke as her answer sent a terrorizing fear down Gabriella and agent Diaz spine. "Gabriella run now! Get to morningst..." blood erupted from agent Diaz mouth as he looked down and saw sherry's arm was inside his stomach. Sherry tosses agent Diaz limp body across the room with inhuman strength. Gabriella runs hard to the exit door but with the speed of a wild animal sherry grabs her while knocking the shotgun out of her hand. "Morningstar!" Gabriella screamed out just before sherry wrapped her up between her arms. "Nooo! Mom why are you doing this? Mom?" "I'm so sorry Gabriella. I have no control over myself." the undead sherry apologizes as tears of blood ran from her eyes. "It's true Gabriella your mother can only obey my will. It's such a pleasure to meet you again young lady." the engineer appear from the darkness. Morningstar heard the cries of Gabriella while feeling an evil presence she never felt before. Finishing off the perverted demon was no longer important anymore. Now she was dealing with one of the falling. Within a instant Morningstar teleported inside of the storage room to bare witness Gabriella's mother holding her captive. That she can handle with ease but the fallen one next to her could be a problem. "Ah, it's nice to meet a beautiful angel such as yourself but we won't be staying unfortunately." "Morningstar!" Gabriella yelled out as all three of them disappeared in to the void of darkness. "Nooo! Gabriella!" No! No! This can't be. I can't feel her grace. I,I don't know where they have taken her. "Koff..koff...Morningstar." Morningstar barley heard the dying voice of agent Diaz. "Mr. Diaz do not worry. You will not die tonight for the heavens have foretold." Morningstar said as she knelt beside his wounded body. "listen I heard him say they was going to use her for a ritual that could bring forth the master. Save her..bring her back..." Agent Diaz blacked out from blood lost. Morningstar puts her hand on his wound as it begins to heal. This is a problem that I did not foresee. If Mr. Diaz heard correctly the fallen angel plans on using Gabriella's body as a vessel to summon Lucifer himself. The only place I can go to get proper help is Valery's sanctuary. A white light flashed in the middle of the storage room. Morningstar was gone in hope's she will get help in time to save Gabriella's life and soul with the rest of the world.

CHAPTER TWENTY ONE

"This is the happiest day of my life Natasha! I can't believe we're going to have a baby. I wonder what's it's going to be?" Jessie rubbed Natasha belly. "it's a girl my beloved husband." Natasha foretold. "wow, a girl. It's a girl I'd always wanted a little girl but how do you know that? It's so early in your pregnancy." Jessie asked his wife in amazement. "She doesn't know why she knows angel of silence. That's because no female angel has never been pregnant by a human before." A very upset Valery interrupted the married couple. "Valery chill out some ok. You telling me in all the time angels been roaming around none been pregnant before now?" Jessie turn his attention briefly to Valery while he still continues to rub the belly of his angelic wife. "No. No female angel never been pregnant never! Look at the abominations a male angel spawns when he mates with a human female. Who could Image what horrors lurk in her womb as we speak." Valery preach with discussed. "you can keep those looks of contempt to yourself Valery. Don't forget those angels slept with those women with lust and disregard of god's command. What we did was out of love not lust, our child will be different." Jessie protested.

Valery crosses her arms over her chest and starts to leave the chapel. "We shall see in due time shall we angel of silence." "Valery! Valery I need your help sister!" Valery heard a voice call out to her from the front of her sanctuary. Valery ran towards the sound of the person who enter her sanctuary along with Natasha and the angel of silence. Prepare for battle if have to be. Inside Valery's main chapel hall they all laid eyes on a beautiful ancient Egyptian angel cover his full angelic battle armor, arms and legs covered in fresh bandages from combat. "Valery it is I Morningstar! I have need of your help please." Morningstar pleaded. "by all is holy what have happen to you Morningstar?" Valery approach Morningstar and saw the fear and horror in her eyes and she knew it had to be something beyond death to put fear in such a angel. Morningstar grabs Valery's arms trying to compose herself. "My...My charge has been under attack by a demon name albert Houston." "the serial killer who died five years ago?" Jessie asked the Egyptian angel. "Yes, he was summoned from hell to kidnap my charge Gabriella but I prove too much for the demon. The fallen angel who summoned him, his self has taken her." Morningstar explain to all of them. "Would you know the name of the trader my sister?" Valery ask her as Morningstar shook her head side to side. "No unfortunately I don't but I have seen his angelic form. He was pale skin with slick black and a goatee. He also wore a human black suit." Jessie eyes widen with mix emotions of fear and excitement once he knew who Morningstar was describing who kidnap her charge. "Jessie what is wrong my love? You're heart has rapidly increased." Natasha worried as she grab Jessie arm. "I know him. The demon in the very expensive suit who tried to get me to sell my soul for a luxury life of sin. Would had accepted to if not for my beautiful wife here who saved me from my self pity and showed me I was worth something. I can show you where I last saw him from our last contact we had together." Jessie revealed to everyone in the chapel. "you mean the Engineer? No! You are not ready to face a fallen one. You are forbidden." Natasha demanded her husband. "Natasha? No there is a little girl's life on the line here. What if that was our daughter Natasha?" Jessie said. "No it's not the same thing Jessie brown!" the couple continues to argue. My god to my ears and eyes deceive me my lord and savior? Is this female angel pregnant? And by a human man? Will there child bring such great evil and destruction up on this world like the seeds of the male angels. If the child is a girl and she's married to this human things already has changed. I am curious to see what this child have to offer this world but if this engineer summons Lucifer there won't be no future for anyone." Morningstar thought. "Enough of this my sister. I will take whomever is willing to help because this fallen one's goal is to summon Lucifer himself among us and force the Armageddon!" Morningstar revealed the engineer's plans. "Morningstar's right there is no time to waste." Another voice interrupted. "Norwell!" they said as he enter Valery sanctuary greatly wounded with third degree burns and deep talon claws slashed across his chest, clothes stain in boiled blood. "Morningstar and the angel of silence is right. I have seen the ritual marks of the beast. Alone I wasn't strong enough to stop my brother but with all of us, we can stop him." Norwell drop to his knees in overbearing pain from his injuries. Valery and Natasha ran to help their wounded brother. "Norwell let me heal your injuries." she asked. "Norwell you will stay here and man the sanctuary while I take your place." Valery said. "No there is no time to heal my wounds. I shall manage Natasha. Valery god gave all of us our duties and objective, my is to stop my brother yours is to watch this place sister. Even if it cost my life I will fulfil my duties." Norwell demanded as he help himself off his knees. "Norwell is correct god has given all of us our duties, my is to protect Gabriella and I'm willing to take who ever can fight." Morningstar agreed with Norwell. "yeah before we do that I have a question foe you Norwell?" Jessie asked him directly. "what could be so urgent Angel of silence that you must delay our departure?" "I notice you looking at Natasha stomach when you arrived. yes she is pregnant with my child and we are married. I know I haven't known you long but it would seem not very like you not to have something to say about that." A sneer grew wide across Norwell's face as he step forward Jessie's face as tension between them was thick and uncomfortable for all. Natasha attempted to intervene but Jessie wave her off. "you grown bold since our last encounter angel of silence. To answer your question my brother reveal this great sin to me when I was in his mercy trying to persuade me to join him. So you see I've had time to deal with this abomination. He smirk. Jessie welcomes Norwell's smirk with a wicked smile of his own. This didn't please the archangel . This shows that he has no respect and fear for the angel known as Norwell. It really pissed him off. Norwell's smear turned in to a frown. "that's another thing I wanted to ask you. I can understand if your brother tried to get you to switch sides even begging, anything to avoid having to actual kill you. but to leave you alive once he realized you wasn't joining his ranks doesn't make sense. Not when he's so close to summoning his master in order to start Armageddon. Knowing full well once you recovered you be hunting him once again. Just seems weird I didn't sense he was the stupid or reckless type but blood is thicker than water right?" this felt more like a statement then a question coming from the angel of silence. Norwell face frowned in anger, his eyes became red with bloodlust. He knew what the angel of silence was replying and Norwell didn't like. This human piece of filth who the fuck do he thank he is to judge me! Too question my loyalty! A human questioning me, me! A angel of god! "how dare you question my loyalty you human piece of filth!" "enough of your petty argument! We must leave now if we plan to stop this demon from rising Lucifer!" Morningstar shouted out. "settle your differences after wards if there is a after!" Morningstar step in between Norwell and the angel of silence. "Morningstar's right. You must go now if you hope to stop the Engineer summoning ritual. Natasha and I will stay and watch from the sanctuary." Valery agreed with guardian angel. "No my sister Valery my task is to aid the angel of silence at all times. I shall not stay." Natasha step forward to leave with the others. "what? No Natasha you can't you're pregnant!" Jessie protest. "I can and I will! There is no debating this matter. To deny me is to deny god's will my beloved husband." Natasha stood her ground. "...fine just stand by me at all times ,understand?" Jessie reluctantly gave in to his wife. "That I shall do my beloved." Natasha stood close to the angel of silence side. "My brother Norwell you lead the way since you just departed this place." Morningstar told the archangel. Eager to enter the heat of battle to save her charge and who has become more of a little sister to her as well. Norwell begins to chant the spell to open the portal gates to journey to the place where the engineer and his hell spawns awaits. "tell me Natasha can I see the aura glow around angels like I can humans?" Jessie whisper to his wife's ear for no other can hear. "yes you can my beloved but you must focus on the angel for thirty seconds and it shall appear. Why do you ask?" "somethings not right about Norwell Natasha. I can feel it in my soul. All my warning are going off, I learned as a soldier surviving black ops to always trust my instants." "you are a soldier of god's now and so is Norwell, and there is no other more faithful to Yahweh our lord and savior then him. Have faith my beloved husband." Natasha assures that everything's ok with Norwell. "....just stay close to me ok." Jessie said again. Natasha and Valery both have blind faith in Norwell. I guess I could understand knowing someone for eons can do that. Morningstar is to worried in saving the little girl to notice the holes in Norwell's story. There's no doubt that Norwell doesn't like human beings but that doesn't mean he is a traitor to god. Best thing I can do right now is keep my wife and unborn child next to me in order to protect them while I keep a eye out for our archangel over there. Since I can't prove anything and I hope there's nothing to prove. I'll keep my faith in Yahweh our lord and savior and my wife Natasha but not in Norwell, because Norwell is a angel and angels can fall. A bright blue light engulf the four warriors of god as they teleport out of the safety of Valery's sanctuary. Jessie brown feels like his body is being boiled alive. Once again a unwelcome feel from teleportation but Jessie feels that his body is starting to adapt to the pain. Once Jessie's eyes clears he finds himself inside an old catholic church covered in weird ancient markings. This must be the ritual that Morningstar and Norwell was talking about. Jessie thought. "Jessie do you need me to heal you my beloved?" Natasha ask as she grab his hand. "No thank you beautiful. The more I make these jumps the stronger my body gets. Save your energy." Jessie explained to his wife. Norwell and Morningstar were just a couple of feet in front of us. "Norwell I can see the ritual markings but I can't sense Gabriella's presences.?" Morningstar said with Agious thanatos in her hand ready to slay all whom would stand in her way from saving Gabriella. "She's here. The dark magic is affecting your senses. She's by one of his creatures, do you sense her now Morningstar?" Norwell said. "Yes I can feel her through the darkness now. I'll save Gabriella while you put a end to the engineer. Morningstar said as Norwell sword appeared from his hand. "Yes I will once and for all." Norwell said with a blink expression but Morningstar was already gone chasing after her charge. Norwell looked back over his shoulder at Natasha and the angel of silence. "Prepare yourselves I can feel the enemy approaching!" Norwell warned but Jessie couldn't stop starring at the archangel as he stood in place. What! No it's real! Jessie thought to himself surprised but know he shouldn't be. All I did was stare at Norwell since the chapel and now I see it. The angel of silence see the red aura around Norwell's body and he knows he's not hallucinating. So you can see my aura. Natasha taught you well, unfortunate for you angel of silence you're the only one looking. Norwell projected his thoughts in to Jessie brown's mind. "Natasha stand back! Norwell's a traitor!" the angel of silence wings sprung out of his back instantly shielding Natasha from any harm. Jessie's vision became a blur as everything became red. There was a hot wave that came across his body from his left shoulder down to his right rib cage. The angel of silence felt to his knees as he looked down and saw his blood gashing out of a wound that ran across his body cause by the sword of Norwell the archangel. Jessie could hear the faint voice of his wife calling out to him as he looks in to the hateful face of his would be murder. "Now the angel of silence will be silences forever." Norwell mock the dying angel of silence as he felt in to the arms of the only woman who loved him. "Jessie please hold on, god please give me the strength to heal his wounds!" I hear my wife pray for my life but the only thing I find myself caring about is for Natasha and my unborn daughter to be safe. Please god just let them be safe. "I love..you Natasha." Jessie brown manage to say and then there was darkness. Jessie brown the angel of silence was no more...

CHAPTER TWENTY TWO

The blood of the angel of silence ran across the ancient markings of the church floors. Phase one of the ritual was completed. Norwell thought. I watch her beg and plead to our god to heal her now dead human husband. Disgusting it takes all of my will and strength to keep me from chopping off her head and simply end this horrific sense before my eyes. Black lights emerge from the ancient marks all over the church floors. "the shadow glows Natasha. This means the ritual is pleases with your dead husbands sacrifice." I finally said to Natasha, anything to stop her continuing howling. "Come back to us Jessie. God please help me please...please." Natasha continues to plead to god for a miracle to save her beloved. Are you ignoring me for a damn dead human corpse Natasha? "plead and beg to god all you want Natasha but his soul belongs to Lucifer now. May be your unborn child can watch her father soul burn in hell when she's born heh heh heh!" Norwell laughs at Natasha with his crew mockery. Suddenly Natasha pleads and prayers stop and Norwell felt slight swagger of fear pass through him as he felt the aura of bloodlust emerging from Natasha. A bloodlust that he never felt from her before. "Jessie soul is to righteous for your master can take but you shall take my sword through your soul as both you and your master will burn in hell in eternal darkness." Natasha look up at me with a dead stare, her words were more of a statement then words of pride or anger. "Heh! I've never seen such a look from you before Natasha but be sure of this when the day come for me to be slay it shall not be by your sword." "My beloved was right about you but we all was to blind to see the truth. I always turned a blind eye towards your hatred for mankind but I never would of thought you would betray our lord and savior. He knew, my beloved knew the truth." Natasha said as she held her husband corpse tighter, Completely drench in his blood. "My love for god is absolute, I'm willing to sacrifices my soul to clean up his one mistake Natasha. The mistake of creating these filthy human beings. Because of his promise to Noah god can't just be rid of them so I'm going to do the dirty work for him. Fore there is nothing I love more than the mighty Yahweh the mighty El shaddai." I explain myself to her. I could of easily executed Natasha as she pleaded and beg god to save her now dead husband life. I 've known Natasha for to many centuries to just kill her and her unholy child without explanation. "Dear Norwell you are truly lost in the darkness. You poor misguided soul, you have no idea what plans Yahweh the great El shaddai have for all of mankind. Norwell your ego is just as massive as your new master's now." Natasha preach as Norwell felt a swollen of darkness burning deep within his soul. "...Natasha I never knew you could me such a whore and now you show me your serpent tongue." a look of complete murdering rage shown on his face. "You stupid bitch who do you think you are talking down to me like some low class demon! I'm going to murder you on top of your dead husband's body and cut open your womb, then slaughter that abomination you call a child." Norwell responded. "Good I'm glad you've shown your true face. God will grant me the strength to..." "Gasp!" then I saw her freeze in shock as the filthy human corpse jerk up in the arms of Natasha gasping for air. I too stood in shock as I witness the angel of silence drew breathe once more. "No it's impossible!" Norwell shouted as god answer Natasha prayers. I see the dark magic rising, getting stronger all around me but I know everything's going to be okay. The light always overcome the darkness. I always knew this but on this day my lord and savior has chosen to show me proof for my faithfulness as he answer my prayers. God bless me with his miracle as my beloved breathes life in to his lungs once again. "Natasha." my beloved first word was to call for my name, I can feel his love for me I am so grateful. "sshhh.I'm here my beloved. Rest let me heal your wounds, god is with us." I tell my beloved husband while I focus healing the wound across his chest. "Tell god there won't be no Armageddon!" Norwell yelled out as he aims his sword to impale Natasha and the weaken angel of silence with a single stroke. No I don't have enough time to defend us, I was to focus on healing Jessie I didn't pay attention to the enemy in front of us now were going to die. Natasha prepares for death as her eye vision becomes black. "stay close to me." Natasha heard her husband say. She did what she was told as she saw Norwell pierce the darkness that covered her eyes. Natasha heard her beloved grunt in pain as she realized that the darkness that shielded her was the wing of her husband protecting her. Natasha quickly use the opportunely to thrust her sword through the gap of the angel of silence wings. The tip of her sword slices out Norwell's left eye. "Ggeerraahh!" Norwell screamed out in agony as he felled back covering his left eye socked where his eye use to be. Even now in my husband weakened state he those all he can to protect me and our unborn daughter. Natasha thought as she felt Norwell's flesh gave way to her blade. I shall put a end to this now by slaying my former partner

Norwell the fallen. "Rest now my beloved husband god has foretold me it is my sword that shall slay this great traitor and send him to the pit my love." Natasha places Jessie's body down as gentle as she could. "No don't! Teleport out of here right now! He's a monster! He's a fucking monster!" Jessie yelled out trying desperately to stop his love from engaging in battle against the fallen angel Norwell. Natasha rises above her wounded husband as Jessie desperately tries to get up in time to protect Natasha because he knows what a true monster Norwell is and always was. "that's exactly why god has given me the pow..uuah?" Natasha's body went in to shock as Norwell's sword rips through her belly. "you always talk too much Natasha." Norwell whisper in to her ear before yanking out his sword from her dying body. "Natashaaa!" Jessie screamed horrified as he caught his dying wife's body. "Natasha what do I do baby, please just tell me what to do, what do I do? I don't know what to do..god please me please..don't die..please don't die." jessie cried and pleaded as he tried to stop Natasha's bleeding with his hands. "Sorry..love you.." hard to talk. I want to let him know how I feel. Natasha tries to express her final thoughts to Jessie. "Wait, wait. I remember now you taught me I have the power to give my life for another." Jessie realized a way to save his family. "No..don't, only works for humans..kiss me." I manage to say. I just want to feel him one more time. Jessie kiss his beautiful wife lips with passion as she gasp, breathing her last air in to his mouth. Jessie looks in to his wife's face and saw that she was dead. Jessie cried and held his wife body tight to his wounded chest and cried out her name with such pain, grief and sorrow it was felt in Valery's sanctuary. Valery felt the angel of silence pain and she knew that Natasha was dead and she weep.

CHAPTER TWENTY THREE

As I fly above I can see the black fire rise from the ritual markings from the ground. I recognizes this type of fire from Egypt so many centuries ago when I was still human. This spell can only be done by spilling the blood of someone whom been touch by heaven and hell. In ancient Egypt this kind of ritual was use to contact Osiris, but this spell isn't strong enough to summon Lucifer alone. Neither is sacrificing a child with the gift of foresight like Gabriella but both of them to sacrifices both a child of light and one whom been touch by heaven and hell is enough to rise Lucifer from his prison. This is why Norwell came to the sanctuary to lure the angel of silence here. The very reason why the Engineer tried to recruit the angel of silence in the first place and resurrected Gabriella all for the purpose of summoning the bringer of light, Lucifer the falling. Morningstar fully recognizes the true purpose of the Engineer plans. I'm so sorry Natasha, I can hear the cries of sorrow from the angel of silence for his now late wife Natasha who was killed by her former partner Norwell. I was blinded by the guilt of losing Gabriella I didn't see the holes in Norwell's story, I just didn't care enough. Now it's too late to help him. The angel of silence blood has started the ritual and once Gabriella's life is taking there won't be nothing that could stop Lucifer from returning to this world. I'm sorry angel of silence I won't be able to save you because if Gabriella's die's all is lost. Morningstar ignore Jessie cries as she fly's towards the church alter to save Gabriella's life. "No!" Morningstar shouted as she saw the engineer standing over Gabriella who was strap down on a wooden cross. The engineer held an ancient dagger that was made from the bones of a fallen archangel wings ready plunge the blade in to Gabriella's heart. "Morningstar help!" Gabriella scream out to her guardian angel. "It's too late!" the engineer yelled out as he plug the dagger in to Gabriella's heart as a yellow beam shot from the hole in her chest. The beam of light knock the engineer back a couple of feet from the child. "I'm not dead! I'm not dead!" Gabriella shouted out over and over again. The engineer turned and saw Morningstar land two feet away from him. "what did you do? You didn't have enough time to chant a spell." an angered engineer ask. "It's a life blinding spell. Only a guardian angel can use it simply by willy it. As long as I live on this realm she cannot die. Morningstar explain as she pulls out her Agious thanatos. The engineer's eyes turns a deep green as his fangs and talons appears, his black wings spread from his back, ready for battle. "Then it simply my lady. You just have to die." "Morningstar behind you!" Gabriella scream out warning Morningstar. Multiple chains with hooks burst out from the darkest shadows with the speed of lighting Morningstar counter just quickly as she took flight dodging as many as she could accept two that hit's it's mark. Tearing the flesh from her left shoulder as she manage to pulls away. Morningstar grunts in pain barley escaping the horde of hell chains as the engineer's using the opportunely for a sneak attack. "Don't get distracted!" The Engineer said as green flames shout out his mouth. Morningstar was to wounded to evade the engineer's attack, all she could do was shield herself with her left wing. Morningstar screamed as her wing began to burn from the engineer's flames. With her left wing damages Morningstar crashed to the ground. With a moment of rest a burst of hell chains emerge from the shadows to tear in to Morningstar's flesh. This time Morningstar is more prepare for the attack this time. "For thy whom hides in thy dark, reveal all in your grace!" Morningstar deflected the chains with her Agious thanatos as she chanted her ancient spell. A bright light descended from the shy in to the center of the darkness of the chains. Blinding all in its radius. "Rrrahhh! Damn finding spell!" The engineer sneers as he shields his eyes from the blinding light. A woman engulf in yellow smoke staggers out of the blinding burring light as a blue blur of light cuts through the air as the staggering lady's head fall from her shoulders. "Mom?" A confuse Gabriella asked. "I'm sorry Gabriella but you see for yourself that she was no longer your mother." Morningstar explained. "I know..I know it's because of this demon my mother was made that way. He's the one who should die." Tears filled Gabriella's eyes but not from sorrow but from anger as she stares down the engineer's wishing that he would die. "such a hateful stare little Gabriella but don't you worry your mother won't be leaving you so soon." the engineer smiled as he pointed at the decapitated body of sherry shuford. "Oh god!" Gabriella scream out in horror as she watch the headless body of her mother rise up and grabs her decapitated head and reattached it to her body. "I'm sorry Gabriella, mommy has no control over herself." whatever was good left in sherry's soul apologizes to her daughter. "No. how is this my Agious thanatos should of killed her flesh?" "That's cause Mrs. Sherry is a necromancy, her flesh is already dead." The Engineer revealed to the guardian angel as Sharpe blades pops out of sherry's scars, turning her in to a walking shredding machine that will rip through anything that she touches. Sherry sprints towards Morningstar with pure bloodlust. "you have to destroy me in order to save my baby Morningstar!" Sherry pleads to her daughter's guardian angel as she tries to peel the flesh from her face. Morningstar manages to dodges sherry's assault, knowing it's only a matter of time the engineer will find a opening while she's distracted defending herself from Gabriella's mother. It takes all of Morningstar's speed and skill to evade necro sherry's attack. But as she's defending herself Morningstar hears sherry's master chanting a deadly spell that would cripple Morningstar, leaving her defenseless for a easy kill while he complete the ritual summoning Lucifer from the pits of hell. "No! I won't let you!" Morningstar throws her dagger towards the engineer's head, the speed of Morningstar's blade was too fast to block with his wings. The engineer intercepted Morningstar's blade by clapping both of his hands together around the dagger stopping it from stabbing him through the head, Interrupting his spell. "you angelic bitch!" sherry's master yells out as she finally sees an opening as she goes' in for the kill, Morningstar won't be fast enough to evade this time. "I'm sorry, Gabriella forgive me." Sherry reaches towards Morningstar's chest inches away from ripping out her heart from her defenseless chest. "Obey me!" Morningstar said in her native tongue as black mist came from her mouth in to the face of the undead sherry. Sherry's attack stop's lest then an inch away from stabbing Morningstar in her chest. "Descend!" Morningstar commanded the undead sherry as she collapse to the ground like a lifeless puppet. "Naughty little angel you are. That wasn't a spell of your lord and savior wasn't it ?" The Engineer smirk. "No it wasn't it's an ancient spell of Egypt that controls the dead. God will forgive me once I rid your head from your body." Morningstar gloated. "we shall see little Egyptian." The Engineer's said as both of them charges at each other in full force. I've been watching from the shadows for the last couple of minutes and best to believe this shit is pathetic. First he botched up the job to kill the nigger and then follows up by taking forever to kill the uptight mouthy bitch. Now he stands there watching the nigger cry and moans over the dead angelic bitch. What the fuck already! Stop talking to the nigger and chop off his fucking head already! I can't stand and watch this shit anymore. I'm coming out of the shadows and show this angelic motherfucker how murder is truly done. "I was wondering when you would kill that talking bitch." Albert Houston said as he emerge from the shadows of the church and stands next to Norwell. "watch your tongue demon, only reason you still breathing is because my brother wishes." Norwell snap at albert. "yeah, yeah. Why ain't the nigger dead yet? He's looking pretty piss now." He ask ignoring Norwell's remarks. "you murdering motherfuckers better kill me now! I swear to god I'm going to kill you both! You hear me! You fucking hear me!" Jessie threating's them while holding his dead wife tightly in his arms. "Your empty treats have no power over me filthy human. I will no longer soil my blades on such filth as you." Norwell looked down on the angel of silence. "don't misunderstand me angel of silence you will die today. This hell spawn would love to soil his hands in your misery. You may kill him now demon." Norwell turns his back as he begins to walk away. "What about the female angel?" Albert ask the former archangel. "what about her? She's dead. You can do as you please with her corpse." Norwell said just before he took flight and flew away. "you hear that boy? I'm finally gonna get some angel pussy. Don't worry you can watch as I fuck your dead wife, best to believe it." Albert Houston put his hand in to his

226

pants and started to stroke himself. "I'm going to fucking kill you. I'm gonna kill all of you. You hear me you all fucking dead!" Jessie scream out as the entire church shock. Jessie's eyes became black as night, his teeth became razor Sharpe fangs. "The fuck? The little dog still have some bark left in him huh." Albert grins unfazed by the angel of silence transformation. He begins to laugh out loud. Jessie's scream became a unhuman roar of rage as he stood up leaving his dead wife body on the floor as talons replace his nails while his wings exploded from his back. One wing of light the other of darkness. "you're fucking dead!" "you think you can fucking scare me with a transformation. Best to believe you ain't the only who can transform motherfucker!" The sound of ripping flesh and bones rings throughout the church halls. Albert Houston demon form completely rips through his human skin. Revealing his new form standing ten feet tall, hands fuse with metal spheres and dragon wings extending out of his back. The ritual black magic has evolve albert's body and power to new levels. "My master has given me power beyond your comprehension. I'm going to rip off your wings and chop off all your limps, so you can watch me fuck your dead wife in half as you beg and plead for me to stop like the little bitch you are." the angel of silence doesn't say a word as he stare down albert Houston with a emotionless glance. "yeah best to believe you're scare shitless so much you can't talk." within a blink of an eye albert's wings speed close the distance between the angel of silence and himself as his spheres extend out to cut off Jessie's arms off.

Slash! Massive amounts of blood splashes in the dark fires. "wasn't you going to cut of my limbs?" Jessie held albert's severed arm in his hand. "what? How the fuck?" How is this possible? I'm stronger and faster but how in hell I couldn't see him? It's some form of a trick, best to believe it.

"just die!" albert's shouts out as he steps forward towards the angel of silence. Slash! Slash! Slash! Slash! The sound of albert Houston's flesh and bones giving way as the angel of silence cuts off albert's other arm and both of his legs. Albert Houston felt hard face first smashing it to the ground. Barley alive without a single limb to support himself. The angel of silence lifts up albert's head so he can look in to the demon's eyes. "look at the infamous albert hou...are you crying? Are you fucking crying, you piece of shit!" Once again albert Houston knew fear but this wasn't fear of excitement of the unknown but fear of someone, Something that was once human and more scary then himself, With all the power he possess he finds himself defenseless just like his victims. This was true fear, For the first time in his life he was the pray. "Please don't fucking kill me man. Please you're a man of god right?" "what was that you said earlier. You was going to fuck the shit out of my dead wife? Don't pussy up now albert." "Fuck you! Best to believe I would and it would have been the best fucking cock she would of ever had dead or alive nigger!" Albert spit in the face of the angel of silence. "yeah that's the psycho killer I know. Since you love your dick so much I have the best parting gift for you." the angel of silence smiled. Horrifying gaging and koffing sounds was heard throughout the church halls. Albert Houston tried to scream but all he could do was gag and koff as his throat extended wider and wider until his eyes pop from his eyes socket, His throat split open as he choke to death. Albert Houston was dead and there was a massage in carved on his chest. Albert Houston loved his dick so much he decided to swallow himself whole the Angel of silence was here.

CHAPTER TWENTY FOUR

Not a single word was utter, Only the clash of blades can be heard throughout the church. Neither of them yielding an inch to each other. The speed of their hands could no longer be seen by humans eyes. Gabriella watches helplessly as her guardian angel fearlessly fights to save her life. Gabriella then looks at the limb, motionless thing on the ground that was here mother and wonders why all of this is happening to her and the ones she loves. Mom I'm so sorry that this has happened to you, it's all my fault. Only if I've never cross that stupid street that day. Gabriella thought. No honey it wasn't your fault, don't you ever think that. You saved that girl Gabriella, you're a hero don't you ever forget that. Gabriella heard her mother's voice inside her head. "Mom is that really you?" a confuse Gabriella said out loud. Ssshhh, don't speak out loud I don't want him to know, I can speak freely to you. This demon left my mind intact on purpose so I would be aware of all my actions knowing I had no control over them. I am his puppet Gabriella he made me hurt that police officer who tried to protect you and made me kidnap my own daughter while attacking the angel who desperately fighting for your life right now as we speak. I'm sorry mom but it is my fault. If I didn't go and get myself killed you would of never made that deal with the engineer. Enough of that Gabriella, I made the deal because I'm your mother and I love you Gabriella. I was supposed to be watching you two that day. The fact you had to put yourself in that situation is my fault you understand Gabriella. I would do anything to save you, I love you Gabriella. I love you too mom, I love you so much. Crack! The Engineer's wings hit's hard against Morningstar's skull knocking her down to the ground. "Morningstar!" Gabriella scream out to her guardian angel. "I must Amit you are better than most archangels, Including my brother Norwell. Lucifer will be proud when I present your heart to him." The Engineer stands over her as he goes in to rip out Morningstar's heart from her back. Morningstar quickly spins on her back stabbing the engineer's through his attacking hand. "you talk to much!" The Engineer's left hand starts to decay with black sores. "No my hand!" No the decay is already spreading up my arm. I have to severed it before the decay reach my chest. "I know what you're thinking engineer, I won't allow you to be rid of it!" Morningstar shouted as she rise up from the ground to deliver the finishing blow. "No!" the engineer's use his wings to shied himself from Morningstar's attack. "Rot!" Morningstar said as her Agious thanatos cuts in to the engineer's wings. Imminently the engineer's wings started to decay as his black feathers felt from the bones of his wings like the pedals of a blossom tree. Shit I have to create an opening to get breathing room in order to detach this arm before it reaches my chest, my wings will fall of the bones before the decay could reach my back. "Rot!" Morningstar continues her war cry as she struck the engineer's wings again completely obliviated what was left of his wings. The engineer grunts in pain as the remains of his wings decays to the ground. This is the opening I need. The engineer's mouth opens wide as an inferno blaze of green flames burst through them. Morningstar rolls out of the way to avoid further damaging her wings by blocking the engineer's attack. The engineer's screams out in pain as he chops off his left arm just below his shoulder to stop the decay from Morningstar's Agious thanatos. "Now you're dead..." the engineer gasp as he looks down and see's Morningstar pushing her blade through his gut. "Rot!" Morningstar said coldly as she pulls her Agious Thanatos slowly from the engineer's stomach. Streams of black blood erupts from his mouth as the engineer collapse to the ground. "Heaven wins demon. Agious thanatos stroke in the center of your body., the decay will spread to the upper and lower side of your body. You're dead." Morningstar said already walking away from the decaying falling angel. "Morningstar I knew you would win! Please hurry and get me out of this so we can go home." A excited Gabriella said to Morningstar as she walks over to release Gabriella from her bondage. "yes and we shall watch more of I love Lucy with cookies." Morningstar said as she began to loosen Gabriella's restrains. "No! Don't!" Gabriella shouted out in terror as she watches her guardian angel and friend Morningstar gets stab through the heart from behind by the falling angel Norwell. "I am truly sorry I couldn't grant you a true warriors death Morningstar but you control one of god's scared weapons. It's very possible that your skills could surpass me, even in prime condition. There's too much on the line to fight you fairly, I couldn't take that chance." Norwell whisper in the dying Morningstar's ear. Gabriella oh god I've failed. I failed you Gabriella..please forgive me, I'm sorry, I'm sorry. Morningstar thought as Norwell pulls out his sword from her back, she falls down in to her eternal sleep. Morningstar was dead. "No! No! No! You murdering coward! You are supposed to be on god's side! How could you do this? God please help me please!" Gabriella pleads to god desperately trying to get out of bondage. "Hush now child. Your body shall die here but your soul will live for eternally in the kingdoms of heaven." Splat! Gabriella spit's in Norwell's face. "Go to hell!" Gabriella said defiant until her last breath. "I will child but not before this world goes first." Norwell responded. "Brother the dagger..of twilight.." The Engineer spoke out to his brother as his body continues to rot away. Norwell picks up the dagger of twilight that his brother drop during his battle with Morningstar. "yes the dagger of twilight made from the bones of a holy and falling archangel. Lucifer could not be summoned without it." Norwell eyes turned blood red, As his body became an inferno that melted away the dagger of twilight. "No what have you done!" the engineer tried to reach out to his brother but couldn't no longer move as the decay deteriorate his entre lower half while it reaches in to the engineer's chest. "sorry brother I never had any intentions to rise Lucifer from the pits. There is another ritual that requires the sacrifice of one whom been touch by heaven and hell and one who have the ability of foresight with a pure heart." Norwell explain to his dying brother. "Death." The Engineer could barely say as the decay makes its way to his heart. "yes Natta, The horse man of death. I shall summon him until this world to correct god's only mistake. Death shall kill every single thing in this world, There won't be no Armageddon because there won't be any soul left alive." the engineer's heard his brother's explanation as his eyes fade in to darkness as the decay spread throughout his heart. He was terrified that his brother hatred for mankind out weighted any evil he had ever done since he felt from heaven. What have I unleashed He though before all he was became consume by the darkness of death. The Engineer was no more. I can hear albert Houston plead for mercy. The angel of silence must of resurrected his power somehow. Let me be done with this before he arrive then. "No! No please don't!" Gabriella's pleads goes through deaf ears as Norwell stabs Gabriella through her heart. "No it can't be!" yellow beam of light shot from Gabriella's chest as Norwell pulls his sword out of her. "Rot!" Norwell barley heard the voice as his right hand was cut off. "Aaahhh!" Norwell howl in pain but imminently create space and burns off the rest of his forearm with his newly found hell fire powers killing off the living cells, stopping the decay of Morningstar's Agious Thanatos. "How can you still be alive? I've stab you clean through the heart." Norwell ask as he continues to step away from her, Holding his maim burned arm, puzzled and confused. Morningstar stands in her fighting stance, alive and ready for combat but clearly very weaken from the fatal black hole in her chest where her heart was. "Osiris learned of your plans and became one with me. He won't allow me to die." Morningstar gave Norwell an explanation of her resurrection. "Osiris? You mean death. He always loved you fucking Egyptian filth. Norwell spits on the floor showing his disgust. "Enough!" Morningstar charges at Norwell and sphere's her sword towards his midsection knowing the slightest cut of Agious Thanatos would mean certain death. Both of Norwell wings cross in front of his body, shielding his body while taking the damage of Morningstar's Agious Thanatos, Imminently killing off his wings as they decay. "Sometimes you must make sacrifices and order to deliver the killing blow!" Norwell purposely used his wings as a sacrifice in order to create a opening to deliver a killing blow, As Norwell reach up high with his remaining hand and split Morningstar's head in half with his sword. "Morningstar! Oh god no!" Gabriella scream out as Morningstar's blood splatter across her face. Morningstar slower in her weaken state but still to dangerous, had no choice to sacrifice my wings in order to be rid of her for good. "Die!" Norwell's leg splits open on his upper thigh. "No!" Norwell yelled out as he watched the flesh a round his leg became black with oozing pose as the decay began to spread. Norwell burns a huge chuck of infected flesh off his left leg. "I told you he won't allow me to die. Burn as much flesh as you want it's only a matter of time before my Agious thanatos hit's a vital area." Morningstar said as her breathing became heavy because of the fatal wounds she received as black blood ran down her face from the splitting gap in her skull from Norwell's sword. "I apologizes for my appearance Gabriella." Morningstar said to her charge. "I love you Morningstar. I don't care what you look like, just kill that evil bastard!" Gabriella rooted for her friend and guardian angel. "Disgusting filth of dirt from the soles of thy feet. You show your true nature just like the rest of your kind." Norwell sneered. "Do not swear child but slay this traitor I shall." Morningstar skull slowly starts to heal while she prepares herself while calming her mind to deliver her ultimate attack that will surly put an end to the falling archangel Norwell. "may the city of Zion opens its gates for thy brothers and sisters in thy holy heavens!" Norwell chanted as a blue aura of light surrounded Morningstar. "If I can't kill you, I'll simply summon back to heaven." Morningstar struggles but slowly starts to break through the blue light. "No you don't possess the power from heaven anymore to cast me back Norwell." "because of your weaken state and tainted with the soul of Osiris, I have just enough grace to pull this off!" Norwell said. "Now be gone!" a beam of blue light shoots down from the ceiling in to the blue aura surrounding Morningstar's body. "Nnnooo!" Morningstar yelled out as she vanished in to the light. Norwell felt to his knees as he grunts in pain as the last of his heavenly grace was gone. The mark of the beast was burned in to the flesh of his chest. "It is done. Now mankind shall finally be cleansed from this world. Norwell raised from his knees seconds away from succeeding his true mission. "you monster! What did you do to Morningstar?" Gabriella cried as she saw her friend and protector vanished from existence . "I used the rest of my grace to summon Morningstar back to heaven. It will take several hours for her to return to this plane, which is more than enough time to send you there as well." this time knowing she will surly die without sharing Morningstar's life force. A loud roar of pain is heard from Norwell's mouth as multiple chains with hooks rips in to the flesh of his back. "the engineer's dead now demon! I have complete control over myself now and I won't allow you to hurt my daughter!" the undead sherry said regaining her freewill. Gabriella listen to me. Once I free you, keep running ahead until you see a African American man, his name is the angel of silence. He can get you out of here. Sherry sent her thoughts telepathy to her daughter's mind. I'm not leaving without you mom, not again. I'm already dead Gabriella, now do as I say now! Sherry's hell chains cuts off Gabriella's bondage. With the speed of rabbit Gabriella was already running past her mother, towards the center of the church. I love you mom. A tearful Gabriella said her goodbyes. I love you too honey, now go and don't look back no matter what. "No! I won't be denied by some human necromancy filth!" hell fire burst out of Norwell's wounds where his wings used to be. The fire travels down sherry's chains evaporating them, burning sherry dead body beyond repair. Gabriella hears the screams of her mother's smelling her dead roasted flesh but she continues to run ahead knowing what's at stake. Mr.li, Mr. Diaz, Morningstar and now my mother all sacrificing their lives to protect me. No I won't let their sacrifice be in vain. Gabriella stop's in her tracks as she see two wings spread before her above the black fires and she knew what he was. "Are...Are you the angel of silence?" Gabriella ask still not being able to make out his face as he approach her. "...yes I am. Are you the brave girl Morningstar sent us to help?" the angel ask, his voice was sad. "yes I'm Gabriella. Are you going to take me out of here now?" I ask him as he knelt in front of me. I could see him now. He wasn't like other angels his eyes where sad, he was a man who's heart was filled with pain and sorrow, it was like looking at myself in the mirror. Gabriella I can see you have the gift to look in to peoples souls. You have lost so much because of this war between heaven and hell. The demon that kidnap you is he still here?" the sad angel ask me. "No Morningstar killed him but the other demon forced her back to heaven." then I saw a flood of anger flash in his eyes, enough hatred to destroy his very soul. "I can and I will take you out of here Gabriella but that thing murdered my wife and put this scare across my chest, he brandish your guardian angel. He won't stop hunting you until he kills you to resurrect Lucifer from hell. Gabriella this is your life so I will let you make the decision of running or fighting." "this demon also murder my mother. She's why I was able to escape... we can't run and hide all our lives Mr. Angel of silence, we stay and fight. But the demon doesn't want to summon Lucifer like the other one, he plans on summoning death to kill every human in this world." Gabriella gave her choice and revealing Norwell's plans to the angel of silence. "killing Norwell it is then." the angel of silence said as he picks up Gabriella and holds her to his chest while he fly's where Norwell a waits. Gabriella and the angel of silence reach the area witness in the new deform Norwell whom stood tall with a wicked smile on his face. His eyes was red, pure as blood his wings on his back was made of hell fire. His left hand was made from fire as well. Norwell was now a true spawn of hell. "mother." the angel of silence heard the little girl mumble under her breath. The angel of silence lands them both by the charred body of sherry shuford. "is this your mother?" he ask Gabriella never taking his eyes off her Norwell. "yes she is. Can you help her? Are you able to help her?" Gabriella cried as she watch her mother dying again, then she saw him knelt next to her mother and place his hand on her body. "I see what I can do...i see she didn't give her soul willingly, she was tricked by the engineer." the angel of silence reveal. "yeah she told me she thought he was a angel sent from heaven to rescues me. Can you bring her back to life or something?" Gabriella look up at him with hope in her eyes. This little girl still believes in hope after everything that's happened to her, I see why see's so important now. The angel of silence thought. "No but I can save her soul." the angel of silence place his hand on sherry's forehead. Her eyes open wide as a blue light glowed from her eyes, sherry's mouth open wide as a beam of blue light exploded out towards the sky. Gabriella with her gift of sight saw her mother teleport in blue light ascending to the gates of heaven's kingdom. I love you mom. Gabriella said to her. I love you too honey, I love you so much, I love you so much Gabriella. Mother and daughter shared their final goodbyes telepathy before was gone for good in the kingdoms of heaven. "Are you done yet saving souls?" Norwell said standing completely composed. The angel of silence carefully places Gabriella behind him. "I've noticed you didn't chase after the girl. I could of easily teleported her a way and ruin your plans to wipe out the human race." "Heh. That would have been the smart move to make angel of silence. Once I knew the little bitch was running towards you for help. I knew you wouldn't leave without your petty revenge." Norwell laugh. The angel of silence fist clenched tightly trying to compose himself from reacting in bloodlust. "you had my blood already, why did you have to kill her? You were partners!" Jessie wanted an explanation. "you're right angel of silence, I cared deeply for her once. Natasha was the most righteous angel I knew until you came along and turned her in to a fucking human loving whore who carries abomination of human cum inside her wound. I had to kill the fucking whore!" Norwell said with a sinister smile on his face. His soul completely taken by the darkness. "I'll kill you for what you done to my family!" the angel of silence flew at him in great speed, consumed in murderous intentions. Norwell's left hand turns in to a inferno of hellfire blasting towards the angel of silence. Jessie screams out in pain as the skin and flesh of his forearms starts to melt from shielding his face from Norwell's inferno blast. "your little hell fire ain't going stop me from ripping out your fucking heart from your chest Norwell!" the angel of silence endures the pain spearing Norwell to the ground. "you killed my wife!" Jessie slashes Norwell across his chest with his talons. "you killed my daughter! My fucking daughter!" Jessie cuts deeper in to Norwell's chest. Again and again and again until Norwell's breast bone was exposed. "I'm going to rip out your black rotten heat you hear me! You hear me!" A in rage angel of silence howls out in bloodlust. Covered in Norwell's blood ready to deliver the final blow. "Off me you human piece of shit!" Norwell shoots hellfire from his mouth, hitting the angel of silence in his chest, knocking him off. Norwell stands back on his feet holding the gap that use to be his chest. "hoff, hoff, how dare..you defile me..you human. Filth touch me a archangel." "I'm going do more than defile you, you delusional mother fucker! I'm going to murder you and some third degree burns ain't going to stop me!" the angel of silence returns to his feet ready for his next attack. "let the void of the ether consume thy enemy's soul!" the angel of silence scream out in great pain after Norwell cast his spell. The Angel of silence vomits chunks of blood from his mouth as his skin from his arms starts to evaporate in to thin air. The angel of silence is experience a high level arch-angels spell that forces a person or angel in to the gates of the ether of heaven, if this spell is cast on a living person it will cause massive organ failure as there body evaporates painfully in to the realm where the dead rest in heaven. "No! I don't understand why are you still here?" a confuse Norwell questioned as he watch the angel of silence contin-ues to spit up blood. "uuhh..Natasha taught me a thing or two about magic..don't you get it you fucking fool? You can't send me to the ether because you're not a archangel anymore!" when the angel of silence reveal this to the fall-ing angel a hot sense of pain flash throughout his body. "what?" was the only response his mind could think of as the realization of his situation finally sink in. He wasn't an angel anymore. "Norwell. Natasha me a great spell from heaven let me show you!" the angel of silence scream out snapping Norwell back in reality. "Heavens grace of light evaporate everything in sight of thy eye!" the angel of si-lence body glow hot with the light of heaven as a massive beam of light shot from his hands destroying everything in its path. The back of the entire church was destroyed. Norwell used all of his strength, speed and agility to fly above the bright beam of death. If it wasn't for the angel of silence misguided taught that snap me out of my thoughts, I would of surly died in that blast. The hell is this? Only the core seven should have that kind of power. The angel of silence is proving himself to be a worthy foe. I can see the damage from the ether spell has greatly damage him and using such a high level spell has further drained him of his strength. A hell beam from this distance will kill him for sure, he doesn't have the energy or power to avoid this attack from here. Fire glows from Norwell eyes as the angel of silence spots him flying above him and he knew he wouldn't be able to evade Norwell's attack. "Burn to ash from the dirt which you came from human!" Hell beams shot from Norwell's eyes towards the vulnerable angel of silence. Black matter exploded in a heap of fire. No it wasn't the angel of silence. something else took that killing blow. Norwell quickly turn around and lookup at the ceiling above him. The shadows are moving, they were alive. The shadows sprung from the ceiling and attack. "No! What are you doing? We are on the same side!" Norwell said as he tries to negotiate with the shadow demons as they tear at his flesh while crashing to the ground. "hell knows about your plans pretender but we don't care cause we don't serve you or hell anymore! The angel of silence gave us the mark of heaven to help him destroy you! "the shadow demons said while Norwell tires fending off their hordes. He can see the mark of heaven on their foreheads, so the angel of silence truly have the power to save the souls of the damned whom been wrongfully condemn to hell. A consuming rage boils deep in Norwell's soul, A rage he's all too willing to unleashed on the redeem souls that's trying to stop him from fulfilling his destiny. Hellfire explodes all around Norwell's body like a bomb, destroying everything around him. "Off of me! No redeem souls won't stop me angel of silence, you have no right to such power!" "God said I have every right!" the angel of silence answer as he thrust his wife's sword through Norwell's heart. "you feel this blade piercing through your heart, it belongs to Natasha my wife. I kept it from your sight just for this moment, god doesn't make mistakes." Jessie whisper in Norwell's ear. The black lights shot high in to the sky as the ground underneath them began to shake. "the fucks happened?" the angel of silence said. "you ain't the only one who can hide things from sight." Norwell laugh as the angel of silence decapitated his head. Norwell dies as his soul descends to hell to be torture for all of eternity. The angel of silence ran back to the front of the church in a panic as the ground began to quake, As the ground breaks beneath his feet. "Gabriella! Gabriella where are you..oh god please." the angel of silence called out for her. He was answer only by the rumbles of the earth until he walk up on her. "Gabriella? Gabriella oh god, oh god no!" the angel of silence felt to his knees as he saw the lifeless body of Gabriella shuford riddle with black holes. "the shadows, he used the shadows. I'm so sorry, I'm so sorry Gabriella." Jessie apologizes while he cried over her corpse. Blood erupted from the open cracks of the earth. What, what the fuck? The earth is bleeding...It's dying, I can feel death making his way through. No I won't allow this to happen, I'm not going to let all of mankind die because of my revenge, I won't let this little girl die for my actions. The angel of silence folds his legs in a meditation stance and place Gabriella's head on his lap. I couldn't use this spell on my wife and unborn daughter because they were angels but I can use it on mortals...I can use it for this girl. The angel of silence closed his eyes and began to start the spell. The earth near him exploded upward as a large black hand of death rose out from the ground as it sank it's talons in to the ground. Every man, woman and child, every beast that flew, walk or crawl the earth within twenty miles of the church instantly died. The world would consider this the worst terrorist attack in history as thousands died in a single night. No it's rising, it's hand a lone just killed sixty blocks, No I have to focus or more is going to die. "Dear god my lord and savior of heaven and earth may I give thy life for one shall live." Jessie chanted. I see you soon baby. I'm coming home to you Natasha, I love you. A bright beam of blue light shot down from the heavens up on Jessie the angel of silence body. Gabriella's eyes open up with new life as her wounds heal in to healthy scars. Gabriella sat up and saw a giant black hand sank back in to the earth, An image that would hunt her for the rest of life. The last thing she remember was shadows stabbing her throughout her body and everything went dark, then she was here breathing again, alive and she knows it was because of the angel of silence. "Jessie are you there?" I don't remember him telling me his real name but somehow I know. Gabriella thought as she called out to him. Gabriella look behind her and saw the angel of silence laid out across the broken ground. His wings and claws were gone but I can tell it was him. "Jessie sir please wake up, please wake please." Gabriella hug the lifeless body of the angel of silence. Gabriella knew just like everybody else in her life, Jessie brown the angel of silence was dead. Everything's so bright, so beautiful. Once in my life I knew there was a place I really belonged. It was heaven. Jessie brown saw the beauty of heaven's kingdoms. Then I saw eight figures approaching me from heaven's front gates to welcome me. Some of the people that approach me I've never seen before but I knew who they all was. It was detective Li with his mother and father then there was Gabriella's guardian angel Morningstar standing next to Gabriella's father and mother. Then there was the ones I knew and loved before I died. My mother Jennise and my grandmother god bless them. The one I was looking forward to the most was in front of all of them. So beautiful and loving stood Natasha brown greeting me with a little...with a little, oh god is that my daughter standing next to her? I know she is, I can feel it somehow and I know her name. I pick her up and grab my wife around her waist and hug them tightly. Thank you god! Thank you so much Yahweh the mighty El shaddai of heaven, praise god. "Her name is Nubian, your name is Nubian! Natasha she's so beautiful like you." Jessie kiss his daughter on her cheeks and his wife on the lips. "come on Natasha, you Nubian, mom and grand mom and show me around the kingdoms of heaven." Jessie never felt so happy in his life. Natasha gently press her hand on Jessie's chest. "No my beloved. God only wanted you to see what a wait's you when you return to heaven there is still much for you to do on earth my husband." Natasha explained to Jessie but he couldn't understand, he was dead, he was here, his journey was done. This was his reward. "No baby no. don't say that I died. I died and saved Gabriella's life, I sacrifices my life for mankind. I ..I deserve this, I deserve you and Nubian." Jessie started crying. "please don't do this I love you please." Jessie pleaded as Natasha and Nubian began to cry. "we love you too my beloved, we will be united in heaven again one day remember we all love you." Natasha and everybody else started to walk back to the gates of heaven. "No wait! Wait!" Jessie scream out as he sat up and saw the little girl's face that he saved. "Mr. Jessie thank god you're still alive. What happened?" Gabriella ask as she held me tight with a hug and I welcome it. "I was in heaven Gabriella." Jessie said. Gabriella just looked at him and didn't say a word. "Detective Li was there with his family so was your mother and father along with Morningstar. All waiting In heaven for you one day." Gabriella smiled and cried with joy knowing every one she cared and loved for was living a better live in heaven.

"Did you see your family Jessie?" Gabriella ask him as he pick her up and started to Carrie her in his arms. "yeah I did and one day I'm going to join them in heaven, but until then I'll continues to be the angel of silence." Jessie said just before they both vanished without a trace.

EPILOGUE

Mr. and Mrs. Ajanlekoko couldn't find a doctor or a priest that could help their little Tafari. Who has been possessed by the greatest falling angel of them all Lucifer. "please, please let our daughter go!" the father pleaded to the demon that was inside his strap down daughter's body. "Never your daughter is being fuck by every demon in hell as we speak while she screams out your name!" the demon laugh then moan as it threw up in the father's face. "Oh god please, help us please help our daughter." the mother continues praying to the lord for a miracle. "He can't help you as I wear your daughter's cunt all through hell!" Tafari thrust the air in a sexual matter as she calls out for her daddy in a moaning voice. "Daddy please help me! Help me like you do when you come in to my room when you tried of fucking mommy daddy!" "Shut up! Shut up!" The father scream as the demon laugh. "Don't feed in to it, that's what's it wants." the priest said. As he enter their home dress in all black with cargo pants and a polo shirt. "who? Who are you?" the mother ask. "I'm the man who's going to get your daughter back." he responded in their native tongue. It's just one of many gifts god has granted this priest. "Who are you demon?" the priest ask.

"I'm chaos, I'm all that is evil with in the world, I am the devil!" Tafari spoke in ancient Latin. "No. you're just a lonely demon pretending to be the big papi. If all it took was a simple possession for Lucifer to rise, he would had done so centuries ago. Zulu the perverse." Tafari body goes' in to shock as saying the demon's name weaken it. "Now it's time to go back to hell Zulu." "Wait my master has a message for you angel of silence." "He said prepare to suffer angel of silence for the days of Armageddon is up on us." the demon begins to laugh while the angel of silence touches the forehead of Tafari and sends the demon back to hell. "Tell your master that I'm ready, There's nothing he can do to make me suffer more than I do right now, Having to wake up every day walking this earth for the rest of my days." The angel of silence disappears in to the shadows before the relieved family could thank him while he a wait's the final battle between heaven and hell in Armageddon so he can finally reunite with his family again.

THE END...